IN FIDELITY

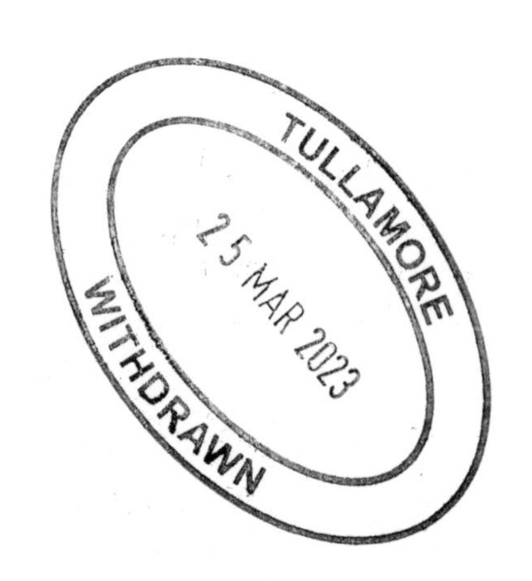

IN(T)FIDELITY

Jack Wilson

Matador
9 Priory Business Park,
Wistow Road, Kibworth Beauchamp,
Leicestershire. LE8 0RX
Tel: 0116 279 2299
Email: books@troubador.co.uk
Web: www.troubador.co.uk/matador
Twitter: @matadorbooks

ISBN 978 1784623 838

British Library Cataloguing in Publication Data.
A catalogue record for this book is available from the British Library.

Printed and bound in the UK by TJ International, Padstow, UK
Typeset in 11pt Minion Pro by Troubador Publishing Ltd, Leicester, UK

Matador is an imprint of Troubador Publishing Ltd

To my former wife, Betsy,
who has endured so much
with grace and courage.

Introduction

A stream meandered for years between the same banks, scarcely changing its course. An occasional drift of ice or fallen branch altered its progress from time to time. But to the observer, the casual visitor who came to fish or cross on stepping stones, all seemed the same.

And then one day there was a storm – an enormous storm – as if the tempest of creation was renewed. The earth cowered under a drumbeat of rain, and the stream swelled, foaming over rocks and washing over its banks. Torn from the sandy soil, overhanging bushes and obdurate stones tumbled and heaved in the angry current.

When the storm subsided, the stream had changed. The exposed roots of still-standing trees gaped over its expanse. New islands and rapids had been formed. The water had carved a fresh channel, and the stream never returned to the one it had known before.

PART ONE

WOODBURY

Chapter 1

A Premonition of Danger
1974

"Look out!" Her voice was sharp and tinged with annoyance.

"It's not me. We hit a rut." His effort to explain was received in silence.

Snowflakes were falling softly in the headlights' beams and in the coronas of each passing streetlight. The macadam surface of the road, black only a half-hour before, was glazed with a film of white that disguised tire tracks packed hard from a previous snowfall. The spiny branches of trees, some now imprisoned fast in the drifts thrown up by plows on either side of the road, groped upward into the milky, swirling darkness.

For a few moments, the silence continued. The car's interior was cold, and the chill insinuated itself into their bundled layers of clothing.

"Did I do the wrong thing?" he asked, shivering. "I mean, at the table, that stupid comment about the Midwest. I forgot Alice and Malcolm came from there."

She swiveled her head in her fur-lined hood to look at him. "You were fine. Everyone thought you were very funny – the life of the party."

"No. That's what they think of you."

"Particularly Carol," she added, almost as an afterthought.

It was only a half-mile, more or less, from the house where they had been to their own house. In the summer they would probably have walked. But it was cold, a biting cold that made nostrils click on exposure and breath dance white on the air; snow had been predicted, and the unshoveled sidewalks in some places had long since turned into lumpy corridors of ice.

He swung the car into their driveway and parked near the street. "No point shoveling out the whole driveway in the morning," he explained. "I'll leave it near the road."

"Oh for goodness sake, put the car in the garage. You'll save ten minutes of work and wonder next year why it's so rusty."

He glanced at her, then silently turned the ignition and drove the automobile forward.

"Are you all right?"

"No."

"What's… what's wrong?"

"What do you think?"

There was silence again. He had turned the ignition off, and they sat in the darkened garage, their features barely visible to each other. The heater had finally warmed the interior, and their breath no longer hung in filmy clouds as they spoke.

"It wasn't… it wasn't something that I did?"

"No." She spoke the word with resigned exasperation.

He looked at her. Filtered light from the house next door played faintly on her features, and a wisp of reddish brown hair hung down from inside her hood.

"Does it… still hurt?" He spoke hesitantly.

His wife sighed and pursed her lips. "What is it, Dick? Why won't it go away? Sometimes… sometimes I think it's nearly gone, but it comes back. I'm worried that it's getting worse. At least," she reached for his hand, "it was worse tonight."

"I couldn't tell. We could've left, if you'd wanted."

She shook her head. "What good would that've done? It was bad this afternoon, though. It really hurt. I called Dr. Sacks and made an appointment."

"Doctor? Who's Dr. Sacks?"

"You know, the one Dr. Tomlinson recommended. He's on the staff of the hospital, and I guess Dr. Tomlinson knows him pretty well. He thinks he's very good. He's a plastic surgeon."

"Why a plastic surgeon?" There was an anxious edge to his question. "Why not go back to that dentist and ask him to look again?"

"Oh, Dick, he was incompetent. They're all incompetent," she added bitterly. "How could he just open up my gum and see 'white stuff' and close it up and say he'd never seen anything like it before? And then have the nerve to send us a bill."

"I never asked you. Did he ever talk to anyone – some other dentist or doctor – about what he saw? Maybe I'd better call him."

"Don't bother. I didn't like him."

She continued to clutch his hand. Both were wearing gloves, and he removed his to improve his grip and feel her warmth. After a few seconds, she did the same. In the darkened vehicle she did not observe him swallow involuntarily, but she could discern his somber, earnest features.

"Why… why a plastic surgeon?" he asked again.

"Because we've tried everything else. That's what Dr. Tomlinson says. And it's not going away."

"And… and so?"

"And so we've got to go a step further." As she looked at him, her voice low, she bit her lower lip. He was struck with a sense – it did not rise to the level of conscious thought – of her beauty, her even, regular features framed by her fur-lined hood. "He says," she continued, faltering, "that we've got to assume now that it may be something more serious. I mean not just an infected tooth or something… something like that."

"What do you mean… something more serious?"

"I was going to tell you. Tonight. Before bed. Dr. Sacks, I mean, I don't know for sure, we're going to talk about it, may operate where the pain is to see if the problem is in the sensory nerve, the one that gives me feeling. Dr. Tomlinson said that if that happens, once it's done, I won't get any feeling back in that part of my face."

"So don't do it! Why would you do such a thing?"

His grip tightened on her hand.

"Dick… they need to for a biopsy. We can't wait any longer. We've got to find out."

"Oh, Christine!" He eyed her with a look of dismay.

"Don't worry. Darling, don't worry. You worry so much of the time. Dr. Tomlinson says the chances of it being something really bad are remote. We've just got to make sure. And we have to think positively. You must promise me… you must promise me that you will."

They were staring bleakly at each other in the darkness, their faces only a foot apart. This time she detected his Adam's apple rise and fall beneath the loose folds of his scarf.

"I'll try," he whispered. "But of course I'm going to worry. Anybody would. Even you would."

Chapter 2

The Dating Game

1953, 1974

The nagging pain had been there for months. It had started as an occasional twinge, as if perhaps a tooth were not quite right, maybe in need of a filling, or the gum were a little sore. It will go away, Christine had thought. But it did not. It got worse, more persistent and intense, and finally in the fall she made an appointment with the family dentist.

That man examined her and noted that in places the gum was slightly red and swollen, no doubt because Christine was long overdue for a cleaning. Diligently, the dentist scraped plaque from the base of her teeth. He counseled her to take aspirin before going to bed and advised that some discomfort would linger for a day or two. After that time, he opined, she would be "as good as new."

She was not. The cleaning, doubtless beneficial, did not remedy the problem. The family physician, Dr. Tomlinson, had been trained in internal medicine; finding nothing amiss, he dutifully recommended that she see an eye, ear, nose and throat specialist. In due course Christine scheduled an appointment with the specialist who, after a lengthy and expensive examination, said that her malady was in all likelihood an infection at the base of one of her molars. He knew an excellent oral surgeon and gave Christine his name.

That doctor, somewhat baffled himself, made an incision in her gum to examine the root of the tooth closest to the locus of pain. When he looked, however, he merely saw "white stuff" which, he confessed, he had never seen before. His bafflement unassuaged, he closed her incision with a comment that he did not know what was wrong.

The pain continued.

Christine was not a complainer, but neither was she a masochist. Besides, unexplained pain – and particularly pain that intensifies over time – has a galvanizing effect. It stalked the hours of her days.

Had one of her children complained, she would have behaved in a similar fashion. That is to say, she would have initially responded to a complaint about a minor ailment with neglectful concern, but if it persisted, she would have devoted increasing energy to the problem's resolution. She and Dick had two children – a boy in his teens and a girl a half-dozen years younger. Christine was caring and competent. With children she seemed to blend love and firmness with a sure instinct, and other women her age – mid to late thirties, early forties – admired her skill.

She and Dick had married when they were young. They had met when she had journeyed to Princeton for a blind date with a young man who lived in a suite of rooms across the hall from the suite occupied by Dick and his roommates. It was the weekend of the Yale-Princeton football game. Dick had had a date from Vassar, but at the last moment the girl had called to say that she could not come. She was disappointed, but a term assignment, deferred too long, demanded her time.

So, readying himself for an afternoon in the stadium with a roommate who was also without a date, Dick had stood by the second-floor, latticed window of his room watching scattered groups of young men and women depart for the game. Idly, he noticed his friend from across the hall exit through the door beneath him. A young woman was with him. She was wearing a light camel-hair coat, a plaid skirt, saddle shoes and an orange and black scarf that was thrown loosely around her neck. She was laughing, and as she turned to look up at his friend, he observed the fresh, freckled regularity of her features. He observed also the lustrous chestnut hair that fell in waves to her shoulders.

Entranced, Dick watched them stroll down the path, he about six feet tall and stocky in a brown herringbone jacket over a Shetland sweater, and she of average height and build in her coat and Princeton scarf. The leaves had long since fallen from the trees, although firethorn in brilliant hue still climbed the gothic buildings, and they walked under the bare branches in animated conversation; just before they rounded a corner, he saw her pirouette in a laughing circle, the scarf flung out, as she kicked at a clump of leaves.

It was an image that lingered in his mind, as if, at just that moment, it had become embedded in cooling, yet still molten, glass. However, when his friend came across the hall late the next morning to invite Dick and his roommate for Bloody Marys before lunch, he had largely forgotten. With a jolt of recognition, he saw her standing by the fireplace when he entered his friend's living room. A student he did not recognize was talking with her.

Dick walked to a makeshift bar – some bottles and assorted glasses on top of a battered, stained chest at one side of the room – and prepared a drink. Several young women and men were present, casually dressed, the women in plaid skirts, the men in chino slacks, dirty white bucks and, like the women, Shetland sweaters. Without stopping to chat, he proceeded to the window seat that was framed inside a bay window and sat down on a tattered cushion. The light slanted into the room across his shoulder. By habit, Dick liked to survey his surroundings before venturing into conversation. Slowly sipping his drink, he looked about him.

The student with whom the young woman had been talking had moved away. When Dick glanced in her direction she smiled at him, and, embarrassed, he attempted hastily to look away. But it was too late. Securing her drink from the mantelpiece, she walked across the room and sat down by his side on an adjoining cushion.

"Did you go to the game yesterday?" she asked.

"Ah… yes, it was good, wasn't it?" Dick hoped that she did not see his Adam's apple rise slightly and fall as he turned toward her.

"No, I was hoping Yale would win."

"Really? You had on a Prin…"

The young woman looked at him keenly and then laughed. "Were you… did you see me at the game?"

"No, I was… I was standing by my window and saw

you leave." He smiled, trying to hide the fact that he was flustered. "So," he ventured more boldly after a moment, "like some sort of traitor, you went under false colors and probably even cheered for Princeton."

"I did nothing of the sort. I was on the Princeton side under duress."

"What kind of duress?"

"Your friend, Tom, bought my ticket, the scarf and dinner."

"Oh."

They both laughed.

"And may I ask, what caused this wrong-headed allegiance?"

"You may ask."

He waited for her to continue, but she did not. A slight smile curled her lip.

"Okay, okay. Let me start over. Why did you root for Yale?"

"My father went there. We've always rooted for Yale. In fact we particularly don't root for Princeton. No offense, we just don't."

"I'm a little hurt," he responded, "but don't worry about me, I'll get over it." Dick made a face and clutched lamely at his heart. She giggled. In teasing banter, he continued, "Do you come with a name? Is there a label on the package? I mean, when people yell at you, how do they get your attention?"

"People don't yell at me. But when they're proper and respectful, they call me Christine."

"My name is Dick. Dick Blodgett." He took a sip of his drink, and she did the same with hers.

"And when you go home, Miss Christine daughter-of-a-Yale-graduate, where do you live?"

"We live in Scarsdale. How about you?"

"Northern New Jersey." He hesitated, not wanting to name the town. Perhaps, he thought, she's never heard of it, but if she has, it's not Scarsdale.

"Of course," Christine giggled again. "New Jersey! I might have known." She uttered this remark as if it explained everything.

Dick looked at her quizzically. "Might have known what? Is there something about people from New Jersey? A stripe, maybe, or a tell-tale left foot?"

"Yes."

Christine sat near him, almost prim in her erect posture. She was toying with her glass, and a smile played upon her features.

"You can't just say 'yes.'" Dick was intrigued. "You have to give a reason."

"No, I don't. But I'll give you a hint. There is something terribly odd about your left foot."

Again, they both laughed. The game of finding out continued, the probing banter to assess compatibility. Yet if on the surface like a game, played over and over in countless encounters, it contained a biological imperative. Dick discovered that Christine's father was a stockbroker, indeed the head of his firm on Pine Street, one block from Wall Street. Christine's focus was on Dick, not his family. Had she inquired she would have discovered that his father was a research engineer at the Bell Telephone Laboratories in Whippany, New Jersey, and that he was attending Princeton on a partial scholarship.

And had she mined even deeper, Christine would have struck a hard, hidden vein of insecurity. Gifted with intelligence and charm, Dick had worked hard to be accepted at Princeton. His life was forfeit to achievement awards, to applause for able performance, and not to an easy comfort with himself. High school had been an uphill race for the very top grades. Recognizing his intellectual ability and the similar ability of his brother, his parents had encouraged – even demanded – outstanding achievement. Luckily or unluckily, he had been able to comply. But at Princeton the hill had become steeper and the best grades more difficult to attain. Moreover, he could not remake his past. Dick could shed his loud ties and jackets with too-wide lapels for conservative attire, but he could not shed his middle-class origins, his limited allowance, or his lack of a prep school background. At Princeton in his day, such things mattered.

"Do you…" Dick inquired, "do you go out with Tom very often?" Tom was the student who lived across the hall, the one who had taken Christine to the game.

"No. I hardly know him, and to be honest, I don't think he likes me that much."

"Why not? I would think…"

"I agree with you," she interrupted, flattered by his evident admiration. "Our mothers play golf together, and he as much as confessed that he had to invite me and buy that silly scarf. I'll give it back. He's very sweet, but not my type."

Dick was impressed by her forthright honesty. It was her beauty that had first attracted him, a visual assault upon his senses. But it was the person who now compelled his attention: the directness, the laughter, the firm clarity of her opinions.

"You didn't tell me… I guess I didn't ask… where do you go to school?"

"Aren't you assuming that I do?" Christine glanced at him with amusement.

"Well, yes, I guess I thought… I mean, do you?" Again, Dick was flustered, continually thrown off balance. He surveyed his now empty glass in an attempt to disguise his confusion.

"Let me get us another," Christine said. She rose and crossed the room to the makeshift bar, threading her way past chatting couples. In three or four minutes she returned and sat again by his side. "The answer to your question is that I go to Mount Holyoke."

"Oh. What year?"

"Junior."

"Me too." Dick sipped his drink and made a wry face. "Wow! That's strong. Did someone bump into your elbow or something?"

"That's the way we make them in my family," she said matter-of-factly.

"I'm surprised anyone ever makes it to dinner." He laughed to dilute the sting of his comment. A friend approached and interrupted with a question. In all likelihood he wanted to be introduced to Christine, but neither of them moved to offer him a seat. After an awkward interlude, unable to penetrate the intensity of their conversation, he moved away.

"Well," said Dick, "if Tom wouldn't mind, maybe you

and I could meet in New York." I could swing it, he thought, if I get that job delivering mail at Christmas. "It's sort of halfway in-between. Or... I could drive over at Christmas... over to Scarsdale."

"Where... what would we do in New York?"

"Go to the theater or something. Just have a nice time. You could come down from Mount Holyoke on a Saturday, and I'd come up. We could meet under the clock at the Biltmore."

"I don't think I could do it before Christmas," Christine said slowly, weighing his suggestion. She brightened. "I have another idea. There's a party at our club every Christmas. You could join me if you'd like. It's lots of fun. My parents would pay, so all you'd have to do is wear your tuxedo. Do you dance?"

"Yes. The tuxedo's the hard part," he said truthfully. "I guess I could rent one."

"Oh, please do! I'd love to have you join us."

Chapter 3

A Fumbling Start
1953–1954

Dick rented a tuxedo and he went to the dance. Following Christine's directions, he drove with muted apprehension along a winding road, large houses on either side set back amidst tall trees, until he came to a dense bank of rhododendron with a small, unadorned sign – Haskins – tucked into pachysandra at the foot of a driveway. It was dusk, and he was fearful he would lose his way in unfamiliar surroundings. A film of snow dappled the leaves of the bushes and the sides of the road, but the bony branches of the trees, a spiderweb of black against the gray sky, had been whipped bare by the wind.

He turned into the driveway with relief. A large, half-timbered house was visible, brightly and cheerfully lit in the gloom, and the long driveway, edged with laurel, curved to it at one side of a spacious, frost-hardened lawn. In such surroundings, Dick fretted about the appearance of his rusted Ford. But he need not have worried. Christine's parents greeted him warmly – he was, as yet, too unsophisticated to detect their practiced charm – and Christine was genuinely delighted. The downstairs rooms were filled with tasteful decorations, and Dick was invited to share a drink before a fire in the living room before departing for the Haskins' club.

To reach that room, he had to traverse a rectangular central hall covered for most of its thirty-foot length by an ornate, oriental carpet. At one side, through half-opened French doors, he glimpsed the rich sheen of a cherry-wood dining room table. On it, amidst sprigs of holly, were silver candelabra; to one side was a large, antique sideboard with red candles at either end in matching, fluted candlestick holders. A painting of an ancestor, his jowls florid with Christmas cheer and illuminated by a small spotlight recessed in the ceiling, hung on the wall between the candles.

For a fleeting moment Dick reflected on the spare dining area in his parents' split-level home. He walked into the living room through another set of French doors on the opposite side of the hall. His first impression was of a Christmas tree decorated with small white lights that stood in the corner of the room. It was ten feet tall, and the glittering star at its apex reached to the middle of ornate molding that girdled the ceiling. Two couches faced each other by the fire, separated by a glass-topped coffee table with burnished brass legs, and two additional couches lined the wall opposite the fireplace. Across the broad, carved mantle were boughs of pine with small ornaments tucked in the needles. Assorted tables, lamps, paintings and an easy chair in a corner completed the room.

"I hear you met Christine at the Yale-Princeton game," the host said affably as he poured himself a generous drink from a crystal decanter. "What'll you have?"

"I'll take the same," Dick answered, not sure what the brown liquid might be. "We call it the Princeton-Yale game," he ventured.

Mr. Haskins glanced at him keenly for a moment, then chuckled. "Ah yes," he said, "Christine tells me you attend a college in New Jersey." He dropped two ice cubes into an old fashion glass. Dick noticed that, unlike his own father, his host poured liberally from the decanter without measuring the amount.

"Water?" the older man asked.

"Yes, sir."

"Call me Bob. Everyone calls me Bob."

"Yes, sir."

Mr. Haskins added a dollop of water from a small, crystal pitcher. A tall man, handsome in his tuxedo and lean despite his age, with a full head of well-trimmed, white hair, he was seated on one of the couches by the fire. The glasses, decanters (a matching set of three), ice bucket and pitcher were on a large tray on the coffee table. He handed the glass to Dick, who had been standing but now took a seat opposite him.

Mrs. Haskins entered the room, followed by Christine. In a striking way, she resembled her husband. Once, it was obvious, she had been extraordinarily beautiful. Her hair, like her husband's, was white but, in her case, tinged faintly with blue. Slender, with erect bearing, and attired in a simple, black gown that contrasted with a gleaming pearl choker, she seated herself gracefully near to Dick on the couch. Christine, attired in a similar gown of blue silk with a plain, gold broach at her shoulder, took a seat next to her father. To Dick, no young woman had ever seemed so lovely or so little in need of adornment.

"Barbara and I had planned to attend the game," Mr.

Haskins said. "We usually go with the Allenbrooks." He said the name as if Dick should know them. "I forget. For some reason we couldn't go."

"We had to go to the Lehman's for dinner, dear. Don't you remember how you grumbled?" Mrs. Haskins turned to Dick. "Bob hates politics. It was simply like pulling teeth to get him there."

For a few seconds the name did not register. Then it did. She must be talking about Senator Lehman, Dick thought. They act as if he's a friend. The name had been dropped so naturally, so guilelessly, that Dick never detected the subtle way it was done.

"I understand, Dick, that you're from New Jersey," Mrs. Haskins said. She paused momentarily as her husband handed her a drink similar to his own – and Dick's – and commenced making yet another for Christine. "What town?"

"Whippany."

Mrs. Haskins looked perplexed. "Where is that?"

"Oh, um… near Morristown or Chatham. West of the Oranges. Not far from Mountain Lakes, if you know where that is."

"Yes, we've heard of Mountain Lakes… haven't we, Bob?" She was relieved. At least Whippany wasn't near Jersey City or Newark – dreadful places. "Is it anywhere near Short Hills?"

"Well, maybe a few miles. Maybe a fifteen-minute drive."

"We have dear friends in Short Hills, but we don't see them very often. Terry works in a bank near Bob. I don't suppose you've ever heard of the Rothmoores."

"No," Dick answered candidly, "I haven't."

"Mother!" Christine interjected with a tone of repressed annoyance. "You're giving Dick the third degree. She always has to play do-you-know," she explained to Dick. "In a minute she'll want the names of all your grandparents."

"I shall do no such thing," Mrs. Haskins said, smiling. "I'll wait and ask later in the evening."

"Barbara has to get the lay of the land," Mr Haskins said rather lamely. There was a long pause of reflective silence.

"Have you, uh, lived here long?" Dick ventured, breaking the spell.

"In Westchester County, probably twenty-five years," Mr. Haskins replied smoothly. "We moved up from the city. Got tired of dodging taxis, and we were starting a family."

"But in this house," his wife interjected, "about ten years. We saw it and simply fell in love with it."

"It's... um, very nice." What else do I say, Dick thought. That you just saw it and liked it and so you bought it? Just like that, no going back and looking in the checkbook or figuring out the mortgage? "It's nicely decorated... I mean, I mean with Christmas decorations... not, of course, that the other decorations aren't nice. They're, uh, very nice."

Christine laughed. "Oh, Dick, they've put you on the spot." She could see that he was flustered, and with barely detectable ostentation, she looked at a grandfather clock near the doorway to the room. "Don't you think we should be going? It's getting late."

"Yes, by God, you're right. Let's finish these drinks."

Mr. Haskins tilted his glass, and the remaining brown liquid vanished. He placed the empty glass on the tray. "Dick, you're going to enjoy the dance. And it's a great pleasure to have you with us. I'll get the car and be around in front in five minutes."

He rose and departed through the French doors. Dick heard him rummaging in a closet.

"I suppose we had better get our coats." Mrs. Haskins also rose and placed an empty glass on the tray. Dick had not observed by what process she had so rapidly consumed its contents. Not being able to emulate his hosts, with some embarrassment he placed his own glass, over half full, next to hers. To his relief, he noted that Christine – from natural inclination or politeness to him, he could not tell – also had not finished her drink.

"Bob is right, Dick," Mrs. Haskins said. "We are so pleased that you'll be joining us."

And indeed, if the beginning was awkward, the Haskins' gracious charm and generosity soon made him feel at ease. Served with wine, the dinner was excellent: shrimp cocktails, beef Wellington, cheesecake followed by Benedictine and brandy. Almost as if he were a member of the family, he was introduced to many of their friends. Dick and Christine danced, then danced again, then danced again and again. In the elegant dining room of the club, chandeliers pointed with myriad lights, it was as if, dreamily, they were at some magic ball in mid-nineteenth century Vienna. Dancers in swirling clouds swept past them as they twirled across the floor. Looking back, Dick decided that it was then that they fell in love. Christine never disagreed. They saw each other again during the vacation, and they did, after all, meet under the clock at the Biltmore in late January.

It was not until the summer, however, that they declared their affection for each other. Christine was working as a waitress in a hotel in Orleans on Cape Cod – her mother had insisted that the experience would be useful preparation for 'life', although how and in what way was never made clear. Dick had a job as a lifeguard at a lake in New Jersey, and after work on a Friday in mid-July he drove to the Cape in his old Ford to see her.

He was too tired after arrival to do much but fall in bed in one of the hotel's cheaper rooms. Christine had arranged a day off on Saturday, and they went to the beach at Truro, then to an inexpensive restaurant in Provincetown for dinner. Perhaps Christine had learned something from her summer experience, because she insisted that they leave a large tip. "That's how the waitress earns her money," she explained with feeling. Afterwards, almost aimlessly, they drove back to the beach where they had spent the day.

The sun, sinking in the west, was riding the crest of the dunes as they took off their shoes and began to walk, hand in hand, along the beach. The sand, now cool to the touch, crunched between their toes. Christine was wearing shorts and a light cotton blouse; Dick, a half foot taller, was attired in a blue polo shirt and tan, denim slacks that he had rolled up in order to wade in the ebb and flow of water from the breaking waves. His face, like Christine's father's, was even featured but with contours too large to be pretty. He had an aquiline nose, dark, rumpled hair and eyes that seemed always to change expression – sometimes crinkly with amusement, sometimes dark and flashing, sometimes enigmatic or alight with wonder. He was blessed with broad shoulders, a slim waist and a loose-jointed stride. Christine liked to watch him from the rear, although she would have been mortified to reveal her secret attraction to even her closest friends.

"Let's climb the dunes," Dick said. "We can look out at the ocean from the top."

The sloping wall of sand rose nearly one hundred and twenty feet above them. Dick trotted across the beach to it and started the ascent. Christine walked after him and stopped at the base, a dubious expression on her features.

Aware that she was not with him, Dick turned, sand cascading downward from each placement of his feet. "Come on! Come on! It's already a great view." He was standing at least forty feet above her.

"What's wrong with walking on the beach?" she shouted.

"We'll do that too." He turned and recommenced his climb.

Christine started after him. She had enjoyed strolling by the water, but Dick's enthusiasm infected her. She loved that quality in him – a boyish, guileless enthusiasm for climbing, or walking barefoot in the water, or running, or seeing the ocean, or a valley, or anything, 'from the top'.

The climb was laborious, and when she reached him, panting, at the summit, he was standing at the edge of an alcove carved into the sand by the wind. Coarse grass framed its upper lip and grew in clumps along one side. From this vantage point, unshadowed by the dune, she could see the warm peach glow of the sunset over the wooded, undulating land to the west. She clambered to his side and took his hand again. For a few moments they stood without speaking.

"Isn't it beautiful," he said. "Look. Look how far out you can see the white line of the waves."

"You certainly put me to a lot of work," she grumbled affectionately. "We could have seen the same thing in one of the Provincetown galleries."

"Not from up here. Not at sunset. You can't paint after dark." Impulsively, he sat down at the edge of the sandy alcove, his legs crossed. "Come on. Sit down next to me."

For a moment, Christine hesitated. Then she sat close to him. He draped his arm across her shoulders, and she leaned her head against the side of his chest. In the quiet, breathless dusk, not speaking, they could hear the tremulous murmur of waves breaking along the thread of glistening sand far below them. A gull, with a sharp squawk, slid across the canting plane of violet sky in a long, curving descent to the beach.

Dick could feel the warmth of Christine's body. "Let's lie back."

"I wondered if that was why you asked me up here." Christine searched his face.

"No, it wasn't. But you feel good next to me."

Dick leaned forward. "May I kiss you?"

"You're not supposed to ask. What if I say no?"

"I don't think you will." With that, he placed his lips on hers. Christine sat rigidly, then slowly placed her arms around his neck. Gently, Dick pushed her back until they were both reclining next to each other. Still kissing, the lips and tongue of each caressed the other. He paused. She pulled his face toward hers, and they kissed again with mounting intensity.

Dick rolled his body half on top of her. "Oh," he murmured, "this feels wonderful." Against the bare backs of her legs, the sand, so unlike midday, felt chill and cold. He slid his hand from behind her back and held it by her side. Did she flinch? He did not think so, and after a minute he moved it further, next to her breast, then on it, cupping and fondling first one, then the other. Dick shifted his hand again, downward across her belly.

"Wait," Christine implored, catching her breath. "I'm not… I'm not sure you should do that."

"Let me. Won't it feel good?"

"That's the problem. I'm not sure I'll be able to stop."

"Let's not stop."

Both were panting. His hand moved upward again and, fumbling, he began to unbutton her blouse. Briefly, she stopped him, but when he persisted, she did not resist. With her blouse open, he slipped his fingers inside her brassiere, then moved his hand down again and placed it inside her shorts and panties. Again Christine resisted, and again her effort, without conviction, was ineffectual. His fingers probed past her soft, curly hair to the warm, wet, pliant folds of flesh between her legs.

And all the time, they kissed. Dick rolled to one side and, unbuttoning his trousers, pulled them down and off together with his underpants.

"Feel me too," he gasped.

"No… no, I don't want… no, not right now, darling."

"Then let me feel myself next to you." He released the

top button of her shorts and began to pull them down her legs.

"Dick… Dick, I don't think…"

"It's okay… it's what… it's what we should do."

She looked at him, her chest heaving and her expression a mixture of passion and consternation. "Dick, I don't think we should do this." With both hands she held fast to the top of her shorts.

"Why not?" His tone was one of pained urgency. "It's not as if we don't love each other. It's what… people who are in love act lovingly to each other."

"I know. And I do love you. It's only…"

"Only what?" Her grasp loosened as he pried her fingers away. Swiftly, he pulled her shorts and panties down and off. She had sat up. He was hardly experienced, and he turned to unhooking her brassiere. But his efforts were uncertain and clumsy. After several moments, with a muted laugh, Christine reached behind her back and undid the clasps. Then she fell back with Dick, his body touching the length of hers, on top. His tongue was in her mouth. Her arms were around his shoulders, and she arched her slender body to feel the hardness of him. Together, kissing with shortened breath, they swayed in unison. It was only a slight shift of his pelvis, a hesitation as she moved, and he found the opening. The motion was so swift that, even had she wished to object, there would have been insufficient time. With a rapid thrust, he forced the passage.

Christine grimaced and uttered a cry of pain. "Stop. Stop it! It hurts. Please. Please, come out!"

Reluctantly, in confusion, he withdrew. "What's wrong?" He looked at her in bewilderment.

"It hurts."

"I'm sorry. I didn't mean to..."

"I know... it's just... oh, Dick, we shouldn't have tried."

"Yes, we should have." He adjusted his weight to one side and slowly sat up, hesitant to resume but unwilling to abandon his desire for her.

Christine had turned away, but he pulled at her elbow, and, resisting, she rolled back. Still panting from their recent exertion, she looked at him forlornly. Her hair hung in disordered strands across her shoulders and around her face.

"We shouldn't have," she repeated, shivering. "I wasn't ready. Maybe... maybe another time. It's supposed to be..."

She stopped and placed her hand between her legs, withdrawing it quickly. "Oh God. Dick, do you have a handkerchief? God, what a mess. I think I'm bleeding."

He fumbled in the rear pocket of the trousers lying next to him on the sand and handed her a folded square of white cloth. She took it gingerly and turned away again. After several moments Dick, reclining backward, pulled on his underpants and pants, stood up, and walked to the side of the alcove. Standing at the lip looking seaward, his ardor ebbing, he attempted to ignore Christine as she also dressed and carefully rebuttoned her blouse. Neither spoke, and she continued to sit where they had been, her head bowed.

After several minutes had passed, Dick turned. Thinking that she was crying, he walked back and, crossing his legs, gracefully lowered himself to a sitting position beside her.

"Are you all right?" Gently, he placed his hand on her arm. This time there was no mistaking her flinch, and she jerked it away. The only sound was her quick, labored breathing, that and the low growl of the surf and the shrill note of a bird from far across the dunes.

"It's okay, Christine. I understand. It'll be better next time."

Her silence continued. The dusk had deepened, and the dark expanse of ocean had begun to merge with the sky.

"Christine, don't be upset. I didn't mean to hurt you."

"Next time?" She spat out the words as if she had never heard his intervening remark. "Next time? We were having fun, and you got me up here on purpose for this, didn't you. You did this… it's all your fault, you and your, 'let's climb up the dune,' as if I shouldn't have known better. I should never have listened to you. I hate you. I hate you for this!"

Dick stared at her.

"Didn't you do this? We could've walked along the beach… or gone back to the hotel… is this what you do with all the girls you go out with? Don't you think we could have waited and done it properly, or just talked it over first?"

"Look, I said I… what do you mean talk it over first? What am I supposed to do, send you an engraved invitation? If I did that, you'd be criticizing me the other way around."

Christine was staring at the sand in front of her. She dug at it with her hands, angrily sifting the grains back and forth between her fingers. It was cold to her touch. Still breathing heavily, she said nothing.

Dick's body was rigid, his scowling features immobile as he looked moodily at the gathering darkness beyond the crest of the dune. Had Christine seen the line of his jaw, she would have observed it clench convulsively, involuntarily twitching.

"I'm sorry you feel this way," he said finally, clipping his words. "When you feel like it, perhaps we should be going."

Christine turned and looked at him. Her face was distraught. In a low voice, she said, "I wasn't very good, was I?" She continued to sift sand between her fingers.

For a moment Dick failed to adjust to the shift in her mood. He had started to rise, but she restrained him by holding his arm. Her eyes met his. He could not tell; the light was too dim. Had she been crying?

"I'm sure the others are a lot better."

"Christine, what others?" His voice was low, almost inaudible, but emphatic in its conviction. "There are no others."

She read his face intently. "Dick, we didn't use any birth control."

"It'll be all right. I didn't do anything. I didn't have time." He snorted in a whispered amalgam of bitterness and growing tenderness, ashamed that for a moment he had not understood, had lost his temper.

"You don't know that," she replied. "It can happen… and it's the middle of the month."

They looked at each other in silence. "What will we do if I get pregnant?" She asked the question, not to him directly but in a subdued voice to the blankness before them.

"You won't tell your parents, will you? Please don't tell them we did this."

"I'll have to, if something goes wrong."

He clutched at her. "No. Please."

"Why does it bother you so much?"

"I don't know… it just does. They wouldn't like me."

"Oh, Dick, you always want to be perfect. My parents adore you. Let's not worry. As long as you say there's no one else."

"No, Christine. I thought it was obvious. I'm in love with you… I really am."

He started to rise, and this time she did not stop him. With a stifled grunt, he pulled Christine to her feet beside him. A slight breeze riffled the grass and brushed his hair. In the lavender-ink emptiness above them, a dusting of stars had begun to emerge.

Christine put her arm around his waist. "Dick, I love you too. And I'm sorry for what I said. You have to realize that. I was angry… I didn't understand. I didn't mean it." She tiptoed upward, kissed his cheek, then took his hand. "It's time we were going back. I may need your help getting down the dune."

Chapter 4

Wedding Vows

1955

Less than a year later, shortly after their graduation from college, Christine and Dick married. Several months before, Christine had insisted that the pin Dick wanted to give her was insufficient evidence of commitment, and so they agreed to become engaged. Her parents gave their full support, and Dick was swept along by the lavish engagement party at their house and then by plans for the wedding. Dick's father questioned whether his son was ready, whether he was mature enough, but once having made a commitment, Dick felt honor-bound to continue.

Once committed to marriage, however, Dick had become prey to doubt. Is she the best for me? He had inquired of himself in a recurring torment of self-interrogation. He had striven to excel for so long that the habit invaded even the promptings of his heart. In a hidden corner of his being, acknowledged but unexplored, he knew that Christine's social position and her family's prominence had influenced his acquiescence to a decision made more by Christine than by himself. He loved her. She was right for him. And yet... and yet, was it Christine the person that he loved, or, though he would not have admitted it, was it Christine the personification of his striving? And if the latter, was she the best? So doubt, the uninvited, unwelcome companion of his drive for perfection, came to infect his waking moments.

And then mere doubt had been obliterated by panic. The engaged couple had attended a dance, and a friend had asked Christine to join him on the dance floor. Dick had thereupon asked that young man's date – a tall, willowy woman with raven black hair – for a dance. She had accepted, and as their bodies touched, and he held her, and he heard her lilting laugh, he experienced a surge of intense desire. Confused, trembling, he returned with her to the table. He wanted her. God, he wanted her. But he must not. In weeks he would be married. How could he marry when he desired another woman so badly? The fear spread in rapid, unobstructed waves throughout his being.

Dick steeled himself. He had made a promise, and he would see it through. No other course of conduct was honorable. His duty was clear, and he was not going to disgrace himself, Christine or their families by backing away. Nevertheless, despite his resolve, he felt compelled to seek help, solace, advice, and without an alternative, he confided his fears to Christine. If she was to be his confidant, she must be his confidant in all things. He had always discussed his problems with his mother. Now, he thought, it must be with the woman about to become his new wife.

"Do you think it's normal," he had asked, desperate for an answer yet embarrassed by the question, "to be getting married and yet, sometimes, you know, have sexual thoughts about others? Do people do that?"

"Dick," Christine had said soothingly, taking his hand,

"you worry too much. I don't know, sometimes you seem so interested in sex, and sometimes you seem to want some kind of sexless perfection. It's not possible, darling. We're sexual beings. That's the way God made us. You can't want me in particular without wanting women in general."

"But is it wrong?"

"No. I do it, too. Everybody does. If you must know, I liked it when George asked me to dance. It felt good. Why shouldn't it? Put those worries in a garbage can and throw them off a bridge into a river."

He tried, unconvinced, to follow her advice. Nonetheless, her confidence and good sense had a calming influence. And as the wedding approached he grew less apprehensive, swept up in the excitement of the preparations. Gifts began to arrive at her house, often several in a day. Some were inexpensive and practical: lamps, bowls and bookends. But others were expensive and elegant, befitting the wealth of the many friends of Christine's family: goldleaf china, silver trays and antique furniture. Christine was delighted, Dick dazzled, as an upstairs bedroom filled with the treasure trove.

They had decided to hold the reception at her parents' house. And why not? In size it rivaled a club with spacious grounds. Two days before the event, workmen swarmed about the place, clipping hedges and manicuring flower beds. An enormous tent was erected in front of the house – in appearance much like a king's pavilion – with a covered walkway to the French doors at the end of the central hall. It would be proof against inclement weather, although none was expected.

On the day before the event trucks arrived with tables

and chairs that were set up by a team of men inside the tent and in the rose garden at one end of the house. Then cases of liquor and soft drinks were carted to locations within the house and to a long table at one side of the pavilion. In the meantime, two maids dusted and cleaned until the interior furnishings gleamed, and the kitchen began to fill with trays and plates and assorted glasses. Not until the morning of the wedding was the food expected to arrive – a mountain of hors d'oeuvres and sandwiches and shrimp and cheese and crackers and salad and, of course, a gigantic wedding cake.

The wedding itself took place in Saint Anne's, the local Episcopal church. Every pew was filled. Christine wore a gown of white lace that had been worn by her mother at her wedding years before. It fit snugly at the waist, accentuating Christine's slender figure, and its elegant whiteness emphasized her cascading, chestnut hair. The bridesmaids wore pink chiffon dresses, with a light floral print of yellow and blue, mimicking the season of the year. It was a Saturday in June, warm and crisp without a cloud in the sky.

Dick, dressed uncomfortably in a morning coat, waited for his bride at the head of the nave. Next to him stood his best man, his older brother, David. His fears had departed in the excitement of the occasion, and as he glimpsed Christine walking up the aisle, her hand linked to her father's arm and a shy smile on her face, he experienced a surge of joy. The minister, in his silken vestments, also stood waiting. As Christine drew nearer he motioned Dick forward, and Christine's father stepped backward and to the side.

"Dearly beloved..." the minister began. He was a tall, bird-like man with a sharp, pointed nose, and the wattles on his neck seemed to droop to his collar. But his voice carried across the vaulted enclosure. "We are gathered together in the sight of God to join this man and this woman in holy matrimony." They were a handsome couple, Christine, standing stiffly at attention, her even features composed, her eyes on the minister; Dick, taller and trim in a similar attitude of attention, his chiseled face turning first to the minister, then to Christine, then resolutely forward. In her white wedding gown and his dark jacket and trousers, they were a stark contrast in white and black. The minister, his opening remarks concluded, motioned the bride, groom and two attendants to the altar rail to repeat their vows.

"Do you, Christine, take this man..." Her voice in affirmation was soft but steady and clear. "And do you, Richard, take this woman..." Without hesitation, he swore to stand by her, "in sickness and in health, for better or for worse, as long as ye both shall live." Christine and Dick were both twenty-two years old. They exchanged rings, he fumbling slightly to place hers on her finger. The assembled congregation looked on and heard, "I plight thee my troth... till death us do part..." Then followed organ music, swelling past the clerestory to the vaulted ceiling, and the recession and laughter and hugging and shaking hands outside the church.

The reception afterward was a blur of activity. There was a receiving line in the rose garden, and it took over an hour for the four hundred guests to walk down the line and murmur, "Best wishes," and, "Congratulations," to the bride and groom. Pictures were taken of the wedding party, the families and newlyweds. Most of the furniture had been removed from the living room, and a combo played dance music in the corner. As was customary, Christine and Dick danced first, then Dick danced with his mother and new mother-in-law. Christine danced with her father. The floor became crowded. The young couple walked to the tent to greet relatives and friends. And soon it was time to cut the cake and make ready for departure. A large limousine had arrived at the door of the house.

Christine's father approached Dick.

"Before you go upstairs to change," he said, "I'd like you and Christine to come with me to the den."

They traversed the dining room and entered a small, adjacent room. The walls were lined with books, and there was a low, stone fireplace at one end. Christine's mother was already there, waiting.

Dick was baffled. What was going on? Had he done something wrong? Were they about to receive a gift?

Bob Haskins reached for a book on one of the lower shelves of a bookcase near the fireplace. It was a bible. He opened it to the beginning, where there seemed to be inked-in names in a genealogy of sorts.

"This is our family bible, Dick. Barbara and I have our names in here, and the date we married. I'd like you and Christine to each write in your full names and then you, Dick, put the date of your marriage underneath."

Christine giggled. She was still holding a glass of punch. "Which name do I use? It's going to be so strange being Mrs. Richard Blodgett." She squeezed Dick's arm.

"Use your maiden name, dear," her mother told her. "If you look, you'll see that's what I did."

There it was: Barbara Emily McWalter, and under the name a date: September 15, 1927. Dick peered at the page. He saw that there was space for 'Issue of the Marriage', but the thought of children was far from his mind. He wrote his full name, Richard Perkins Blodgett, and next to it, in a round script, Christine wrote hers: Christine McWalter Haskins. Underneath, Dick wrote the date: June 27, 1955. The small ceremony was complete.

"We're so pleased, Dick, and proud, to have you as a member of the family." Barbara Haskins spoke, not quite concealing the glisten in her eyes.

She kissed his cheek, then kissed her daughter. "She speaks for us both," Bob Haskins said. "And remember, and I mean both of you, that marriage is a sacred covenant." He paused. "There is something else." Reaching inside his jacket, he withdrew a long, white envelope that he handed to Christine. "Here's something to help out as you get started," he said gruffly. "You can open it later." He embraced Christine, then shook Dick's hand. "Wonderful, wonderful wedding… well… it must be about time that you two were leaving."

They opened the envelope in the limousine on the way to the Waldorf Astoria. Inside was a check for ten thousand dollars. After they arrived, scattering remnants of rice on the pavement, they decided to take a walk in the city. It was not late, perhaps eight o'clock, and they were both excited and unwilling to stay in their room. Arm in arm, they walked to Rockefeller Center and partook of a late supper in a nearby cafe. Only then, exhausted and tired, did they return to the hotel. The bed covers had been pulled back by an unseen maid, and a mint-covered chocolate had been placed on each pillow. The room contained a large double bed with a gleaming white headboard. In addition it had a white desk and dresser with gold fittings, and two upholstered chairs in a soft floral print next to a large, circular glass table. The carpet in which these furnishings were set was a rich, emerald green.

Christine undressed in the bathroom behind a mirrored door. When she emerged, dressed in pajamas, Dick had turned off all the lights except for a small lamp on the desk, and he was waiting for her in bed. He too had on pajamas. She sat on the bed, hesitating, then slowly swung her legs under the covers and rolled next to him. Quickly, Dick fumbled for her breasts under her pajama top, unbuttoning it finally with impatience. When he placed his fingers between her legs, however, Christine admonished him to be careful. "You're hurting me," she whimpered as her body stiffened. She said the same thing again when he tried to enter her too soon. They did not experiment with different positions; the act was experiment enough, and Dick found release quickly. Christine, puzzled, did not, though she enjoyed their loving caresses; and in the morning, complaining that she felt sore, she declined to renew the activity. Instead, she drained his ardor with her hand.

Loath to rise and see other faces, they ordered room service. When the bellboy brought breakfast, coffee steaming in two Pyrex decanters, they were still in their pajamas. Christine hastily donned a silk bathrobe and ushered the bellboy with his cart into the room. She had requested Eggs Benedict; Dick had ordered an omelet with English muffins and marmalade. They sat in the upholstered chairs, the food before them on the glass table, and enjoyed their first breakfast as a married couple. Both had misgivings about the night before. I hope I've married the right man, Christine wondered, but she kept this fretful thought to herself.

Instead, she poured Dick his coffee and tenderly kissed him before helping herself. They talked about the excitement of the preceding day and the helter-skelter bustle of their arrival at the Waldorf. Christine laughed as Dick described the drunken antics of one of the ushers while Dick was changing for their departure. They discussed, in a more serious tone, the seeming discomfort of his parents, who had appeared ill at ease and out of place at the reception. Just as Dick had done a year and a half before, his father had rented a tuxedo and purchased a white, pleated shirt for the occasion. The collar was too large, which made him seem like a farmer in city clothing. He and Dick's mother had hung back shyly, not moving forward to meet strangers with the sophisticated charm of Christine's parents, and they had even seemed diffident when they were called forward for family photographs.

"We should get going," Dick said at length when the breakfast was nearly finished. "We've got to be at the airport in a couple of hours."

Christine rose and started for the bathroom. "I'm going to take a shower," she said.

"How did I do?"

"You mean last night?"

"No… I meant, you know, at the wedding?"

The question reached Christine as she was halfway to the mirrored bathroom door. "Dick, you weren't taking an exam," she said emphatically. "Darling, I'd give you an A minus."

"Why the minus?"

Rolling her eyes upward, Christine turned, her bare feet sunk in the green pile of the rug. "Because no one is perfect, that's why."

Two hours later, after a cab ride to La Guardia Airport, they boarded a flight for Martha's Vineyard. For all that the world could see, they were a happy, carefree, newlywed couple. And so they tried to convince themselves.

Chapter 5

Carol and Walter Revisit the Past

1970

Carol and Walter were sitting at their kitchen table. The table consisted of varnished pine planks and thick, round legs of Wedgwood blue. It was large enough to seat them and their two children and more besides. They had purchased it two years before in an upscale antique shop that occupied the bottom portion of a red barn on the outskirts of Doylestown, the Bucks County, Pennsylvania, town in which they lived. The shop featured pine tables and cupboards and cane chairs of assorted shapes and sizes along with brown crockery, white porcelain rabbits and, outside on a brick terrace, cute birdbaths and iron patio furniture of metallic gray. It had been, as Carol exclaimed, the perfect place for them to start the renovation of the kitchen.

The job was nearly complete. A linoleum floor had been removed – the task had taken Walter two weekends of backbreaking toil – and a local carpenter-cum-bricklayer-cum-farmer had been hired to install a new floor of Mexican tiles. A country kitchen, that was what they wanted, and so of course a cupboard had to be added to display some of the crockery from the shop. It had been Walter's idea to add both a potbellied stove and a large, restaurant-sized, cast iron Wolf range, coal-black in hue;

and it was the man who laid the tile who suggested breaking out the old, wooden back door and substituting French doors, double-paned for winter, leading to a brick terrace surrounded by yew bushes. For a model, they had returned to the shop to examine the pattern of the brickwork there, and they bought some of the outdoor furniture at the same time.

The result, typical of Carol, was a charming and functional kitchen, a room that could be occupied comfortably by the entire family. They had enlarged it by breaking down a wall to an area that once sufficed for storage. In the new, open space that had been created, Carol had placed an overstuffed sofa with a long, pine coffee table in front of it that was piled with magazines and catalogs of every description. She had wanted a kitchen where people could gather and where, in idyllic contemplation if not reality, she and Walter could sip coffee and read *The New York Times* on wintry Sunday mornings.

Not that the farmhouse in which they lived had been neglected in the process of creating a new kitchen. Carol's energy had also been directed to the living room and formal dining room. Walter had inherited a long mahogany table and sideboard from his parents, who, in their later years, had lived near Schenectady in upstate New York. As a successful accountant, he and Carol had enough money to furnish the remainder of the room with a matching set of antique chairs, and through Carol's family in Ohio they had acquired the prim, gold-framed portraits of an aunt and uncle who had sat for the paintings, veritable symbols of successful, middle-class rectitude, at some time in the latter half of the nineteenth century.

They were an interesting contrast. Carol, in tight-fitting slacks and an open-necked blouse, looked younger than her thirty-seven years. Of average height, slightly buxom, she had a languid, sensuous quality that was accentuated by long blond hair that she wore loosely to one side, usually over her left shoulder. Educated at Sweetbriar College in Virginia, she had acquired a slight Southern manner, a grace in her hospitality and a direct confidence with men. She enjoyed repartee, and her passion was poetry. By the standard of the day she was attractive, not beautiful, but she was invariably an object of attention from the opposite sex at the parties to which she and Walter were frequently invited.

Walter, on the other hand, was quiet, and he usually sought out other men at these social occasions to discuss business. He had met Carol sixteen years before when she was twenty-one and he twenty-nine. Then he had been square set, of above average height, with a keen interest in tennis and jogging. Since that time his athletic interests had waned, his open face had acquired lines, and his once flat stomach had become a protruding paunch. Only his hair, sandy in color, had remained the same with a mere wisp or two of gray at his temples.

Walter had been working in the garden. It was spring, and a fresh pale green had begun to cling to the branches of the trees. Daffodils were in bloom. He had seen pussy willow by a creek near their house only a week before, and a day later he had spied his first robin. It was warm – or, rather, warm by comparison to winter – and Walter had on only a flannel shirt, covered by a worn sweater, corduroy pants and a pair of old, battered sneakers. His hands were brown with fresh dirt.

He had responded willingly to Carol's shouted suggestion, through the open French doors, that he stop for a few minutes and have a cup of coffee. Without reluctance he had thrown down his trowel, batted some lumps of dirt from his knees and walked into the kitchen, first stamping his feet at the door. Two mugs of coffee, freshly brewed, were waiting on the table.

"Where are the children?" he asked.

"They took their bikes. They've gone to the fair down by the library. I gave them each a couple of dollars."

Walter slumped in a chair, took the mug in both hands and slowly sipped. It tasted good, and he inhaled the smell of it. "I thought you were going to join me out in the garden," he said genially. "What's the matter? Drink too much last night?"

Carol gave him a sidelong glance. She too had been sipping her coffee. She lowered the mug an inch or two from her lips and looked at him steadily. "I was in the back room, washing the shelves. It took more time than I thought it would. It's called spring cleaning, Walter."

"No offense. I just wondered where you were."

"Then you didn't need to add that crack about drinking."

Carol sipped her coffee again, and he did the same. For several moments they sat in silence. Walter shifted in his seat, adjusting his chair so that it was sideways to the table, and glanced out the window.

"It's really nice out," he said at length. "You should finish that cleaning and come outside."

Carol said nothing. He tried a different tack.

"That was an enjoyable party last night, wasn't it?"

"Yes."

"You seemed to be the center of attention. But then, you always are."

Again, Carol gave him a sidelong glance. Walter's cheerfulness – was it forced? – annoyed her. She had asked him in for coffee, not ruminations on the night before. But then, they had not had a chance to talk, as he had risen early and was already clattering around in the tool shed when she finally got up to go to the bathroom. They had not, in fact, spoken to each other in a long time, except at dinner with the children present. Was it weeks? Perhaps she had been unwary, inviting him in for coffee with the children gone.

"Is there something wrong with me being the center of attention?" she asked edgily.

"Not at all. Of course not."

"You don't enjoy small talk at parties, Walter. You've said it yourself. Sometimes I wish you did. Just go over to some of the women and ask them how they are. It doesn't take much." She exhaled, then added with finality, "I like it, I guess, and you don't."

"I'm just not good at it. I'd like to be, but it doesn't make me feel comfortable." Walter coughed into his hand.

"Still have that cold?"

"No," he answered. "I don't really think so. It went into my chest, but the cough now is more a habit than anything. If any's left, it'll be gone in a month."

They fell silent. Outside, a robin alighted on one of the patio chairs and cocked its head, first one way and then the other.

"Look at that robin," Walter said.

Carol glanced in its direction, saying nothing. The silence continued.

"It was a delicious dinner, wasn't it?" Walter finally ventured. "But I'd rather sit at a table than balance plates and napkins – and glasses of wine – on a couch."

"You seemed to be enjoying yourself," she responded.

"Well, yeah, sure. I didn't ask Joan to sit next to me. You see, there's an example. If a woman will come over and start the conversation, then I'm fine." He hesitated. "What were you and Joe talking about? You were like a couple of conspirators over there in the corner."

"Nothing. You know what he's like. Why, did it bother you?"

"No, not at all.... But I think it might have bothered Larry."

There it was. The remark, delivered in such an off-hand way, shot like a bolt from a crossbow toward her. She almost recoiled. Then slowly she shifted in her chair, placed her mug of coffee deliberately on the table and faced him. "Are we back to this again?"

"Well, yes. It seems so." Walter sipped from his cup. He had not lost his genial expression. "Or maybe not. It's too nice a day."

"It won't go away, will it?"

"Well, most of the time... I mean, sure, when you first told me, but I tried not to think about it... Carol... it's hard, going to these parties, and knowing other people there know too. Certainly... Larry does, and I think others. And this morning... while I was digging... well, I admit, I was thinking about it, trying to be sensible."

"If nothing else, you're always sensible." Carol frowned. "Maybe it's time we really talked. Now that the bad part is mostly over. You didn't just walk out, is what I mean."

"I wouldn't do that. Anyway, we're all human... me too, you know."

"I wish I'd met her, just once... just to see."

"You wouldn't have learned anything. She wasn't nearly as pretty as you are."

Carol half smiled. Walter's comment was so predictable, as if looks mattered. She reached out and put her hand on his.

"Walter, honey, what were you thinking? I think we'd better talk. This is a good time."

Carol looked at him, almost, he thought, as if she could see through him, could pull parts of him – parts he wouldn't recognize himself – out onto the table. He sighed, his genial expression gone, and looked out the window as if something extraordinary, something fascinating, were happening in the freshly dug flower bed. The robin had flown away.

"I'm not very good at this." He coughed again.

"I know."

She patted his hand, then stopped. Neither spoke. Carol rose, walked to the stove, and retrieved the pot of coffee. She refilled Walter's mug and then her own, returned the pot, and sat again near him without, this time, touching his hand.

"There's sugar on the table," she said unnecessarily.

Walter reached over and pulled the sugar bowl to him. "I need a spoon."

"There's one in that drawer. Sorry."

Walter turned, opened the drawer in the cupboard behind him, and took out a spoon. Carefully, he measured a half spoonful of sugar and stirred it into his mug.

"I guess… I guess what I wanted to know," he averted his eyes, "is why. What I did was so long ago… I thought we'd gotten over it. I never did it again. I was stupid. None of the men I know at the office would have said anything. I just… I couldn't stand not having everything right between us. And this time, I was thinking… if I knew why, maybe we could make everything right again."

"Is there ever one simple reason?" Carol also averted her eyes, and her voice dropped, although it remained clearly audible. "I don't know. Maybe for some people there is. I've… I've thought a lot about it, Walter, trying to get it straight in my mind. Like others, I guess, I thought no one would ever know… that it would be, you know, quick and simple and over." She smiled wanly. "I suppose, in a way, it was, and I… we… were lucky it didn't go any further. I've wondered. Do people try to get caught… leave some clue to get them out of a situation that's wrong? Why else would Larry have left his watch? I'm surprised, I really am, that he can even look at you."

"Carol," Walter said gently, "you're not answering my question. You're saying what – sort of – but not why. I was thinking, if you don't mind my saying it – promise me you won't mind if I just say what I'm thinking."

Carol nodded.

"I was just thinking," he continued, "that you've been more of a flirt in the last two or three years. It's, I think, kind of a come-on. And Larry would be just the guy to respond. He's a real conceited asshole, if you ask me, and God knows he has a lousy marriage. The way he plays tennis… well, anyway, what I was thinking was, why would you need to be a flirt? I mean, there has to be a reason. And then it came to me, while I was out there digging, that… well, of course… I'm older, and after several years of marriage you'd want some excitement, something that says to you that you're still a beautiful woman."

"Oh, Walter, I don't need to know that!"

"Not at one level. You can look in the mirror and see that you still are. But I thought, maybe…"

" I told you, it's not that simple," his wife blurted. "Walter, don't try to find just one reason. It was circumstance… that was a lot of it… and perhaps I was a bit bored, and human beings, I read somewhere, I know it sounds trite, but they need variety. It just caught me off guard, that's all."

Walter looked at her and nodded his head slowly. He rubbed the back of his neck. "I suppose so. I can imagine being in your late thirties and restless and me no longer young and handsome, and…"

"It isn't that."

"How so? How…?"

"It isn't just you being older, Walter, or that we've lived together for so long. Do you really want to hear it? I guess I should say it. I guess I should."

He looked at her dumbly. "Say what? Yes, I think you should. We need to get this talked out."

Carol took a deep breath and faced him. "It isn't just you being older. It's… it's the way you're older, Walter.

Don't you see? You've gotten… well, maybe not fat, darling, but overweight. I've reminded you, but you don't care. You just go and sit in front of the TV and eat crackers and peanuts, and every night – every night, not one ever missed – you have a drink. Or two. Usually two."

"I didn't know it annoyed you."

"It's not that it… oh, Walter, it isn't as if I don't know we're going to get old. And I'm not trying to change you. But you don't… you could, just a little, try to be… try a little to stay in shape… like Joe, or Les."

"Like Larry?"

"Yes, if you have to bring it up. Yes, frankly, even like Larry."

Walter sat quietly, slowly stirring his coffee. His gaze, still averted, was directed at the floor. "I guess that's good to know," he said after an interlude of silence. "It's something I can fix. You should have told me before."

"I did," Carol answered softly. "Maybe just hints, but in lots of different ways."

He looked at her. "Anything else?"

For a moment only, Carol's eyes wavered, but she held them steady. Get it all out, she thought. This is the moment; don't let it pass. "If we're talking candidly, yes, there is more. I'm sorry, I don't want to hurt you, Walter, but if we're having this talk, I guess we'd better talk about all of it."

Walter cocked his head to one side. Did his squinted eyes seem wounded? She could not tell. He had slumped further into his chair, his posture defeated. But his voice was firm. "So say it all," he said.

Her words came in a rush. "You come home, you go

and watch television. Sometimes you talk to the kids. But not much. All you talk about is business. That's all you talk about with our friends, too. Don't you see? It's so dull, Walter. You never talk about what's really going on at work. How you feel and things like that. And, darling, you're so tired all the time. You get home late, night after night. I know you'll take this the wrong way, but you get home late, and tired, and… there's never any time left anymore for making love. Night after night. I know, when people get older, well, we're not that old, Walter. It should be better. And it's not."

"What do you mean, I don't talk about my feelings?" He avoided the comment about his lovemaking – dared not ask, dared not, indeed, ask himself.

"Oh, Walter!" She was exasperated. "What feelings? Sometimes, I wonder. Do you have any?" She looked at him, the expression on her face a mask of pent-up frustration. "Feelings?" As her voice began to rise, he seemed to shrink further into his chair. "Yes, Walter, feelings – not just whether the accounts balance for the day. I mean little things like were you happy, or sad. Did someone annoy you or, perhaps, tell a joke? Things to talk about when you come home and we're having dinner. Things to share, for God's sake. We're not two people who live in a hotel. For all anyone out there knows," she swung her arm in a half circle, "this is Camp Happy Farm. Well, maybe for you it is. But not me. Sometimes I feel like I'm strangling to death in this house. I know one thing. I've decided I've got to get a job, get out the way you do, so maybe I'll be tired, too, at the end of the day."

She stopped. Her expression of frustration was now

forlorn. Nervously, Carol sipped her coffee, but she stared directly at him, waiting for his response. There was none. He, too, sipped his coffee and, once, sucked in his breath and exhaled quickly. His mouth, puckered, was set in a line that curled into his cheek. After a short time, Walter rose and walked to the French doors where he stood, looking out. Minutes drifted by while neither spoke.

Finally, clearing his throat, without turning, he said, "I thought this was going to be a nice day."

"There's no reason why it can't be," Carol answered. "Maybe it will be the best day we've spent in a long time."

"Why?"

"Why? Because I feel... well, sad, sure. And relieved. Relieved, Walter. It's long past time we spoke to each other instead of dancing around pretending nothing has been happening. I feel like I've been a prisoner in a masquerade. It feels good to get it out, to say honestly what's been bugging me. I feel a little like I just crawled out from under a rock, and it's nice to be in the sunshine."

Walter turned around. "I had no... no, I take that back. I knew something was wrong. I guess I thought it would take care of itself. Was it that bad?"

"Yes."

"Then," he said firmly, "we have to do something about it. I do... and you do too." He returned her gaze. "We can end this marriage. I don't want that, and we have children."

"Walter, I don't want that either. Not without trying. We can go for counseling, other people do. There's no reason why we can't."

"Oh God." He made a wry face. "Counseling? Sitting

there and pissing and moaning to some shrink who'll be our friend for seventy-five dollars an hour. I can't stand the idea. Why can't we talk like this?"

"Because you won't talk. You never want to."

"I did this time."

"You had to. The next time – if there is one – you'll run away. That's the way you do things, Walter."

"I won't, if it means the marriage. Come on, Carol, I'll go, if you really want me to.",

She looked up at him, his bulk silhouetted against the French doors, his coffee barely steaming, sitting half consumed on the table. "Would you?"

"Yes. And something more, something that will probably do us more good than talking. You should think about it. We both should think about it."

'What?"

"We should get out of here. I've wondered about it before... after what happened. We should move and start over."

"Why would buying another house help? You mean as a distraction? We have enough to do as it is."

"I don't think you understand," Walter said slowly and emphatically. "I mean move away – far away. Go to New York, or New England. We could even think about going to California, really far away."

"Going to Cal...?" Carol stared at him blankly. "What? Are you serious? Walter, the children are in school. We can't take them out of school. And we love this place. We just started fixing it up, and we have friends here. Look at all the work... Walter, don't be silly. We can't move. You have a job here."

"So what?"

"So… what are you talking about? So plenty what. I don't want to leave my friends. And the kids. They've got friends. Would you just take them away?"

"It wouldn't kill them. Lots of kids do it. Hell, half of corporate America does it, or used to, anyway." Walter left his position by the French doors and strode to his place at the table. He stood, grasping the back of his chair with both hands. "I can change jobs. It would be easy. They're plenty of accounting firms in New York. Or Hartford. I've always thought living around Hartford would be nice. And, you know, I don't even have to quit, just change locations in the company I'm in."

"You've… you've thought about it, haven't you?"

"No, well, maybe a little. Look, Carol, things between us aren't so good. You just said it. You want us to stay here, always reminded of our past, and get a divorce? Would that be better for the kids? Just think about it, that's all I'm saying."

"But," Carol said beseechingly, "I love this place. It's our house. It's our home. Look what we've done with it."

"If we did it once," he answered forcefully, "we can do it again. We own it, remember. It doesn't own us. I could lose weight. We could have a better life. Carol, just think about it."

"I, I… Walter, it's a crazy idea. I will, but it's a crazy idea."

Chapter 6

Unforeseen Trouble

1971

"How was church?" Walter was sitting in the living room in his favorite, overstuffed chair. Loose pages of a financial report with jotted numbers were strewn around his feet and heaped haphazardly on a table next to the chair. Unshaven, still in his pajamas, he was wearing a blue, Scotch plaid dressing gown. On his feet was a pair of worn, fur-lined slippers.

"It was wonderful," Carol responded exuberantly. She had walked into the living room but now retreated to the front hall closet to hang up her coat. He heard her muffled voice as she shouted from the closet: "You should come with me next time."

"I should come with you?" he repeated loudly, making sure he understood.

"Yes," Carol said, as she re-entered the room. "Next time don't be a stay-at-home. It's time you got out and met people." She knelt and picked up the Book Review section. "Anything interesting?"

"Not really."

"Is there any coffee left, or should I make some?"

"I saved you about a cup. Don't get any for me. I've had more than enough."

Still holding the section of the paper, Carol left the

room. He heard clattering in the kitchen and had just begun to resume reading when she reappeared, a steaming cup of coffee in one hand, the Book Review section still clutched in the other. Carol sat at the end of a leather couch and balanced the cup on a pile of magazines on a coffee table in front of her.

"Thanks for keeping it warm."

Walter lowered a page he had started to read, carefully noted his place on it with a stub of pencil, and dropped it on the floor. "So tell me about it. Don't read yet. Why did you like it so much?"

"You mean church?"

"Yeah."

For a few moments Carol paused, reflecting. "Well, for one thing, it's different, but in a way I like. It's simpler, the service, I mean. And the building, too," she added quickly. "I didn't feel as if I had to make a lot of internal reservations, and I didn't have to say words I don't really believe. I hope you'll come with me the next time and see for yourself."

"Are you going to become a Unitarian?"

"Let's not move too fast. Maybe. If I ever become anything."

Carol had been raised an Episcopalian, as had Walter. She had loved the church of her youth. It sat back from the road next to a graveyard from which it was separated by a low stone wall. In the summer, gnarled oaks partially obscured its brown stone, ivied exterior. The building lacked a steeple and had, instead, a square, crenellated tower. As a child she recognized that the architecture of the church differed from other buildings in town, but the difference seemed natural for a church. Only years later did she see it as a tangible, cultural link to an earlier time and different place. After reading English history she never approached the church and its squat, forbidding Norman tower without imagining rough, bearded archers on the battlement in green broadcloth and leather jerkins.

The interior matched the medieval quality of the exterior. The foyer was separated from the nave by low, stone arches. Within, over the congregation, heavy, timbered beams supported the roof. A rose window seemed suspended in the gloom behind the choir, and narrow windows on either side of the pews were checkered with oblong panes of colored glass held in lead casings.

There, in that church, she had sat dutifully as a girl, flanked by her parents, and recited the morning prayer. She had loved the pageantry, the swelling organ music and the hymns. It was in college at Sweetbriar that she had begun to doubt. During vacations at home, when she attended church services, she noticed her growing reluctance to recite the Nicene Creed without questioning its language. Was God really a father? Was Jesus Christ a begotten son? How? Was he born of a virgin? Again, how? Was it necessary that there be a remission of sin? If God made us did He not make the good and bad alike, and, if so, how could the bad not be good if it emanated from God? She began to drift away; by the time she met Walter, Carol rarely attended church except at Easter and, occasionally, on Christmas Eve.

When she and Walter moved from Pennsylvania to Massachusetts, Carol decided that a good place to meet people would be at church. She sat through an Episcopal service with the same old doubts and reservations. Shortly thereafter, she resolved to attend the ten o'clock service at the Unitarian church.

It was, from the moment Carol parked her car across the street, a different experience. Instead of a medieval building, redolent of sin and the decay of the flesh, she was confronted by cool New England rationality. The edifice before her gleamed white in the sun. Of simple, clapboard construction, it stood without adornment, save for its steeple, at one end of the town green. The church could have been the village meeting house, and indeed, in former, less affluent times, it had often been used as such.

When she arrived, a throng of people was ascending the half dozen steps to the front portico and square, dark green front door. She entered a building as different inside from her former experience as the outisde had been. Tall, ordinary windows of clear glass flanked the congregation so that the interior was diffused with light. Greek revival columns, not stone arches, were the architectural motif. The rough, uncompromising pews, however, were still divided into the sections that had been constructed for families in years past. And the altar! It was the altar that interested her the most. Gone were the cross and any hint of elaborate, carved ornamentation in wood or stone. A lectern stood before a curtain. Two plain, wooden chairs were behind the lectern. That was all.

The service, in its pace and style, was plain Protestant. There were hymns, lustily sung. But all allusions to the

Trinity had been carefully excised. This was a house of worship for Deists – a loving Deity, not otherwise described. Its intellectual antecedents were the Enlightenment and the probing, Harvard-educated rationality of post-colonial New England. Carol absorbed its thought and flavor without internal dissent.

After the service, as Carol explained to Walter, the congregation had been invited to gather for refreshments in a meeting room located in a rear wing of the church building that also contained the minister's office.

"I hate that," commented Walter. "Everybody knows everybody else, and you just stand there. Like the stranger you are."

"It wasn't like that. I felt a little uncomfortable, but a nice, older woman came up and talked with me for a while. She was interested in gardening. She had just planted some seeds for a vegetable garden."

"I guess it's getting to be about that time," Walter said. He glanced out the window.

The stark, bare branches of trees were etched against a clear, blue sky. It had been on such a day, almost a year before, that he had first broached to Carol the idea that they move. Finding a position in the branch office of his accounting firm in Boston had not been difficult. Convincing Carol to move had been another matter. She had, finally, relented. The house in Pennsylvania was sold for a profit. The protesting children were relocated to new schools. And Walter and Carol had begun a new life in a harsher clime. At this time of year, in Pennsylvania, the ground was soft and pliable. In Woodbury, their new community southwest of Boston, the fallen needles under the pines were still gripped in slowly melting ice.

Yet they loved the town with its simple village green and quaint shops. Contrary to their reputation for reserve, their new neighbors had been welcoming and cordial. They had found a new house – another structure to renovate gradually – that backed onto a small pond. It was located on a radial street about a half-mile from the center of town.

"Meet anyone else?" Walter inquired.

"Yes, the nicest woman came by and said hello to me. She asked if I was new. I think she'd been talking to some older man over where the coffee and tea were being served, and she was walking past me on the way back to her husband. We chatted for a minute or two, and she asked me to come over and meet the others.

"I went over, and Walter, they were the nicest people, her husband and another couple. They're all about our age. I spoke for a while with the husband and found out that they live in town – both couples – and have children nearly the same age as ours. I'm pretty sure he said his name is Dick."

"New Englanders?" he asked.

"No, I don't think so." Carol sipped her coffee, then replaced the cup gingerly on top of the magazines on the table. "For some reason I got the impression they're from around New York."

"What're they like?" Walter did not want to fall in with compulsively cheerful, churchy people. At root, although he would never admit it, he was a snob. Slightly cynical, well-educated people with money were the kind he preferred.

Carol knew him well, and she guessed the probable reason for the question. "Not what you think," she laughed. "Like us. That was my impression. I do remember her name. Christine. She's the most beautiful woman, very open and friendly with a wonderful laugh. She was dressed, you know, the way they dress in New England. Sensibly, I think I heard someone say. Flat shoes and tweed."

Walter did not disguise his suspicion. "I suppose he was handsome."

"You mean her husband? Not really." She ignored the motive for his comment. "Dark hair. Good looking, but not symmetrical. He was very friendly, and he said he'd like to meet you. He told me to bring you the next time."

Walter made a face. "You know it's not my bag. Maybe once or twice," he sighed, "to get to know people. I'd… sorry, I'd rather read the paper."

"And you should, if that's the way you feel. But the next time, just once. For me, please."

"I dunno." He hunched his shoulders and squirmed in his chair. "Let me think about it. Did this guy say what he does?"

"The way his wife talked, I got the feeling he's a teacher."

"What about the other couple?"

"Very nice, too, but I didn't really get as good a chance to talk with them. She's kind of plump and cheerful, but in a pretty way, and he's very tall. Sort of thinning blond-brown hair. A bit like yours but without gray at the temples. They're from the Midwest. I did ask that. And they've lived here a couple of years. They all acted like pretty good friends."

"Did you get their names?"

"Hers is Alice. I don't remember his. You know how I am. If you're with me next week, you'll remember them."

Chapter 7

A 1970s Conversation

1973

"Are they nearly done?" Christine had shouted her inquiry into the gathering gloom of the backyard. Three men were standing, talking, by an outdoor cooker whose orange coals were now visible in the dark. Two of the men were wearing shorts; all were wearing polo shirts and holding drinks.

"Give me a couple more minutes," Dick shouted back. He began to turn the steaks on the grille with a long-handled fork.

"Don't overcook them," Christine admonished. She had been standing by the open kitchen window, but she turned to busy herself with a large salad she had been preparing. "Would you check the corn?" she said to Carol. "I've got to get Malcolm or Walter in here to open the wine."

"Are we going to eat in the dining room?"

"No, it's too hot. I asked Alice to set up the little tables on the porch. It'll be all right, and a lot more comfortable."

Christine returned to fluffing the salad. In a moment, Dick appeared with a platter of barbecued steaks. "Where shall I put this?" he asked. The other two men had followed him.

"Malcolm, would you open the wine?" said Christine.

"I said, where do you want me to put this?" Dick's question was more insistent. "This platter weighs a ton."

"On the porch."

"Not the dining room?"

"Dick, I said the porch. It's too hot. We'll eat at the little tables."

"I hate those little tables," Dick muttered. But he turned dutifully and proceeded to the porch, trailed by Walter, who was holding a rum and tonic and Dick's tall, nearly empty glass of beer.

It was a hot, late summer evening. Although the temperature had dropped slightly with the setting sun, the air was oppressive, sticky, without a stirring of breeze. In the queasy, green stillness while the men had been standing outside, Malcolm had remarked after swatting a mosquito that he had heard a low muttering of thunder on the horizon.

Carol and Walter had lived in Woodbury for nearly three years. Through the Unitarian church, they had become close friends with Carol's early acquaintances. The families had enjoyed each other's company from the beginning. They often spent time together on the weekends.

Tonight they were at the home of Christine and Dick. It was near the center of town where old, comfortable houses were clustered together on tree-shaded streets. Bushes and hedges had long since provided privacy to each backyard. The wooden house was ramshackle and in need of fresh paint. Dick had become a professor – he taught law at a nearby law school. There had never been sufficient income to furnish their home properly, despite occasional assistance from Christine's parents. A large, screened porch at the rear of the house off the living room was its saving amenity.

Alice had brought two pairs of brass candlestick holders from the kitchen to the porch, and the candles in them burned tall and bright in the sweltering, quiet air. Their glow softly illuminated the gathering. The lights had been turned off inside, except for one in an upstairs bedroom to which their son, feeling unsocial, had retreated.

Dick had placed the platter of steaks on a rough, wooden table at one end of the porch, and Christine and Carol soon followed him with, respectively, a large bowl of spinach salad and another platter heaped with ears of corn. After retreating to the kitchen, Christine returned with sturdy paper plates, plastic glasses and utensils, and Dick fetched beer and two bottles of inexpensive Chianti wine from a kitchen counter. The guests, and then Christine and Dick, helped themselves to food and liberal libations and then took seats in the wicker chairs – a gift from Christine's parents – that were scattered about the porch.

"How can you say he hasn't done a good job?" Walter spoke in the direction of Malcolm, continuing a conversation that had started while the men had been standing by the outdoor grille. Malcolm, with his receding sandy hair and beaky nose, was seated opposite Walter, his long, hairy legs stretched out and crossed in front of him. "He got us out of the war in Vietnam," Walter continued, "and he got us, for Chrissake, to recognize that China actually exists."

"Was it him or Kissinger?" Alice interrupted, defending her husband.

"Oh please. Give him credit for hiring Kissinger. In the end, only one person calls the shots."

"Walter," interjected Carol with exasperation in her voice, "you'd defend Herbert Hoover. You still think Social Security was a mistake – and we don't need another discussion about why Medicare is going to make us all go bankrupt someday."

"On that score, I started early," Dick said quietly. "Thought I'd beat the rush." Carol laughed.

"What I was saying," Malcolm said firmly, "is that there's something about him I don't like. It isn't just that I'm a Democrat and you're not. Well… I'm pretty sure you're not, Walter. I'm not sure about Carol."

Carol shook her head.

"Who did you two vote for?" Malcolm directed his question at Christine and Dick.

"McGovern," said Christine. "And Dick too. McGovern was honest about getting out of the war, and he supported a minimum income for the poor. The American people crucified him for it."

"That's because," continued Malcolm, "Nixon played on the fears of the American people. He told blue-collar workers and the folks in the South and West that all their tax money was going to pay welfare to the Negroes in the northern states."

"Negroes?" Christine laughed. "Oh, Malcolm, where have you been? Could you possibly be referring to Blacks?"

For a moment, Malcolm appeared abashed. "Anyway," he said lamely, "you know what I mean."

Clearing his throat, Dick said softly, "The point is that the middle class is tired of being taxed and then perceiving that their money is all going to social programs for the poor. And they think the more they… or perhaps I should say we… the more we're taxed, the more the Democrats simply start new programs and add to the bureaucracy." Walter nodded his head in assent. "Nixon was smart. He figured out that the demographics of the country have changed. People who vote have moved out of the cities to the suburbs or have gone west where they think there's more opportunity. The old Democratic coalition has…"

"The professor has spoken," said Christine.

"Hey, come on," sputtered Dick. "I had something to say. The old…"

"Don't talk that way." Carol turned to Christine. "I always like the way Dick talks. He has a wonderful way of expressing ideas."

"I know," Christine smiled. "Just kidding, darling. You do express yourself well, always have."

Malcolm had been busily attacking his corn, chewing deliberately down the cob. With his mouth half full, he rejoined the conversation. "Anyway, this isn't where we started when we were talking outside." He swallowed. "I was saying there's something fishy about that burglary at Watergate, and Walter thinks I'm full of it. I think he's wrong. There's something very fishy about it."

"Like what?" Carol tossed her hair as she spoke.

"I don't know. But don't you think it's strange that Republican types should be trying to get into Democratic Party Headquarters? Someone high up had to authorize it. This wasn't some break-in to steal a TV set for drugs. Funny thing, a lot of people were involved, yet the President didn't know about it? I'm not buying that. He's lying."

Walter rubbed his hand over his eyes. "Come on, Malcolm. The President can't know everything that goes on. It would hardly be the first time something's happened like that. You're making too much of it."

"I don't think so," Malcolm grumbled.

"You know, it's interesting," Dick said, "that if it really had been a routine burglary for drugs, no one would pay any attention." He rose and walked with his plate to the table at the end of the porch. "Hey, everybody. There's plenty more of everything. Just help yourselves." Dick scooped some salad onto his plate and returned to his chair.

"Nobody pays attention to anything anymore," Alice said. "Like the Kleins separating." A petite woman with blond hair and a pageboy haircut, she bobbed her head emphatically.

"The Kleins have separated?" Christine seemed shocked.

"Yes. I heard a couple of days ago."

"Why? They seemed so happy together." The tone of Christine's voice conveyed her distress. "And they have children. Are you sure?"

"Well, that's what I was told. Malcolm heard that Bud was having an affair with his secretary."

"Oh God! How disgusting."

"Why is it disgusting?" Dick barely concealed his annoyance. "All you saw was their public face to the world. You don't know what was going on behind their bedroom door."

"It's disgusting because it's wrong."

"Oh, come on, Christine. You kinda made fun of Malcolm because he said the word Negro. Haven't you heard there's a sexual revolution going on? Kids are having sex now all the time without getting married. I saw a dirty magazine at work the other day. I mean, it was all there, nothing hidden, and the guy it belonged to had just bought it in a store. Right out in the open."

"Dick, when a married man has an affair with his secretary, that's disgusting. I'm not taking it back. And with children..."

The group fell silent. Walter fidgeted in his chair and concentrated on spearing a piece of steak with his fork. Alice and Dick sipped their drinks.

"What happened to them?" Carol ventured quietly. "Did Bud move out?"

A pulse of light behind billowing clouds lit the sky.

"Did you see that? A storm is coming," Alice said. "It must be far away. There's no sound."

Several seconds passed. Like the guttural roar of artillery at a distant front, a low, gravelly rumble reverberated in the air.

"I suppose Bud moved out," Carol remarked, rephrasing her question.

"He took an apartment in Boston," Malcolm said. For a few moments, the group fell silent again. Then Malcolm resumed speaking. "You know, times really have changed, like that magazine Dick said he saw. I've never seen one, and I missed the blue movies in the fraternity I was in. I guess they were illegal. And now look. Bought it on a rack in a store. A few..."

"Which may be good," Walter interjected, "or bad. We were awfully repressed about sex, but I'm not sure it's so healthy to swing completely in the opposite direction. Didn't you do some work with some obscenity commission, Dick? What do you think about it?"

Dick had been about to rise and refill glasses from a jug bottle of Chianti on the table. "I'll tell you what I think while I'm getting the wine," he said. He walked to the table, picked up the bottle, and poured some of the ruby liquid into Carol's glass. "I think it's hard for people in our generation. We grew up with one set of values, and now we're being asked to learn another. I don't mean there wasn't fooling around while we were in college. It's not as if no one ever got knocked up. But abortion wasn't available, or the pill, or anything like that."

"Jesus," Malcolm laughed, "do you remember how embarrassing it was just to ask the druggist for a pack of rubbers? I remember going into a drug store for some – Trojans or something... hell, I only knew one brand name – and some woman walked up to get a prescription filled, and I got all red and practically ran out of the place."

"It must have been mortifying," said Dick, "having to ask for the small size in public."

"Seriously," he added after the laughter died down, "what Malcolm said about buying condoms is exactly what I'm talking about. Those were our values. And if we misbehaved, and we did, everyone knew it was wrong. Everyone. There weren't doubts or gray areas. But with young people today it's all changed. And we look over our shoulders at them and wonder if we missed something."

"You look at women a lot," Alice teased. "Do you think you've missed something?"

"Sometimes." Dick's Adam's apple rose and fell. He cast a sidelong glance at Christine. "I mean, if I were young and single, well, sure, it would be like being in a candy store. Who wouldn't want it?"

"And what about an affair? Like Bud Klein," Malcolm asked. "Would you do that?"

"No, of course not. No." Dick finished pouring the wine and returned the jug to the table. He felt uncomfortably the center of attention. Carol was gazing at him intently.

"And why are you clear about that?" Walter queried. "And yet you say you'd act differently if you were single. Can you really keep those two worlds apart? Isn't that, maybe, part of what may have happened to Bud Klein?"

"Sure, but..."

"Dick, I'm not going to quarrel with what you said." Christine's voice was steady, controlled, on the verge of anger. "We aren't talking about kids in college. We were talking about a married man with children who had an affair with his secretary. That's different... and it's wrong."

Malcolm turned his lanky body in a quarter circle and faced her. "Christine, I think that, maybe, that's the second or third time I've heard you say it's wrong. Flat out. No explanation. Simple conclusion. You're going to have to tell us why you're so sure. What do you mean, 'it's wrong.'"

His last words were nearly drowned by a crack of distant thunder.

"Don't you go to church?" groaned Christine. "How could you even ask?"

"Because I am."

"Because people get hurt, that's why. Sex isn't some kind of toy you can play with for a while and then put back in the toy box. For some people, I suppose, only bodies are involved. The ones who meet in those new dating bars I've heard about. For most people, their heads – and their hearts, too – get involved. Should get involved first, actually. And it isn't just the people who do it. Usually they have families – mothers and fathers and even friends. Everyone is affected. And it's the worst when there are children."

"What if no one finds out?" said Carol. "If the couple just keep it to themselves. If you don't tell anyone else, and so you don't hurt anyone, how can it be wrong? Aren't we allowed to express ourselves in any way we want as long as nobody else gets hurt? And can't people take risks? According to you, no one should ever climb a mountain because if they slip and fall and get hurt, they may bring grief to a child or parent."

"If you climb a mountain," Christine answered slowly, "and if nothing goes wrong, you grow from the experience. You may press yourself to the limit of endurance. With sex suppose no one finds out, then you've still hurt yourself. You've broken a vow if you're married, or you've run the risk of bringing a bastard child into the world, and so someone does get hurt – yourself."

"How?"

"You'd always be worrying that someone would find out. Like my darling husband. He always worries about what other people think." Christine smiled. "Keeps him in line. I'll say that for it."

"Now wait a minute." Malcolm had been leaning forward, listening intently. "You mean to say you can grow somehow from climbing a mountain, but you can't grow from having sex. I'm not buying that. What if you have a lousy marriage? What if you don't care what other people think? And frankly, I'm a little offended that you tie this in with church."

Christine faltered, pursing her lips. "Maybe that was a bit unfair. Sorry, Malcolm."

Dick shifted in his chair and also leaned forward. He interrupted Christine as she was about to continue. "Don't be so fast to apologize. I think I know what you meant. Christine is more of a Christian than I am, so I don't want to put words in her mouth. But I think there is a relationship to church. The first commandment is to love God and the second is to show that love by loving each other. Why? I mean, so what? Why care about others? It's so they will grow to their fullest potential, and if people do the same for you, then you'll grow to yours. When you climb a mountain, you expand your capabilities. When you have sex," he paused, "well, okay, I admit, it may also expand you as a human being. It may also be a loving, creative act."

"Dick," Christine urged impatiently, "come to the point."

"I'm trying to say that with sex we're playing with something that can destroy us as well as make us grow. It can be like wanting Thanksgiving dinner every day of the week. You know, a little alcohol is okay, but overdoing it will kill you. And sex, when it gets out of hand, can rip apart families."

"But," Walter said, "climbing a mountain can also destroy as well as make you grow. Like Carol said, if you fall and kill yourself, children can be left without loving fathers and mothers, yet we permit it and no thought of sin is involved. So with sex it seems to come down to God commanding abstinence."

"Oh, come on. Get off it!" Christine sputtered. "It comes down to commitment. There's no commitment in mountain climbing."

The night was still, as if a shroud had been flung across the earth. The chattering insects had fallen silent. Then a faint, quickening breeze ruffled the air, and for a moment the conversation ceased, as if the small gathering was listening intently for something – something near and ominous.

Malcolm broke the silence. "No commitment? What about the climbers? Isn't there at least an implied commitment among them to protect each other?"

"And then what happens," Dick added quietly, "if one of them has to cut the rope holding another in order to survive?"

Exasperated, Christine turned toward her husband. "Dick, darling, we were talking about the Kleins, not extreme cases."

"But it's an interesting…"

Alice giggled. "My God, this has gotten awfully serious. And confusing. Can't we talk about something else – even football."

"Not for another month," said Walter, as he clutched at his paper napkin. A gust of wind had nearly blown it from his lap.

"You're right, Alice," Malcolm said from across the porch, putting his glass down on a side table. "But I want to come back for just a moment to something Dick said earlier, assuming," he laughed, "that I understood him. He said, I think, that it was easier when we were younger and everyone knew the rules. Isn't that Christine's position? Now we're all confused and everything seems to depend on the situation." He picked up his glass again and sipped from it. "Confused or not, that's my point of view, and until we know more, we should feel sorry for the Kleins and support them. There's no point in…" A flicker of lightening illuminated the porch. "Wow, that storm is a lot closer than I thought."

"Maybe we should go inside," Christine said anxiously. The low grunts of thunder to the west had become louder, and the tops of the trees had begun to sway in sweeping arcs against the dark sky.

As Christine rose, she touched her cheek quickly with her hand. "Get the wine and paper napkins," she cried. The candles had begun to sputter, and she stopped to blow them out.

"Are you all right?" Walter asked.

"Yes… I must have chewed something the wrong way. Would you get that platter with the corn on it and the plastic cups."

A paper plate scudded across the porch floor and slammed into the screen siding where it clung tenaciously.

Grabbing the remnants of dinner, folding the small tables quickly and clearing the dishes from the wooden table, the group stumbled indoors from the porch. Christine was the first to reach the kitchen that was at the other side of the house from the living room and an adjacent front hall. She flicked on the light. Its glow shot out the window into the murk and softly illuminated the way from the porch through the living room.

Carol and Dick were the last to leave. As she brushed by a table next to a couch, Carol turned. "I love the way you talk," she said, placing her hand for several moments upon his arm. No one else was in the room.

Dick saw her oval, upturned face, her blond hair, now wavering slightly in the wind, draped over her shoulder. In his hands he was carrying a stack of plates. He stood, rooted, as if a fragment, a shock of electricity had passed through him from the storm.

"We're going home," Alice yelled as she entered the hall. "Malcolm didn't shut any windows. I hope you guys don't mind if we leave you with the dishes."

"Don't worry about it," Christine shouted back from the kitchen. The entire scene, indoors and out, was lit by a streak of white light. Almost simultaneously, a clap of thunder shook the house.

Walter emerged from the kitchen. "Carol, we're going too. I need to shut the window in the study."

Large drops of rain had begun to spatter the lawn, the paths and the leaves of the trees.

Carol walked to the entrance to the kitchen. "Sorry to leave you with this mess. Thanks for a wonderful evening. Thanks to both of you."

"It's mostly paper. No problem," Christine replied. Dick had entered the kitchen and was standing by her side. "You two had better get going."

The revving noise of car engines sounded through the rain.

Chapter 8

The Pain Continues

1974–1975

The pain was not from something that Christine had chewed the wrong way. Over the next six months – intermittently at the beginning – it continued. And worsened.

She visited her doctor, her dentist, an oral surgeon in Boston, and an eye, ear, nose and throat specialist. As a physician later told her, when you hear hoof beats on Commonwealth Avenue, one does not normally suspect the presence of zebras. The doctors kept searching for a horse, or less likely a donkey or mule. As a far-fetched possibility, an elk or moose. But a zebra? Never!

And yet as options were slowly eliminated, the unthinkable gradually became a remote possibility, something, at any rate, to check off the list on the way to a definitive diagnosis. Dr. Tomlinson, her family physician, recommended that she see Dr. Sacks, a plastic surgeon. An appointment was scheduled. He examined her thoroughly, although from the outside there was not much to see. Then he left her alone in the examining room for nearly twenty minutes. When he returned, white coat open and stethoscope dangling from his neck, he sat down on a stool near a sink in the small room. Christine sat with her legs over the edge of the examining table. Her chestnut hair fell in soft waves to her neck.

Dr. Sacks shook his large head as he frowned at her, puckering his lips. A nurse stood immobile by the door, her emotionless face a practiced mask. "It's hard to know," the doctor began. "I must advise you that there is a possibility that you have cancer. I don't think it's a good possibility, but you did have skin cancer on your lip a year ago. It wasn't far from the site of your pain, which makes me suspicious. Maybe – just maybe – it could have gone inside."

Christine returned his gaze without flinching. "So what do you think should be done?" she asked.

"It's a tough call. If it is cancer we should move quickly. We shall need to take a biopsy of the locus of pain, including the sensory nerve in your jaw. If it isn't cancer – which, as I said, is certainly the more likely possibility – then, well, we'll know it's not cancer, but, for the rest of your life, the lower part of your face on that side won't feel anything. Like novocain, only permanent."

The doctor paused. The nurse standing near him stared impassively at Christine.

"If you had come to see me three or four months ago, I would have been very hesitant to recommend a biopsy with such consequences. But you say the pain is getting worse. Under the circumstances, after this length of time," he cleared his throat unnecessarily, "it would probably be a good idea to make certain."

"What would you do if you were me?" Christine inquired quietly after an interlude of silence.

"I would do it," Dr. Sacks responded. "This kind of

cancer, if it's there, is far more likely in an older person with a history of drinking and cigarette smoking. That's not you. But after this much time has gone by… Christine, if I were in your shoes, I'd get it done. That's my judgment. And I wouldn't delay."

"Then do it," Christine said.

"We shall need to schedule an operating room. I'll ask Nancy," he nodded in the direction of the nurse, "to get on the phone right away. We can probably find time in two or three days or early next week."

"That soon?" For the first time, Christine betrayed alarm.

"If we're going to do it, we might as well do it quickly. We'll get back to you with the time – probably by early this afternoon. You'll need to come in beforehand to speak with the anesthesiologist, and you'll get more instructions then. We'll have to keep you in the hospital for the night."

* * * * *

Dick was sitting at a table in an alcove of the kitchen – a cheerful kitchen, flooded with light through windows on two sides now that the trees were bare of leaves. Following Christine's instructions, he had painted the walls yellow and the cabinets white. Spring colors she had called them. An open cereal box and carton of milk stood on a counter. Coffee simmered on an old, dilapidated gas range, a constant, sometimes irritating, reminder that their renovation of the kitchen shortly after they purchased the house had been largely cosmetic. Christine's parents, however, had provided a new washer and dryer that had been installed beneath shelves in an adjacent pantry.

Holding *The Boston Globe* before him with both hands, Dick had finished his breakfast and had pushed his plate to one side. Befitting his role as professor, he was wearing casual slacks, desert boots and a turtleneck sweater. However, compared to the deliberately ragtag clothing of their teenage son, Allen, who was seated next to him, Dick was a model of sartorial splendor. Christine, clad in a bathrobe, had left the alcove to open a packet of muffins that she had just secured from the refrigerator. The intended recipient was their young daughter, age ten, whose clumping, thumping steps could be heard as she descended the stairs.

Allen was noisily eating his cereal, slurping the milk-covered flakes with each spoonful.

"Why don't you sit up," Dick said after dropping the paper slightly so that he could see above it, "and try to make a little less noise."

Allen ignored him, but he modified the slurps to audible, crunching sounds. Molly entered the room. It was not a sedate appearance. It never was. She half bounced and half walked to the table where she took a seat opposite her father. Dick had always liked the name Molly, and Christine had thought that naming the child after herself would be too confusing. So Molly she had become.

"Oh, Mom! Muffins again?" Molly said plaintively. She had on a skirt and heavy sweater. The house was chilly. Outside, there was snow and ice on the ground.

"You can have cereal if you'd prefer."

"Here, twerp," Allen interrupted. "You can finish mine." He pushed his bowl toward her. Molly made a face. She sighed.

The English muffins, which Christine had placed in the toaster, popped up, and she transferred them gingerly to a plate. Christine had already removed jam from the refrigerator, and she began to spread it generously on the muffins.

Allen finished his cereal. "Mom," he said in a flat voice, putting down his spoon, "what time do you go into the hospital?"

"I have to be there by ten o'clock."

Anderson Hospital was a regional medical center in the next town. It had begun, years ago, as a clinic started by a Dr. Anderson and had grown to service a region comprising several towns southwest of Boston. Serious cases were transferred to the major medical complexes in the city.

"What happens then?" Dick asked, even though he knew the answer. Christine had seen Dr. Halpern, the anesthesiologist, the preceding day and had carefully answered his questions. She had also filled out a bewildering multitude of forms. After returning home, she had been at pains to reassure the children that the procedure was minor, that it was only exploratory, that it was a step toward making her better, and that she would be home again in twenty-four hours. Fidgety, the children had listened to her in silence.

"They'll assign me to a room," Christine said. She handed Molly her muffins and stood by the entrance to the alcove. "I'm told that always takes time. Then I guess

I'll put on a funny gown and wait for Dr. Halpern or a nurse to come and make me feel sleepy."

"What does the gown look like?" Molly chirped.

"It comes to about here," Christine indicated a point about mid-calf, "and ties in the back… if it's like the ones I wore when you children were born."

"Is it a nice color?"

"Light blue or white," Christine told her.

"Mom," Allen queried hesitantly, "why is it going to take so long? What's the big deal? When you saw the dentist, it was just for the afternoon."

Dick had stopped reading the newspaper and was sitting, immobile, listening to the conversation.

"I'm not really sure, Allen. The doctor's going to cut into my gum and look around." Molly scrunched up her face. "They want to really find out what's wrong… where the infection is. They're going to knock me out for it, thank goodness, so it won't hurt." As she said this, Christine looked at Molly. "It takes a long time to wake up from the anesthetic which is why they're going to keep me in the hospital for the night."

"Can we see you?" asked Molly. "Can we come to your room?"

"Maybe. Late in the afternoon. I'll leave that up to your father."

Allen looked at his mother. He wanted to ask again why it was such a big deal. What was the doctor looking for? He did not know. It sounded as if his mother did not know either, and he was afraid to ask.

"Mom," Molly spoke, "will your bed be like the ones I saw on television that move up and down?"

"I think so," Christine glanced at Dick for affirmation.

"Can I work it?"

"Yes, honey, if I'm not too sleepy." Christine moved from the entrance of the alcove to replace the jam and carton of milk in the refrigerator.

"Before you leave the house this morning, Christine," Dick said, "would you take a look at the phone bill on my desk."

Christine turned, the milk carton in her hand. "What's wrong with it?"

"Actually, it can wait. I think maybe we shouldn't go into it right now."

"Maybe we should." Christine's voice was hard and metallic.

"It's too high again. I just want you to look at some of the calls."

"Look at them for what?" Christine spat sarcastically. "So I can find out that I called my mother two weeks ago. The same mother who sends us checks to help us out. Or perhaps I spoke with a friend. Is that what you object to?"

"Hey. Slow down," Dick implored. "I just wanted to..."

"I'll make as many phone calls as I damn well please. If you don't like it, get a proper job."

"God damn it," Dick shouted. "What the hell... what the hell kind of answer is that? You know we can't afford these big telephone bills."

"They're cheaper than a psychiatrist, Dick," responded Christine sweetly, her eyes blazing. "You should look at it that way. And just think. While I'm in the hospital I won't be near the telephone."

"What is this?" He was still shouting. "Is there some

reason you can't write a letter? Poor little rich girl. Is there some reason... some reason you can't help out? And if... if you didn't like me going to law school, you should have said so at the time."

Allen rose from his place at the table and silently left the room. Molly sat still, frozen, staring at her half-eaten muffin.

"Dick," Christine said slowly, quietly, implacably, "I'll make as many phone calls as I please. That's all there is to it. I'm not looking at that bill, now or ever."

Eyes wide, panting slightly, Dick also rose. "I'll see you at the hospital later this afternoon," he mumbled. "I hope it goes all right." Then he too left the room.

Chapter 9

Temptation
1975

In his office that morning, Dick soon forgot the quarrel. Their disagreements about money, though often bitter, were not uncommon.

Christine was cheerfully frugal, but she always believed that wherewithal would be found somehow. Perhaps because of his different background Dick did not share her basic confidence, and he worried about the looming cost of education for their children.

He was glad he was wearing a sweater. The office was situated at the second-floor corner of an old, ivy-covered building, and even with a radiator clanking in a corner, the cold found its way under and around the rattling windows. His desk was cluttered with books and papers, as was a battered leather couch, purchased second hand from a retiring colleague, that filled one wall along with an equally battered filing cabinet.

He prepared for class and met with students in the late morning to discuss criminal law. Thoughts of Christine, now in the hospital, possibly in the bed in her room, continued to intrude. He had been through this before when she had consulted physicians and dentists about her condition, and he was not fearful. Indeed, from what Christine had told him, he looked forward to a firm diagnosis and final resolution of the problem.

Still, this time was different, what with her being in a hospital having an operation. The doctor had called it a minor surgical procedure, befitting its low level of intrusion. He knew, though, that even with the predicted likelihood of a favorable outcome, she would lose sensation in the lower left quadrant of her face. To use Allen's phrase, that seemed like a big deal. And so, while the students had discussed the differences between types of homicide, his mind had wandered to Christine. He thought of her checking in and wondered what her feelings might be as she was wheeled to the operating room. Would she be frightened or, after medication, merely groggy? He did not know, and he longed to be there to provide comfort and, perhaps selfishly, to allay his curiosity and sense of disquiet and unease.

After a late lunch – a sandwich eaten in his office while he tried vainly to concentrate on an article in a professional journal – he went to his car and drove to Anderson Hospital. When he arrived, it was slightly before three o'clock, and he knew the operation had been completed.

A kindly, older woman at a reception desk told him the floor and number of Christine's room. A nurse seated at a station at one end of the corridor informed him that Christine was still in recovery but would be returning soon. Her manner was brisk, impersonal, efficient. She also told Dick that he could wait in the room for Christine's arrival.

He went there and sat down on a chair next to the

bed. Idly, he examined the motel-like simplicity of the furnishings, the sink in one corner, the apparatus at the lower end of the bed which, with its chain and dangling hook, he surmised must be used to hold up damaged or broken limbs. The telephone on a stand next to the bed rang. Uncertain, Dick reached for it and picked it up.

"Hello. Is this Dick?" The voice was Dr. Tomlinson's.

"Yes, how...?"

"I tried to reach you at your office, but you'd already left. I thought you might be waiting in the room. I've had a chance to speak with Dr. Sacks. Can you come to my office?"

A medical office building, which housed the offices of many of the doctors on the hospital staff, was adjacent to the hospital and connected to it by a gleaming, elevated glass walkway. Dr. Tomlinson's office was there, only five minutes away.

"Ah, sure." Dick was surprised by the call and the request. "Is... is everything all right?"

"Let's talk when you get here. See you in a few minutes." Dr. Tomlinson hung up.

Dick did likewise, but slowly. Following the directions of the nurse, he took an elevator, then walked across the glass-enclosed walkway to the medical office building. When he arrived, Dr. Tomlinson emerged almost immediately from his office and asked him to come inside. Apparently, he had been waiting. He shut the door.

"Take a seat."

"Thanks."

"Dick, I have some bad news. I spoke with Dr. Sacks right after the operation. He called me. They did a frozen section on the bit of sensory nerve they took from Christine's jaw. She has cancer."

Dick knit his brows. Despite warning, the news was unexpected. Like an explorer who has sighted an island at the edge of a continent, he neither knew of nor could he imagine the enormity of the land mass that lay beyond. Nevertheless, the name of the disease itself was an alert to danger.

"Are you sure?"

"Very sure. Dr. Sacks is an old hand at these things. The specimen will have to go the lab for confirmation, but he didn't have any doubt."

Dick rubbed his hand across his mouth. "Is it… how bad is it?"

"We don't know. But there's no reason for you to be pessimistic." Dr. Tomlinson's tone shifted from grave to encouraging. "We've caught it early, and that's good. Dr. Sacks did say that a section of the jawbone will have to be removed. Not much, though. Probably no more than this." Dr. Tomlinson held up his hand and indicated a distance of approximately an inch between his thumb and forefinger.

"Won't that disfigure her? Leave a big scar?"

"Not necessarily. The operation could be performed inside her mouth. And reconstructive surgery these days is very good. Dr. Sacks could do it. I recommend him highly, as you know."

The two men sat for several moments in silence.

Dick spoke: "Does Christine know?"

"Not yet. I think it would be best if you let Dr. Sacks convey the news. She should be getting back to the room any time now. Why don't you go and say hello, and then... well, of course you can stay. But I think he may want to speak to her alone. She'll still be pretty sleepy, so he won't get there for an hour or so."

"Can I bring the children?"

"There's no reason why not." Dr. Tomlinson's voice was kindly. "Wait till late afternoon when she's woken up a bit."

Dick retraced his steps, and ten minutes later an orderly opened the door and wheeled Christine into her room on a gurney. Carefully, the orderly assisted her onto the bed. There was no bandage on Christine's face. The operation had taken place inside, and only a fleck of dried blood at the corner of her mouth betrayed the fact that something had happened.

Dick leaned over the pillow where Christine's head lay. Her eyes were half open. The orderly had rolled the gurney into the hall and was closing the door.

"Hi, piglet," Dick said.

She tried to focus on his face. "Hello, you boar," she whispered in return.

It was an old joke between them. Dick took Christine's hand and patted it. A nurse entered the room to straighten the bed and check on the patient. "She'll probably sleep some more," the nurse said.

Dick looked at his wife, so peaceful and unaware. Her eyes had closed. "I'll come back later in the afternoon," he said to the nurse.

"You might as well. She's going to rest for a while."

"I'll bring the children," he added. The nurse nodded in affirmation. "Goodbye, honey," he said tremulously to the recumbent figure. "I'll be back soon." Christine did not stir.

As he walked outside, Dick could not have described his feelings. It was as if, in some strange way, he had been transported from one plane of existence to another. He was dazed, trying desperately to cling to known and familiar parts of his former life. He concentrated on the task ahead: telling Allen and Molly what had happened in a way that would best preserve the continuity of their lives. As yet, he did not – and could not – perceive the impossibility of this goal. A persistent angst tugged at his gut. But at a conscious level, if he was aware of anything, it was the dread caused by the wave of potential change breaking into his life. To the tragic consequences of that change, to the sharp turn his life was taking, he was numbly innocent.

Dick got in his car and started the engine. The noise was familiar. He drove to the high school. Allen was playing soccer on a field ringed with scattered clumps of snow. He was a picture of young, vigorous health: smudged face, bright jersey flapping loose at his waist and heavy wool socks fallen in bunched folds to his ankles. Dick watched his lithe, hard form run up and down the field, his dark, tousled hair so much like his father's at the same age. During a break in the play, Allen ran to the sideline.

"She's okay," Dick said, faltering. "I'll pick you up after practice so we can go directly to the hospital." There was time enough to tell Allen the news.

"Okay, Dad," Allen yelled as he ran back to his position on the field.

Telling Molly, Dick knew, would be difficult. He intercepted her as she was walking home from school. Molly was surprised to see his car stopped by the curb.

"Hop in, sweetheart," he shouted as he pushed open the passenger door.

Her eyes questioned him as she clambered onto the seat. "Daddy," she asked, "why… how did you know I would be coming home this way?"

"I didn't. I just left the hospital and guessed you'd be leaving school. I thought I'd pick you up."

Molly settled into the seat, secure but now uneasy in her ignorance.

"Is Mommy okay?" she inquired tentatively.

"Yes," Dick responded. "She's sleeping right now. I thought we'd go home for a few minutes so I can make a couple of phone calls. Then we'll pick up Allen and go visit her." He was not used to uttering half-truths, even though he regarded an unspoken falsehood as less deceitful than a verbalized one. He squirmed in his seat.

"Molly," he ventured. "Everything is going to be okay. But the doctor found something he didn't want to see. Dr. Tomlinson told me that they found some cancer in her jaw that they're going to take out to make her better."

"Isn't cancer very bad?" The child looked stricken.

"No, no," Dick stumbled, half trying to convince himself. "No, it can be, but not if you catch it in time. Which they did. No… Dr. Tomlinson said she's going to be all right." Again, the thread of a lie, but one he chose to cling to himself.

Molly hunkered into the seat. He pulled the car into

the driveway, and, after he turned off the engine, they both got out and walked in silence into the house.

There Molly dumped a book and her jacket into a cubby in the back hall that was crammed, helter-skelter, with boots, a rain jacket, sweaters, a ball and an assortment of other items. Christine had had a cubby built for each child as a place to isolate and collect apparel and toys that would otherwise have been scattered throughout the house. The idea had been partially successful.

The young girl ran upstairs to her room. Dick, after loosening his tie, walked into the kitchen and picked up the telephone. He dialed a number and waited. Christine's mother answered, and he told her the news, this time accurately but in sparse detail. "I'll be back in touch, maybe tonight," he said in closing, "when I know more."

He tried to reach his own parents, but without success. Next, his brother. They spoke briefly. David tried, unconvincingly, to be positive and encouraging. "Look, Dick," he said. "Concentrate on what the doc told you. He's got no reason to bullshit you, and anyway, most of the time, what we worry about never happens."

"I know, Dave. I know." But his worry persisted. He dialed again.

"Hi, Alice. It's Dick. I'm afraid I have some bad news." She responded, anxious and ready to commiserate. Again, he described what he had been told. Molly was still in her room. "No," he said, "that's very nice of you. But we can fend for ourselves." She spoke in reply, urging him to reconsider her offer to bring dinner. "All right," Dick relented. "That'll give us time to see her in the hospital and not worry about it." He paused, listening. "Sure, ask them to come too, if you'd like. We can all sit and cry together." He hung up the phone and walked to the foot of the stairs.

"Let's go, Molly. It's time to pick up Allen and get going." The girl emerged from her room, ran across the hall, and jumped down the stairs. If she was distressed, there was now no sign of it. His explanation, Dick thought, must have been successful.

"Will she be awake?" Molly asked.

"I think so." Dick took her hand and swung it in the air. She looked up at him. "My favorite daughter," he said with a smile.

"I know, Daddy. And Allen is your favorite son." She ran to the back door.

"When we get back," he shouted after her, "Alice and Malcolm will be coming over with dinner. Isn't that nice? We won't have to do any cooking. They may ask Carol and Walter to join us too."

They fetched Allen at the high school. As they arrived he emerged from a side door, laughing and talking animatedly with two friends. On the way to the hospital, Dick broke the news in much the same language he had used with Molly. Despite the reassurances, the boy's exuberance drained from him. Older than Molly, more experienced, he had more reason for worry and a better facility than his sister for detecting the soft ambiguity in his father's soothing explanation.

Christine was still sleepy when they walked into the room. Dick had cautioned the children in the car not to talk about the cancer until she returned home. They filed silently to the side of the bed, and Dick turned on a bedside light. The room had been dark. Christine, with groggy animation, greeted them and hugged each in turn.

"I spoke with Dr. Sacks," she told them, her speech slightly slurred. "He said I have cancer in my jaw." Forthright Christine was never one to evade reality or gild the truth.

"Oh, Mommy!" Molly cried.

"It's all right, Molly," Christine responded with conviction. "It's the shits, but it's going to be all right. Dr. Sacks thinks we've caught it in time."

Dick took her hand and squeezed it. "We weren't going to talk about it until you came home," he said.

"Why not? It's not something to hide."

"Are you okay?"

"Yes, I really am. It's good to know. Now we can deal with it." Christine looked at her children. "Tell me what happened today."

They stayed briefly. It was obvious she was sleepy, and after desultory conversation Dick suggested that they leave. "I'll call in the morning," he said.

As she kissed him goodbye, Christine murmured, "I'll let you know when it's time to come and get me." Her eyes closed.

* * * * *

Alice was waiting for them in the kitchen when they returned. An aroma of spaghetti sauce filled the room, its source a large pot on the stove. Malcolm showed up shortly thereafter. He had already been told the news, and he shook Dick's hand firmly and silently. Fifteen minutes later Carol and Walter arrived with a long loaf of French bread and two bottles of red wine. They too shook Dick's hand, and Carol bustled into the kitchen with manufactured cheer. In the breakfast alcove, only Molly and Allen sat silently, on the periphery of the activity, unwilling to be alone.

"When's she coming home?" Walter asked.

"Tomorrow morning. I'll pick her up after she calls." Dick opened a cabinet and offered drinks. He poured a liberal portion of vodka into a glass for himself, then rapidly sipped a third of its contents.

"Malcolm, I need some help," snapped Alice. "Would you drain that spaghetti and serve it on the plates."

Walter had fished through implements in a drawer and finally found a corkscrew. He stood by a counter opening the bottles of wine while Carol set the table in the breakfast alcove. Dick felt like a supernumerary, as if, in some odd way, he were a guest in his own home. I'm not the patient, he thought. He fetched a breadboard from a lower cabinet filled with trays and selected a long knife from a drawer. But at that moment Carol returned, having taken the bread from the oven.

"Here. Let me have that," she said to Dick. She took the knife from him. "You go and sit down. Dinner will be on the table in a minute."

Obediently, Dick walked to the alcove, his drink in hand, and pulled out the chair next to Molly. This is going to be like a funeral, he thought, all activity for two or three days and then silence. Nevertheless, he did not resist.

Malcolm began putting plates heaped with spaghetti at the places set at the table. It would be crowded. Walter followed with glasses filled with Cabernet Sauvignon and one bottle, still full, which he placed in the center. Next to it, Alice plunked down a large bowl filled with spaghetti sauce. There was no room for the bread, so Carol cut individual slices for each plate and returned the breadboard to the top of a cabinet in the kitchen. She came back to the table. The others were already sitting down.

"Will someone say grace?" Walter asked.

"Malcolm, you do it," Alice urged. Again, Dick felt like an invited guest. The assemblage bowed their heads and held hands.

Malcolm cleared his throat. "Father," he mumbled, "thank you for this food and this fellowship. And thank you for all the blessings of this day." Aware that the remark might seem inappropriate, he hurried on. "And bless Christine… and make her well, and bring her back among us soon. Amen."

Everyone looked up. Allen picked up his piece of bread with its hard, flaky crust and began to chew noisily. This time, Dick ignored him. Alice was twirling spaghetti against a spoon. "How did she seem, Dick?" she inquired gently.

"Sleepy. Otherwise fine. No nonsense. You know Christine."

'She'll beat it," Malcolm said. "She's too tough."

All of the adults were conscious that the children were present. There was, however, little point in trying to discuss some topic other than Christine's illness.

Moreover, except for Alice, who had spoken with Dick only briefly, they were uninformed and curious.

"What did the doctor say?" Walter asked. "If..." he added, "you want to talk about it."

"Oh, sure. No problem." Dick related the little that he knew, sanitizing the account to emphasize the likelihood of a positive outcome. However, this time, in the presence of the children, he added that a further operation would be necessary.

"When will that be?" Carol inquired.

"I'm not sure. Probably soon, wouldn't you think?"

"Do you have a surgeon to do it?" Carol inquired further. "I suppose that choice will determine whether it'll take place at Anderson or someplace else."

"I'm not... I never thought of that," Dick replied truthfully. His glass of vodka was empty. He poured himself some red wine and filled the glasses of the others. "I suppose we'll decide that soon. I'm sure Christine will want Dr. Tomlinson's opinion. I dunno. Maybe he'll decide it."

"Will there be other treatment?" Alice wanted to know.

"Other? Oh... I've no idea. You mean like chemotherapy or something like that?" Dick sat back in his chair. The implications of Christine's condition, and his, were beginning to emerge.

"All in due time," Malcolm said cheerfully. Molly was staring at her father, eyes wide in an inexpressive mask. Malcolm had seen it. "The important thing... the important thing is that she's going to be all right. Thank God for that."

"Yes," added Walter, "thank God for that." He raised his glass.

Slightly befuddled, Dick's mind left the table, left the house, and fixed on the hospital room and Christine's sleeping form. What was going to happen? He had never contemplated another hospital or thought of other forms of treatment, of long, sick days and long, sick nights. His future was unfolding. He had caught a glimpse, but his habit of mind had stopped on the threshold of thought. Instead of dread speculation he was numb, yet not even conscious of his numbness.

Walter filled the glasses again. The bottle was nearly empty. Alice and Malcolm had drunk very little, so most of the consumption had been by the others. The conversation turned to events in the town, but the discussion was without spirit. The spaghetti was eaten. Carol emptied the last of the red wine into her glass.

"We've got some cookies," Dick said, "if anyone wants dessert." He asked for a show of hands, then rose unsteadily. "There's some beer in the fridge, too." However, he was the only one interested. After placing the cookie jar on the table, he reached inside the refrigerator and groped about on the bottom shelf.

"Damn," he said. "I think they're all gone."

"It's just as well," Alice said. "We've got to be going soon." She rose and bustled into the kitchen, carrying plates with her. Soon thereafter, there was a sound of running tap water and dishes clattering in the sink.

"Malcolm," Alice said, "I need the rest of the plates." Both Malcolm and Walter rose.

"Okay, kids," Dick said to his children. "It's time,

young lady," he addressed Molly, "for you to be getting to bed. And you'd better get your homework done," he said to Allen, patting the boy's arm. "I'll be upstairs in a minute."

Molly and Allen left the room. Dick walked to the cabinet where he kept his liquor and refilled his glass half way with vodka. But he did not drink. He put the glass down and quit the kitchen to go upstairs, leaving the others to clear the table and wash the dishes and cooking utensils. On the way into the hall, he lurched into the side of a table.

When he returned Alice and Malcolm were already at the front door, preparing to depart. Malcolm was struggling to fit his arm into the sleeve of a heavy overcoat.

"Thanks. That was really nice of you," Dick said, blinking his eyes.

"Oh, Dick," Alice responded. "We're so sorry. We'll have dinner again soon. Let us know how we can help. We can have you all over and take pressure off Christine or... or you." She hugged him.

Walter crossed the front hall and opened the door to a closet. Dick turned to him. "If you're going, let me get my drink."

As he walked into the kitchen, Carol was stowing the last of some silverware in a drawer. "It looks like you're going," he said, picking up his glass.

Carol walked toward him. Her blond hair hung loosely over her shoulder. "You'll be all right," she said, placing her hands on his shoulders. She reached upward to kiss him, and Dick felt the softness of her lips on his.

The kiss lingered; Carol's hands slid from his shoulders so that her arms were around his neck. For a few moments, Dick stood stock still, passive, befuddled. Then he reached blindly behind him, placing his glass on the counter. With both hands now free, he grasped Carol around the waist and pulled her to him. Through her blouse, he could feel the softness of her breasts. Their tongues caressed.

"Hey, Carol," they heard Walter shout. "Let's get going."

The couple disengaged. Carol straightened her skirt. "Do I look all right?" she whispered. "Is my lipstick okay?"

He peered at her. "Yeah, fine."

"Dick… darling. You'll be all right." She shook her head. Carol also was tipsy. Inclining her face upward, she kissed him quickly and lightly again.

"I'm coming, Walter. Just finishing up." Carol walked out of the room, Dick following behind her.

Chapter 10

An Attraction Remembered

1975

I wonder what Carol would be like? Dick was in his office again. He had picked up Christine in mid-morning and brought her home. She was vibrant, seemingly without change, and there had been little point to staying in the house for the rest of the day. Another appointment at Anderson Hospital, this time with a cancer specialist from Norfolk General Hospital in Boston, was scheduled in two days in the evening. After that meeting, Dr. Tomlinson had told Christine, they would all have a much better idea what should be done. Until then, everyone would wait.

So Dick had returned to his office in the afternoon. He was hopeful, and the reaction of two of his colleagues, when he told them the news, had surprised him. Both, unsmiling, had commiserated, and their worried responses had not changed when he told them that only a small operation, its effects easily corrected by cosmetic surgery, would be necessary.

After these encounters, he had retreated to his office to read. There he sat, feet propped on his desk, his coat and jacket hung on a hook protruding from the back of the door. Dick was wearing a brown Shetland sweater, one sleeve torn at the elbow, and he had loosened his tie. He had on duck boots over heavy, warm socks. There was still some snow on the ground, and the sky against the dark trees was a sickly, brooding gray. It was cold outside, but without a wind to search out and penetrate the cracks around his windows, the office was comfortable.

I wonder what she would be like. He had tried to concentrate on his reading, but his mind strayed. Often, prompted by a small knot of anxiety that gnawed in his gut, it turned to Christine. More often, as yet outside any limits of conscious self-censorship, it strayed to Carol. He thought of her hair, and he wondered how it would look draped over her bare breasts. Maybe, he thought, she does the kinds of things those women were doing in that magazine he had seen months before. The photographs, once glimpsed, were vivid in his memory. How exciting that would be!

And the more exciting, because he and Christine had never done those things. Their wedding night was emblematic of the marriage: fumbling, awkward, hesitant, shy. Neither knew an alternative nor recognized their covert needs striving for satisfaction. Different positions always hurt, or were uncomfortable, or seemed too flagrantly erotic. Both would have been embarrassed to suggest the possibility of change. Had Dick purchased skimpy undergarments for Christine, red and frilly like the ones in the photographs, she would, he had little doubt, have responded with scornful derision. They both claimed to worship sex, but theirs was the adoration of clerics, not sinners.

Dick's mind wandered back across the sometimes grassy, sometimes stony path of his life. His early anxieties about marrying Christine had largely departed, although from time to time he was aware of them like a retreating echo, a dim claxon that could still resonate in the recesses of his mind. The demands of early married life absorbed their energies and interests. After much worried soul-searching, Dick decided to attend law school, and there he did reasonably well. Not long after graduation, he secured a teaching position in New England, a part of the country where he and Christine wanted to live. By the time they moved to Woodbury, Allen had been born. They purchased a house shortly after their arrival – the ten thousand dollar gift from Christine's father was used as a down payment – and a few years later, when Dick was promoted to Associate Professor, Molly was born in Anderson Hospital.

Dick remembered the time well because another event took place that rooted the promotion and Molly's birth in his memory. That event, which took place over a period of a year, began during the last months of Christine's pregnancy. There had been a secretary in the law school who was assigned to work for Dick and three other professors. Her workstation was directly outside Dick's office; as the junior faculty member, he was the one required to tolerate the most disruption and noise. She had been an elderly, crotchety, gray-haired woman, who performed her duties well but with a minimum of charm and civility. She treated Dick, as the youngest of her superiors, with poorly concealed disdain.

And then, one day in April, she announced abruptly that her services would terminate at the end of the academic year. No explanation was offered, although she mentioned a sister who lived in Florida and who inexplicably had asked her to come and stay. In late June a perfunctory farewell party was organized for her and attended by those who could not concoct a reasonable excuse for their absence. The following day she departed without visible regret on her part or the part of anyone else.

The personnel office conducted a search for her replacement. They selected a young woman, recently graduated from a college in Colorado, who had worked as a research assistant, could type, and wanted to explore living in the East. Dick first saw her as he was returning to his office after lunch. She was seated at her desk, and he was struck immediately by her appearance. She had reddish-blond hair that hung loosely to her shoulders, freckles and blue-green eyes that danced when she laughed, which was often. And she was 'leggy', that is to say, she had long, slender legs so that Dick sometimes thought she walked like a young colt.

In the ensuing weeks and months, her laughter could be heard often in his office. The young woman's name was Cathy, although Dick gave her the nickname 'Colorado'. She performed her duties diligently and soon became appreciated by those for whom she worked. But it was obvious to all but the casual observer that Dick Blodgett was her favorite supervisor. In his mid-thirties, Dick was as trim and muscular as he had been as a recent college graduate. The only sign of middle age, aside from a slightly fuller face, was a patch of thinning dark hair at the rear of his head. He examined it every morning in the bathroom. Cathy knew it troubled him, and occasionally she would walk behind him while he was seated and feign amused horror or concern at the sight.

Their days acquired a familiar pattern. When he arrived in the morning, she was invariably at her desk working. Perhaps because she had grown up for part of her life on a farm in Colorado, Cathy liked to rise early. "Hi, Cathy," Dick would say as he walked toward his office, removing his overcoat at the same time. Then he often added, "Today you seem to be looking Boulder, Colorado." Invariably she would laugh. And as invariably, he would say, "Why don't you get a cup of coffee and join me. Let's see what we have to do today."

It became a routine. They would both get cups of coffee from a pot on a hot plate in a utility room down the hall. Cathy, as the first to arrive, would have made it. They would go into his office, leaving the door ajar, and she would sit on the chair by his desk. Any discussion of work, if there was any, was deferred while they chatted about the events of their lives, the news of the day and office gossip. It did not occur to them, as her laughter drifted out by her unoccupied desk, that they might become a subject of gossip themselves. Each was fascinated by the background of the other. Dick came to romanticize the West and the Rocky Mountains. Cathy was intrigued by his life as an undergraduate at Princeton, his youthful experiences in New York City, and the birth of Molly.

Neither forgot that he was a married man. His status was an invisible barrier, and for a long time it immunized them against the consciousness of a growing attraction. To Dick, Cathy came to represent an idealized image of woman: vibrant, intelligent, nurturing, beautiful. He looked forward eagerly to seeing her each morning and their cheerful teasing and banter. She reciprocated his interest. And yet the boundary between innocent infatuation and sexual expression – between a glance and a kiss, or shared coffee in the morning and dinner in the evening – was never crossed.

Nevertheless, their longing became evident to them both. Slowly at first, they became self-conscious of their exclusive times together each day and the impression they were making on others. Without a word spoken, they became more distant and formal when students or faculty members were standing by her desk. Even this behavior, with its unstated assumption of a silent pact between them, drew Dick closer to her. Yet for Cathy, who acknowledged her feelings to herself and recognized her role as an interloper, the tension became increasingly unbearable. As a young woman starting life on her own, she had no intention of luring Dick from his marriage, even if it were a possibility.

And so, nearly a year after her arrival, Cathy announced that she was leaving to pursue graduate studies at the London School of Economics. On the day of her departure, late in June, Dick felt as if a gigantic, unalterable void had opened in his life. For a few moments she sat, laughing, in his office, as if nothing had changed. Then it was time for her to go.

"Aren't you going to give me a goodbye kiss?" she had asked, teasing him. "It's your first and last chance."

They kissed, a formal peck. He hugged her. They kissed again, with awakening ardor. Cathy pulled away, her face stricken. In silence, she collected a few personal belongings. They walked outside to her car without speaking.

"Stop by when you return," he said finally. "I'd love to see you."

"I'll try," she answered. He hung on her ambiguous assurance. "But, Professor Blodgett… or Dick… is that what I call you now that you're not my boss? I probably won't write… at least not right away."

Dick stared at the ground. "Why not at least drop me a postcard after you've settled in?"

"All right." The spell surrounding them still held. She climbed into her Volkswagen and waved cheerfully as she backed the car out of the parking lot. He watched until the small automobile reached the crest of a low rise, where tall elms lined the sides of the road, and vanished from view.

For the rest of the day Dick tried to read in his office. But he could not. Cathy's replacement had not arrived. There was no welcome clatter of a typewriter outside the door. She would not, ever again, come to his office door at the close of the day to say goodnight. He was glum at supper, too. Christine noticed. Even Allen noticed and asked his father what was wrong. Dick passed it off; a bad day, too much work. Like a whispered warning in the night, Christine connected his mood with the departure of his secretary whom she had met many times. She had long since sensed Dick's attraction to Cathy in the animated way he spoke of events at the office. She let it pass. They had rented a cabin on a lake in New Hampshire for a two-week vacation, and they were due to depart for it in five days. The time away, Christine thought, would do him good.

His depression, however, continued, although he faked conviviality at appropriate moments. On the drive to New Hampshire, Dick was silent. Usually, on a first night away, they would make love. This time he was, he said, too tired from the drive. The next afternoon Christine found him sitting on a rock by the water, staring vacantly at an island in the middle of the lake.

"Dick," she said, sitting down next to him, "tell me what's wrong. Something's bothering you. It's obvious."

He looked at her, took a deep breath, and exhaled slowly.

"Come on, Dick," she continued. "We've come here to enjoy a vacation. What's the matter?"

"It's nothing, Christine. Really, it's nothing."

But she knew it was more than nothing, and, from her perspective, a great deal more than nothing. They sat together in silence for several minutes. Across the water they could hear a loon. She too stared at the island, and Dick became uncomfortable, uneasy that he had not received her usual maternal response.

He inquired nervously, "Is everything all right?"

She looked straight at him. "No, Dick, it's not. I wish we could go home. If it weren't for Allen, I would. I don't want to be here with you." She rose from her seat on the rock. "Don't follow me," she said huskily. Slowly, without looking back, she walked to the cottage and around it and down the dirt road on the other side. It was not until early evening that she returned. She never revealed her thoughts or said where she had been.

Between them, afterwards, it was not the same. A strand of trust had been broken. Christine's idealized image of him was torn away. For a moment, a horrifying moment, a door had opened and she had seen him standing on the other side, naked and vulnerable. If only he had been laughing and proud of his nudity, but he was not. He was so unlike the strong if distant father she had known. Her manner toward Dick acquired a hard edge, a protective coating, and she became less tolerant of his choice of profession, with its vow of quasi-poverty, and his thoughtful ruminations which she increasingly construed as academic posturing. Cathy would have liked them; she did not.

Nevertheless, after a few days the door began to close. The comfortable pattern of their lives re-emerged – a slow groping toward the familiar and known. They were a family – she and Dick and Allen and Molly. When Cathy's postcard arrived, Dick experienced an intense pang of affection. She had signed it, 'Fondly', and he savored the potential meaning of the word. However, when she returned after a year, and stopped by to see him for lunch before resuming her journey to New York City where she intended to relocate and find work, they were like old friends. Dick said goodbye without regret. Weeks later another postcard arrived. On it she had written that she had secured a job and found an apartment, and she included an address and telephone number. Idly, Dick filed the card in a side drawer of his desk, and he did not respond. The tempest had passed.

* * * * *

Dick did not equate Carol and Cathy. Carol had kissed him and had woken his sexual longing. But it was a mere spark, not a flame; he regarded her as a fantasy and their drunken groping in the kitchen as a momentary aberration. It was fun to spin his thoughts into a daydream, divorced from responsibility or the tugs of the real world, but the reality of her touch, her smell or the wetness of her kiss would never return. He knew that. Besides, he had far more important things to think about – looming fears of possibilities that might shatter the placid comfort of his world forever.

Chapter 11

Diagnosis
1975

For a few days southern New England had basked on the hopeful lip of spring, but harsh winter, not to be trifled with or ignored, had roared back and held the land in an icy grip. The sky had turned a metallic gray, the temperature had plummeted, and it had snowed. His breath frosting the air as he cursed, Dick managed to sputter his car's engine to a coughing start and then drive cautiously through silent, empty streets to the hospital.

When he arrived the probing beam from his headlights glittered off a large mound of snow, then swung past. It was reflected again from the side of a parked automobile as Dick maneuvered his own next to it and parked. He snapped off the lights and sat for a moment in the darkness. An hour earlier, he and Christine had arrived at Anderson Hospital together. They had said goodbye at the front entrance, he promising to come back at eight thirty, and she had walked inside for her appointment with Dr. Tomlinson, Dr. Sacks and the cancer specialist from Boston. Dick had returned home and had sat with Allen and Molly, aimlessly fiddling with the television set every five minutes, before donning his overcoat and wool watch cap for the trip back to the hospital.

Slowly, he got out of the car. A chill wind caught the lapel of his coat and tugged at it. The parking lot was near the front entrance and, in the section where Dick parked, illuminated by a solitary lamp atop a slender aluminum pole. A previous snow had thawed, then frozen in icy ruts on the parking lot's ebony surface, and Dick nearly fell as he slipped in the shadowed area beside the car. Groping along the side, he emerged into the soft glow cast by the overhead light and began to trudge toward the building, his boots crunching against brittle ridges of ice.

A figure emerged from the entrance, bulky against the brightly lit opening. It was a man wearing a heavy coat and fur hat. He peered in the direction of the parking lot and, seeing Dick, let the door swing shut behind him. Groping his way down the short flight of steps before the doorway, he started walking toward Dick. A doctor leaving to get his car, Dick thought. Then he recognized Dr. Tomlinson.

"Hello, Dick. Thought that was you."

"Hi, Dr. Tomlinson," Dick answered cheerfully. He stopped as the other man approached. "I guess this means the examination is over."

"Well, almost. Christine should be out any minute. There wasn't anything more I could do." And, he might have added, but did not, that he hoped to intercept Dick and speak with him privately.

"How did it go?"

Dr. Tomlinson answered him obliquely. "Dr. Bader is one of the leading surgeons in the world when it comes to operations on the head and neck. He has a great deal of experience with situations like Christine's."

"Is that his name? The cancer specialist. Bader?"

"Yes, Henry Bader." Dr. Tomlinson paused. "Dick, after Dr. Bader examined Christine, he and Dr. Sacks and I consulted about her case." A sharp gust of cold wind struck them both, and Dr. Tomlinson adjusted his scarf snugly around his neck. "I'm... I'm sorry to tell you this, but... well... Dr. Bader thinks the situation is a great deal more serious than we first thought."

"How so?" Dick's stomach muscles tightened.

"It's his opinion, which, bear in mind, is based on a tremendous amount of experience, that radical surgery is necessary. You can talk with someone else, of course, and get another opinion, but Dr. Bader thinks we should remove her left jawbone... all of it. The cancer may have spread by now along the sensory nerve in the bone. He also thinks that we should remove the lymph nodes on that side of her neck."

Dick cleared his throat and rubbed his gloved hand across his chin. "What are lymph nodes?" he said, stunned.

"Places where infected cells get caught. If any have escaped from the end of her jaw bone, that's where they'd most likely be. If none are there, that'll be a very good sign. They'll be sent to a lab right away to be examined after the operation."

"One whole side of her jaw?" Dick's voice began to rise. "I mean, won't that... how will she eat?" And how will she look, he thought dimly but dared not ask.

"Let's just take one step at a time, Dick. She'll eat just fine on one side." Dr. Tomlinson was a kindly man, about fifteen years older than Dick and Christine. He had a large frame, slightly stooped, and the overhead light accentuated his creased face and jowls. Only his deep-set, drooping eyes, with their constant look of sadness, were shielded in darkness by cranial bone. "It's too early to say," he continued, "but I should think a prosthesis, and false teeth, might be possible so that she'll be almost as good as new."

Dick heard the words and the reassuring tone. They were not proof against his rising recognition of peril. In the preceding three days, he had reached a plateau of adjustment to his new, altered circumstances. A minor operation, he had thought, and the placid comfort of his life would return. Plastic surgery and the miracle of modern medicine would banish the problem to the darkness whence it came. Those fantasies lay shattered on the icy pavement, and the chill, bony fingers of fear began to tighten their grip upon him.

"How serious is this?" he stammered. "Will she... could she die?"

"I don't think so. We'll have to wait and see until after the operation, but you could still have many years together. Dick, as I said, just take one step at a time."

He doesn't think so! He doesn't know! He can't say she won't. He's just trying to soften the blow for me, ease me into this pain. Dick's thoughts tumbled, half outside conscious awareness. His reality was a tightening in his gut even as he struggled to maintain his composure, to speak calmly and deliberately and not shout, or whimper, or run, or do something, anything. What will happen to Molly? She's too young. I can't raise her alone. What will happen to Allen? What... what will happen...?

He heard Dr. Tomlinson speaking. "One good thing you have going for you. Christine will receive excellent medical care."

"But… Christine's parents live near New York. They know a lot of people. They may want… I mean, would we be better off going to New York?"

"No." Dr. Tomlinson's voice was quiet, confident. "Dr. Bader is among the very best in the world, particularly for this kind of problem, this kind of cancer. And Christine seemed to like him."

"You say he's had experience with these kinds of operations?" Dick was still struggling to master the situation, although he knew that, in the end, Christine would make the final decision.

"No one's had more. I advise you to stay with him. Look, Dick, this is a very bad cancer, one of the worst. When skin cancer goes inside, and that's what's happened here, it's very dangerous. It's… it's not a good one, if there is such a thing. Christine can go under Dr. Bader's care at Norfolk General with the least disruption to the family and where you can visit and be close at hand. She'll start with radiation for a couple of months. Immediately. I've asked her to call me tomorrow and let me know her decision."

Chapter 12

Entangled Emotions

1975

Dr. Tomlinson was correct. Christine liked Dr. Bader. His calm, unruffled manner and his obvious concern impressed her. She made a couple of inquiries about his reputation, although she relied heavily on Dr. Tomlinson's recommendation, and she quickly discovered that he was held in high regard. Moreover, she had no desire to leave her family and go to New York, particularly when care of equal quality was available in Boston.

Her radiation treatments began immediately. With some amusement she showed Dick the new tattooed dots on her face and neck that were used each day by the technicians to align their equipment. Her introduction to the world of the seriously ill – a world she had joined without any outward sign of disability – was swift and, at the beginning, disorienting. Every day she drove from Woodbury to Boston, parked in the hospital parking lot, and walked to the radiation clinic in a basement wing of the hospital. After informing a receptionist of her arrival, she took a seat in a large waiting room that, on one side, abutted the corridor without an intervening wall or partition. The room was painted white, with cheery red and yellow diagonal stripes at one end, and it had blue-upholstered couches and chairs on which patients and visitors could sit.

Christine invariably selected a chair near the receptionist, who sat behind an opening cut in the wall opposite the wall with the stripes. At the beginning, focusing on the novelty of her own experience, she did not particularly notice the others in the room. But after a couple of weeks she began to recognize those who had regular appointments at approximately the same time as hers. There was an old man, stooped with age, and his elderly wife, who always brought him, hobbling on her arm, and then tenderly kissed him goodbye. There was a young woman, perhaps a decade younger than Christine, who Christine came to know. She wore a wig, worked as a waitress and had no money to pay for her treatments. The young woman had a brain tumor, and her prognosis was poor. Because she lived alone, she was frightened that the end for her would come without anyone being present. And invariably there were patients left to wait their turns on gurneys in the corridor. Often very old, they lay quietly under their white sheets, staring at the ceiling, locked in the silence of their thoughts and fears.

By comparison, Christine felt healthy. But after four or five weeks, the daily treatments began to take a toll. She felt noticeably weaker, sometimes sick, and spent increasing time at home. Her friends volunteered their help, each taking an afternoon during the week to drive her to the hospital. Awkwardly at first, Dick assumed the duty of cooking. He had to work during the day, but he put his research project aside and, on most days, left in mid-afternoon so that he could be home when Allen and Molly returned from school.

Neither Christine nor Dick disguised her condition. Gradually the house became a magnet for visitors. In the mornings, Christine disconnected the telephone in order to have time to read, nap and be alone with her thoughts. She forthrightly told her friends to leave when she needed to rest. Yet they came without hesitation, and on weekends people thronged into the house. Their presence was a tonic, a distraction from the insistent, corrosive fear that lurked at shallow depth beneath the surface of their lives.

On one Saturday afternoon Christine sat in the living room. Her face, on one side, had acquired a slight tan from the radiation treatments. Alice and Malcolm had stopped by, ostensibly on their way to a local building supply store, as had another couple that lived only a block away. The wife had come earlier to deliver a book of inspirational prayer – the kind of reading that seemed to occupy Christine more and more as the date of the operation approached. Molly was seated on a couch next to her mother; her brother had left early in the afternoon to play soccer.

"May I have another cup of tea?" Alice asked.

"Sure." Christine started to rise, but Alice interrupted her.

"I know where everything is," she said. Alice rose from her chair and started to walk toward the kitchen.

"Just look at you. Stop, turn around." Alice paused at the doorway, and Christine continued, "You can tell spring is here. No more tweeds and sweaters! I love this time of year."

"Only you have it wrong," the male half of the couple from a block away broke in. His name was Bob, and he had come over to join his wife without changing after a game of tennis. "It's not spring. It's early summer. There is no spring in New England."

"What're you talking about?" Malcolm looked amused. "We had spring for a couple days last week, but unfortunately I was away and missed it."

Christine giggled. Mary, the neighbor's wife, cracked her face slightly as if the effort to smile would permanently rearrange her features. She had dropped by to be sympathetic, to offer support in a time of tragedy, and the boisterous conversation seemed to throw her off guard. "The flowers are all up," she said somberly.

There was a momentary lull in the conversation. "No kidding," Malcolm said, glancing at her quizzically. "When did you notice?"

"The lilacs are in bloom all along Fisher Lane," Mary added, oblivious to Malcolm's remark. "They smell beautiful. I walked by them yesterday on the way downtown."

"Say," Malcolm said, pointing to a vase filled with lilacs on a table in the corner, "You weren't walking that way yourself yesterday, were you, Christine? I'm sure the folks on Fisher Lane won't miss a branch or two."

"Malcolm!" Alice had returned with a cup of tea and was standing again in the doorway. "Stop it! I picked those for Christine yesterday. They came from our backyard."

Christine laughed, as did Molly and Malcolm and Bob. Malcolm made a face of mock chagrin.

"How was the tennis?" Dick asked Bob.

"Good. It's great to be out again."

"Who'd you play with?"

Bob mentioned the names, all known to the group. "I thought we were going to win. It was tied after two sets. But that damn Tom was all over the net. God, he's good. You can't get anything by him."

"I know," Dick replied. "He played in our group several times this winter."

"Is that facility still open?"

"I don't know. I don't think so. We only play there through March."

Alice resumed her seat by a window and placed her teacup carefully on a nearby table. "Can I get tea for anyone else?" she asked. "It's all ready."

No one responded. Bob looked at Dick. "How about a beer? I'm awfully thirsty after playing three sets in that sun."

"No problem." Dick had begun to husband the liquor supply, what with the added expenses of parking in the city and, recently, a cleaning woman to come once every other week. But he rose without hesitation to honor Bob's request.

"You know," Mary said, "school will be out in less than a month. What're you going to do, Molly, with your vacation?"

Molly shifted in her seat. "Mommy says we're going to Cape Cod after her operation." Almost imperceptibly, she shrank closer to her mother. "Aren't we, Mommy?"

"We've been going up to Deer Isle for years," Christine said. "But this year we'll stay closer to home. We're also going a little later, probably in late July." She looked at Dick, who had just reentered the room. "Honey, have you called yet to make sure we have the place?"

"Yes. They're supposed to call me back. I'd better remind them."

Bob was still thinking about his wife's comment concerning school. "Isn't that something," he said, "about that gym teacher at the junior high school."

"The damned fool," growled Malcolm. "If he's going to take kids on a field trip, it's his responsibility to make sure they all stay together."

"Oh, Malcolm," Christine turned toward him, "That's so easy to say. Have you ever tried to get children in line?"

"And they weren't children," interjected Alice. "Those boys were old enough to know better."

"Who's going to pay for it?" Bob added. "Not that son-of-a-bitch. You can bet he doesn't have two dimes to rub together. Once that boy's parents find a good lawyer, the whole town's going to have to pay."

"No, we are not!" Christine did not retreat from an argument, particularly when she felt confident of her position. "I'm not a lawyer, but I know enough to grasp that the boy was the major source of the problem. He kept sneaking away. The other kids said so. I don't think Mr. Bradford could have done anything, no matter how hard he tried."

"He was the one in charge," Bob replied. "It was his responsibility."

"So what?" Christine spoke heatedly. "That's the whole point. He was being responsible."

"Hey," Dick said. "Stop it! You're disturbing the patient. Don't you know she can't stand excitement? You're supposed to be quiet during visiting hours."

Christine laughed. "That's right. Here I am, a poor cancer victim, and you're picking on me."

Mary looked confused. The conversation had taken

another baffling turn. How could Christine and her husband joke about her predicament? Yet they were, and with explosive laughter besides. Christine's eyes were twinkling with merriment. Even Alice and Malcolm had joined in the laughter. And Bob… Bob had actually smiled. Unless she was mistaken, so had the child.

"Okay, okay, Christine," said Malcolm, holding up his arms in mock surrender. "We'll come back to this argument when you're all better. And then you'll be sorry."

"No, I will not. You will be." She laughed again.

The conversation drifted away to neighborhood gossip and an anecdote, related by Christine with relish, about the new minister of the Presbyterian church. Another friend arrived, a woman with whom Christine had done volunteer work. Alice asked if she would like a cup of tea, but the woman declined. Dick, who had not resumed his seat, stood watching from the doorway. He observed his friends and the conviviality of the gathering. Once, he exchanged a shy smile with Molly. But most of all his gaze fixed on Christine, who was happily joined in the conversation, animatedly discussing each subject as it arose. And slowly, the incongruity of the scene began to overwhelm him. He saw her seated on the couch, vibrant and alive, her child snuggled next to her. In six months, in a year, would she be there? Or would the room be silent and empty?

"I'm going to get a beer," Dick mumbled. "How about it, Bob? Would you like another?"

Bob held up his hand, palm outward. "No thanks. Mary and I should be going in a few minutes."

When Dick reached the kitchen, he did not stop to

open the refrigerator door. Instead, he unlatched the door to the cellar and walked downstairs. And there he stood, at the bottom of the stairs, his arm against a steel, cylindrical post, his head against his arm. He began to cry, silently, his teeth biting his lower lip, his chest heaving with rapid, convulsive sobs.

My God! What will happen? What will happen to Molly? To Allen? What will we do? She seems so happy. How can she be so brave and cheerful? Oh God, please help us. Make her better. Oh please, please make her better and keep her with us. Make this go away. Make this awful, awful thing go away. I can't. I can't do it. I can't.

With the back of his hand, he wiped his tears away, tried to compose himself, took a step to the foot of the stairs. And stopped. And turned, and again wept convulsively.

Malcolm found him there, still crying but hastily attempting with his handkerchief to blot the wetness on his cheeks and around his eyes.

"How... how did you know I was here?" Dick stammered.

"I came out for a beer. You weren't there, saw the open door." In fact, Christine had asked, perplexed, what had happened to Dick. And Malcolm, also wondering, had said he would find him.

"Are you all right?"

"Yes... yes I am. This is so embarrassing. Please... you won't say anything?"

"Of course not." Malcolm put his arm around Dick's shoulders. "You'll be okay. It's hard, Dick. It's hard for us all, but mostly for you. We know that."

"No. No, it's hardest for Christine. I was just looking at her, and she looked so beautiful and she's… she's so brave. I… I couldn't stand it."

Malcolm nodded his head. "C'mon. Let's go upstairs."

"What'll I say?" Dick dabbed at his eyes.

"You don't have to say anything."

"It's just… oh, Malcolm, I love her so."

* * * * *

A week later, finishing a hike through woods after a brief visit with friends, Dick walked past Walter and Carol's house on the way home. He was alone. Christine had not felt well and had decided to stay in bed for the afternoon and nap.

It was a warm day. Dick was dressed for it, wearing exactly the attire he would have worn years before as an undergraduate at Princeton. The trees were laced with budding leaves, and their shiny, newly minted green was an intoxicant. With delight, he observed that the openness of the sky was closing in as the hitherto bare branches spread their foliage over the sidewalks and streets.

Why not stop in, he thought, and say hello. The house, with its Victorian facade of interlaced molding and shingles and its broad, shaded porch, looked inviting. A screen door, not yet hung, stood canted at an angle against a pillar of the porch. Walter must be putting up screens, he mused. It's time I got to that job myself.

Still strong and nimble, Dick cleared the front steps two at a time. He rang the bell, then remembered that it did not work. The door was open. Peering into the dim interior of the hall, he shouted, "Is anyone home? You have a visitor."

In a moment he espied a figure whose contours quickly took shape as she advanced to the door.

"Dick!" Carol exclaimed. "What an unexpected surprise. Please. Come in." She was wearing a light summer dress, covered by an apron. A wisp of hair fell across her moist forehead, evidence that she had been working at some physical task.

"I'm back in the kitchen," she said. "Please join me."

Dick followed her through the gloom of the interior hall, dark because of the new shade outdoors, through a door and short passageway and thence into a bright, cheerful kitchen. It had been recently redecorated and refurbished with a subtle, floral print wallpaper on a white background; broad, imitation marble counter tops; and a new stove with an oven recessed in the wall. The pine table with blue legs from Pennsylvania, with its accompanying chairs, graced a far corner by a window. Dick noticed that Carol appeared to have been making bread. The dough and a rolling pin were on the counter near the sink that was under a large window framed by plain blue curtains.

"What're you doing?" he asked.

"Making bread. I always think I'm going to enjoy it, and halfway through I always end up hating it. Can I get you a beer or something?"

"No, thanks. I just had one at Roger's." He paused. The house was silent. "Where's Walter? I saw the screen door out front and figured I could stop by and watch him work."

Carol shrugged. "You missed him by half an hour. He

took the kids to a movie they've been dying to see. His turn to play parent."

"Anything to get out of chores. I was just thinking, I'd better get to them, too. Last night we had the window open, and we already got bothered by a mosquito."

He was partially sitting on, partially leaning against the pine table. Carol stood across the room, her buttocks pressed against the counter that rimmed the sink.

Dick tilted his head, searching her face, then said, "Have you been crying? Your eyes are red and kind of swollen."

"No… well, yes… you weren't supposed to notice."

"What's wrong?"

"Oh, Dick, it's not the kind of thing you talk about."

"Well, maybe you should."

She looked at him forlornly, then shrugged again. "I hope I can trust you… I think I can. It's Walter. Years ago he had a girlfriend – an affair during the early years of our marriage. It was all over. So I thought. And then, entirely by accident… I was in the city, shopping… I saw him in a restaurant having lunch with another woman."

"So?"

"I mentioned it to him that evening, and of course he claimed that it was nothing… that he didn't tell me about it to save me from needless worrying, but it was the old girlfriend. He admitted it. She works for a Philadelphia consulting firm but has a client in Boston."

"You should take his word for it," Dick said. "I'm sure it really was nothing. There's no harm in lunch."

"I know, I know. And yet he seemed so guilty, and I can't help wondering. I'm pretty sure something's going on." She clamped her mouth into a straight line. "I don't want this discussed, Dick. It could end up being vicious gossip. You just caught me in an unguarded moment. And anyway, it's you we should be worrying about. You have far worse troubles."

Dick stared at her, saying nothing.

"How is Christine?" Carol's tone was gently inquisitive. "I haven't seen her in three or four days."

"Uh… okay. Okay, I guess."

"You guess?"

"Well, you know, she gets tired a lot now. I mean, it's not as if she's unhappy or something like that. In fact… in fact we almost seem to be having fun. Lots of kidding around, and she never complains. But sure, it's taking a toll. I'm almost glad she'll be having the operation in three and a half weeks."

"It's not like her to complain, is it? She's a brave woman."

"Yeah. You can say that again." He smiled. "Does swear every now and then, though. She says cancer is the shits right out in public, doesn't care who's around."

"Everybody talks about Christine. And that's natural. But how about you, Dick? How're you doing?"

"Me?" For a moment he was silent. "Gee, I dunno. Fine, I guess. Well, of course, I've been better. This is a pretty anxious time, but, no, I'm okay. Thanks for asking," he ended lamely.

Carol looked at him, her hair, as usual, pulled over to one side. She shook her head. "Why is it so hard," she said softly, "for men to know their feelings?"

"I guess we're just like that."

She smiled fleetingly. "Sure you wouldn't like a beer? You can sit there and we can talk while I finish up."

"No thanks. I should be going. Just stopped by to say hello."

But he continued to lean against the table. And Carol continued to lean against the rim of counter before the sink, gazing at him. There was a prolonged moment of silence. Their eyes met and did not waiver.

Trance-like, an explorer in unknown territory, driven by urges and fears he did not comprehend, Dick stood and walked toward her. Carol did not move. "I think we both need a comforting hug," he said, placing his hands on her shoulders and then dropping them to her hips. He kissed her, briefly, awkwardly. She did not resist.

"Cheer up," he said. "It will be all right."

"And you, too, Dick. Have courage."

Sliding his hands to the small of her back, he kissed her again. This time she responded, reaching up to hold him around his neck. Then his arms embraced her, crushing her. His body pressed hers against the counter top, and, in a frantic, blind, groping passion, they struggled against each other. Her mouth, half open, covered his, and his tongue slid into the orifice. And searched it, as Carol's mouth worked slowly back and forth across his, then slid to his neck as his right hand, freed from her back, clasped and cupped her breasts.

"Dick!" Carol finally gasped, "Dick, stop, we're right by the window. People can see us."

He straightened, relinquishing his grip.

"Then we could…" he started to say.

"No, Dick. No. We mustn't."

They kissed again, slowly but no longer pressing their bodies together. The trance was ending. He stepped back.

"My God, you are beautiful." He looked into her eyes and, for the first time, noticed their smoky-green color. "What wonderful eyes you have."

"They're just eyes, Dick." Carol straightened her apron and ran her hand down her hair. She looked at him, at his worried, chiseled features. She noticed that he was panting.

"I think you'd better go," she said.

For a frozen moment, he stood still, looking at her in return. "Okay." He turned and walked back to the table, then turned again. "You won't tell? You won't tell Walter we did this."

A frown creased her features. "Dick… of course not. This is our secret. C'mon, I'll walk you to the door."

She saw him out the way he had come in. Before leaving the house, Dick tucked in his shirt, which was hanging loosely outside his trousers. Waving goodbye with feigned indifference, he walked casually down the front steps. But his chest was still heaving from the encounter. I must not… I must not ever do such a thing again, he thought. I must not… ever. I must not.

Chapter 13

The Operation

1975

Two days before the operation, Dr. Bader met with Christine and Dick in his office. In his kindly, avuncular manner, he summarized his conclusions about the course of the disease and the efficacy of the radiation treatment. He then told them that, in addition to her left jaw and the lymph nodes in her neck, it would be necessary to remove half of her lower lip and the surrounding tissue in her cheek and chin.

Christine and Dick were seated on chairs next to each other. She reached for his hand. Neither spoke. Continuing, Dr. Bader said that he would only perform the first part of the surgery, the part involving the removal or the tissue and bone where the disease was presumably present. He did not ask for permission; their informed consent was implicit in the face of his experience, and he calmly described what would happen as a forgone conclusion.

Once Dr. Bader's phase of the operation was completed, a new team of doctors and nurses headed by a Dr. McNaught, a world-famous plastic surgeon, would take over in the operating room for the reconstructive stage of the operation. He and Dr. Bader had obviously consulted, and a visit with Dr. McNaught had already been scheduled for the following day.

Dr. McNaught, they were told, planned to cut a shallow incision from the middle of Christine's breastbone over the nipple of her left breast to the outer part of her shoulder, and thence back to a point approximately three inches below her throat. A layer of tissue, anchored to a blood supply in the middle of Christine's chest, would then be peeled away and formed into a roll with the end – the skin that had covered her shoulder – attached to her face as a graft in the area where tissue would have to be removed. Half of her upper lip would be curled around so that a portion of it would form a new lower lip, leaving her with a mouth three quarters of its former size. As almost an afterthought, Dr. Bader mentioned that once the graft had attached to her face in a couple of weeks, it would be cut from its former blood supply. The rolled up, remaining tissue would then be returned to its place across her breast. Because no tissue would be returned to her shoulder, a patch of skin would be removed from her thigh to serve as a graft in that location.

The procedure seemed so complicated, and the planning for it so thorough, that they had few questions at the end. Radical neck surgery, it seemed, was required to stem the progress of the disease. Neither asked whether continued radiation might achieve the same result. Christine had placed her trust in Dr. Bader, and her trust did not waver. Thanking him, she and Dick left his office and, in the warmth of an early June evening, drove home in silence. Christine's parents were scheduled to arrive the next day. Time for her and Dick, for their children and her parents, for their friends, had begun to assume a curiously plastic quality. It froze in vignettes, remembered long afterward, yet hurtled them forward to the dreaded culmination of their waiting.

* * * * *

Christine checked into Norfolk General Hospital late the next day. The inevitable forms were filled out in the admitting office. She met with the anesthesiologist and answered his questions. A room assignment had been arranged; with the help of her parents, she was placed in a private room in a posh, older wing of the hospital. She would be there, she had been informed, for nearly a month, and the Haskins had agreed to pay the extra amount not covered by insurance. The room had tall, wide windows, and they afforded a view to the west along the Charles River to the low hills of Watertown and beyond.

Barbara Haskins drove Christine to the hospital and stayed until her daughter was settled; after helping to unpack Christine's small suitcase and stowing her belongings in a spacious closet, she left in the late afternoon to return to her husband and grandchildren. Dick had said he would arrive after work and stay with Christine for a couple of hours.

When he arrived and was told her room number and its location, he took an elevator to the floor and walked past nurses down a broad corridor. He found the room. It had a tall, solid wooden door, as befitted the entrance to a room in a hospital wing built to accommodate Boston's wealthy citizens. The door was ajar, and the footfalls that might have announced his arrival had been muffled by the murmuring bustle in the hallway. Christine was seated in an armchair by the window, reading a treasured book of prayers. The sun, sliding to rest over the Watertown hills, had caught and burnished the trace of red in her hair. She did not notice his arrival.

Dick stood transfixed, not uttering a word. There she sat, in a pose of total tranquility, as beautiful as the day they had met so many years before. Moments passed. Christine paused, turned a page, and continued reading. Still he did not speak but only stood, aware that at the next setting of the sun, this scene would be gone forever. She seemed so whole, so untouched by disease. For the remainder of his days, the image stayed, etched in memory. It seemed impossible that their lives had been, and would be, completely changed.

Like a stone thrown in a pond that ripples its placid surface, Christine looked up, saw him, and smiled. She folded the book and placed it on a table as he crossed the room to kiss her. It was a chaste kiss, on her cheek. He asked how everything was. She said fine. Did she like the room? She answered that she did. Christine said that she had arranged to join him in the hospital cafeteria for supper; thereafter she would be permitted nothing but water until after the operation when she would be fed intravenously.

Supper was the usual hospital fare. Chatting animatedly, they enjoyed their time together. Dick noticed the other diners, wondering what turns in their lives had brought them to this place. He also observed an attractive nurse and tried to banish the thought from his mind.

When they returned to the room, Christine resumed her seat in the armchair. Dick sat on the bed, dangling his legs over the side.

"Dick," Christine said seriously, "I want to say a couple of things, and then I think you should go. We don't need to say very much."

He nodded, not speaking.

"I think everything's going to be okay," she continued, "but realistically, there's a chance it won't be. Darling, we have to face that."

Dick looked down, nodded again; his Adam's apple moved up and down.

"You're going to be all right. I just want you to know that. You're a very attractive man. Lots of people love you, and you'll find someone else to adore you within a year."

"I don't want anyone else. I want you."

"I know that, darling. And I couldn't have made it this far without you… I simply couldn't have."

They sat for a long while in silence.

"You're going to be fine," he said finally.

"You sure?"

"Yes."

Christine held out her hand. Dick eased himself from the bed and took it in his. She kissed the back of his fingers, then looked up at him.

"It's time for you to go. Molly and Allen will need to be with you."

"Are you going to be all right?"

"Yes, Dick. I'll see you in the morning. I need some time by myself. Please be here with Daddy by seven, like you promised."

"I will."

He held her, embraced her, kissed her cheeks, walked to the door, turned, waved, and was gone.

* * * * *

In the morning, as promised, he was once again in Christine's room. Bob Haskins was with him. All three were convivial, talking about the hospital food, the view, or anything other than the subject most on their minds. Christine asked about the children. Dick played briefly with the bed, pressing the buttons to raise and lower its different sections. They were play actors, products of a culture that, in countless subliminal messages, had taught them not to whine or shiver or moan or cry in the face of danger. Pretend it isn't there; pretend that life is under control, particularly in moments when life's fragility is most apparent, when a peek under the curtain might reveal a glimpse of the yawning chasm to eternity.

Moreover, as human beings do, they were experiencing life at the moment. Now, right now, there are stairs to climb, or a shirt to button, or food to eat or even an injection to be received prior to an operation.

A nurse entered the room with a tray of needles and requested Dick and his father-in-law to step into the hall. When she left moments later, she advised them that Christine would begin to feel groggy and that an orderly would come shortly to get her. A few minutes later he arrived, and after securing Christine on a gurney, a sheet pulled over her legs, he proceeded to the operating room with Dick walking by her side, holding her hand. In a confusing tangle of passages, they turned right, then left, then right again and down an elevator. Christine was sleepy. They did not speak. At length they came to a set of swinging doors, and the orderly informed Dick that he could go no further. Leaning over, he kissed Christine. She squeezed his hand. The orderly pushed open the doors with the gurney and, while Dick watched through a small glass window in one of the doors, wheeled Christine down a short corridor and around a corner.

Dick returned to the room. He and Bob Haskins read books in silence, and later they had lunch followed by a long walk on the south bank of the Charles River. It was a warm, pleasant day with fluffy white clouds in the sky. Barbara Haskins called in mid-afternoon. Any news? No, none. Dick began to grow apprehensive but took solace in his father-in-law's stoic demeanor.

But at five o'clock he voiced his fears. "Don't you think we should have heard something by now?"

"Not necessarily."

"It's been nine hours. We said goodbye before eight o'clock."

"My boy, these things take time. Believe me, we would have heard fast enough if something had gone wrong."

Dick lapsed into silence. He picked up a magazine, riffled through its pages, then put it down with a sigh. What if something has gone wrong, he thought. Maybe something awful has happened. At glacial speed six o'clock arrived. The minutes ticked by while, with growing fear, Dick stood by the window. It was not until six thirty-five that Dr. Bader walked into the room.

"Well, well," he said cheerfully. "I'm sure you've had

an anxious day. Christine is in recovery, sleeping. The operation went smoothly. I'm sorry I was delayed getting here to tell you."

"How is she?" Both men said the words, almost as one.

"As well as she could be under the circumstances. I took a little more of the cheek than planned, but not much. Dr. McNaught told me that his part of the operation went very well. We've sent everything we removed to the lab for tissue analysis, but on visual inspection I didn't see any problem in her lymph nodes. Keep your fingers crossed. I think we may have gotten it."

"Wouldn't that be wonderful!" Dick was still standing by the window, his hands clasped in front of him. "I can't wait to tell the kids."

"Why don't you go home now," Dr. Bader said. "She won't be out of recovery until mid-morning, and you can meet her here. I'll drop by around noon."

Bob Haskins held out his hand. "Thank you, Dr. Bader. Thanks ever so much. I'll just call Christine's mother – who I can tell you is a pretty anxious woman right now and will be awfully pleased to hear this news – and we'll be on our way."

* * * * *

The next day, Dick arrived early at the hospital room, this time alone. Nurses' aides were clearing trays of breakfast from the rooms. He nodded a greeting to a nurse at a station in the center of the hall and repaired to the room, a newspaper tucked under his arm. Outside, it was cloudy; there had been showers at dawn, and beads of rain streaked the windowpanes. He took a seat in the armchair by the window and tried to read.

But he could not, and at nine o'clock, an hour remaining until the approximate time of Christine's return, he put down his newspaper and walked to the door. The long hallway was clear except for an occasional cart and an old woman, a patient in a bathrobe, who was walking slowly with hesitant steps, a nurse by her side. He decided to walk to a window at the far end. This he did, returned, and paced the corridor again. Nearly back at the window, he heard a small commotion at the opposite end, a noise of doors opening onto the corridor from another hallway and a murmur of voices.

He saw the gurney and a form on it. There were two orderlies, one pushing and the other guiding a pole on wheels – a kind of thin, metallic hat rack – that had bottles draped like ornaments from its arms. Tubes hung from the bottles and were attached to the patient. The orderlies stopped, looking at the number on the door, then wheeled the gurney and its accompanying contraption into Christine's room.

Striding rapidly, Dick retraced his steps. When he entered, the men had already lifted Christine from the gurney onto the bed. She was awake but dopey with medication and was trying to indicate a problem, a sheet caught under her, with her hand. One of the orderlies rectified the problem. He was a large, black man with beefy hands; he spoke to her in a gentle, soothing voice, "Jus lie back now. Thas right. You going to be jus fine. Jus fine." He adjusted the bed so that her upper torso and head were slightly raised. A tube from a bottle in the metal hat rack ran into the back of her hand, another into her arm. At a slit in her throat, yet another tube, part of a tracheotomy, permitted her to breathe.

Dick saw the tubes, and at a glance he took in her head swathed in bandages. Were they not so bulky and white, she might have resembled some turbaned Arab, face shielded from the sun. His attention was instantly riveted, however, on the grotesque roll of white skin that rose out of the bandages on her chest and disappeared under the bandages on her lower face. She looked like... like an elephant, with a chicken white trunk hanging as an appendage from her lower face.

The orderlies finished their work, gathered the sheets onto the gurney, and left. Dick approached the bed and, for the first time, entered Christine's field of vision. The movement of her head from side to side was almost completely restricted. She saw him. He knew, because she followed his movement with her eyes. There he stood next to the bed, patting and stroking the arm that did not have a tube running into it. He noticed her eyes that were almost the only visible part of her face. They opened, then closed, then opened again and fixed on him. Perhaps it was his imagination, but they seemed infinitely tired and sad.

Chapter 14

Homecoming and Recuperation

1975

After two weeks the elephant's trunk was removed because the graft – the skin that had once covered Christine's shoulder – had acquired a new blood supply from the surrounding tissue in her face, and it was possible, therefore, to cut it free of the blood supply in her chest. Her face and upper torso still remained covered with bandages, but after this second operation she was again able to move her head from side to side.

At first, visitation was strictly curtailed. The children were permitted to visit her only once in the early post-operative days. Afterward, Allen, it seemed, had one hundred questions, but Molly said nothing. She had stood in silence by the bed, staring at her mother, while Christine, in a thick, husky voice, assured her over and over again that she was now going to be well.

Bob Haskins returned to Scarsdale and his work. Barbara stayed to care for the household and, in the mornings when Dick had duties at the law school, to provide companionship to her daughter. For long hours she simply sat in the chair by the window, knitting or reading, a quiet source of support. In the late afternoon and evening, Dick performed the same role.

By the third week the tube to her arm was removed,

the one that had supplied nourishment intravenously, and she began to eat soft foods. The tracheotomy in her neck was also removed, and the incision in her windpipe was closed. They began to take slow walks along the corridor, Christine holding fast to Dick's arm while he, with his free hand, pushed the wheeled contraption that still held a single, inverted bottle suspended from one of its arms, with a clear, plastic tube running to a needle inserted into the back of her hand.

On a Friday at noon, a few days before Christine's discharge, Dick received a telephone call in his office from Dr. Bader. He had been eating lunch at his desk.

"I have some encouraging news," Dr. Bader said.

"What is it?" Dick had absorbed bad news for so long that, hearing Dr. Bader's voice, he was braced for more.

"I heard from the lab yesterday afternoon," Dr. Bader continued. "The lymph nodes were clean. This was the first opportunity I've had to call."

"You say no cancer?" Dick's voice rose.

"No, I didn't say that. I said no cancer cells in her lymph nodes. There's a good probability that we've gotten it."

"You mean she's going to be well? Oh, Dr. Bader, this is wonderful! This is wonderful!" He was standing and, tethered to the telephone receiver, began to walk in a circle, nearly dance, in excitement.

Dr. Bader tried to inject a note of caution. "We'll need to talk, Dick. It's a good sign, but we still have a lot of waiting and watching to do. Still, as a preliminary indication, I'm very pleased."

Dick heard the words, but he rushed by them. "Thanks for calling. I understand. I understand. Oh, this is wonderful. I'll call your office next week… yes, I'll call her mother… yes… Thanks again. Thanks again for everything."

He stood for a few moments, took a deep breath, then called the hospital and told Christine and Barbara the news. Then Bob. And then Alice and Carol. Later in the day when he returned home he told Molly and Allen. The three of them were seated in the kitchen.

"That's really great, Dad," Allen said. "Wait 'till Tom hears about this!" Tom was his closest friend, his rival in soccer, his closest buddy when school and sports were at an end. "He said she wasn't going to make it. Said his Mom told him. Boy, is he going to be surprised."

Dick was shocked. "He said that? Why would he… his mother had no right to say that. We all hoped… Allen, is that what people were saying?"

"I dunno, Dad. You know Mrs. Cahill. She's kinda, you know, like that. Sorta gloomy. Tom and I were talking one day. That's all." The boy was smiling, his joy sufficient armor against his father's concern.

"Did you… did you mention it to your sister?"

"Naw." Allen stopped smiling. "Well, maybe a little. Not really." He looked at Molly. "She's too young to understand."

Molly jumped up. "I am not! I am not!" she protested loudly.

"Hey. Hey." Dick advanced toward his daughter, throwing his arms wide. He picked her up. "The point is, your Mom's okay." He swung her around in a circle. "Who cares what people thought. She's coming home soon, and she's going to be okay!"

* * * * *

There was a small celebration at the house that night. Carol and Walter brought a bottle of champagne. Neighbors stopped by. Afterward, when the guests had gone and the children were in bed, Dick sat alone in the living room with Barbara.

"You have some wonderful friends," she said.

"Wasn't that nice of them to come by. I didn't… I don't think I realized how concerned everyone was. I thought it was, you know, just mostly me. And you and Bob." He hesitated, sipping the remnants of champagne in a wine glass. "Did you… did you ever think the outcome would be really bad?"

"I tried not to think about it," Barbara answered simply.

It was a warm night, and the windows were open. But the street sounds had ended except for the occasional rumble of an automobile on a nearby, main thoroughfare. Their only illumination came from a standing lamp near the couch on which Barbara was seated and the slanted, indirect light through a half-open door into the kitchen.

"What happens now?" he said quietly.

"Just take a day at a time. And be thankful." Barbara was a religious woman, and from that source Christine had imbibed the same convictions. "For now she's going to need all your love and help and support. The future will take care of itself. Take one day at a time."

* * * * *

A week later, Dick drove Christine home from the hospital. The last tube connecting her to the contraption by the bed, and thus to the hospital, had been removed. But her face, by the side of her now exposed, curiously small mouth, remained covered with gauze packing sheathed in a bandage that circled her head. A small plastic tube that served as a drain protruded from the lump of packing.

When the car entered the driveway and stopped near the back door, Allen and Molly emerged from the house and ran to the front passenger side. Allen opened the door.

"Hi," Christine said. "What a greeting!" Her voice had reacquired its former timber. Fumbling, she placed her legs outside the car. Allen started to pull her to her feet.

"Easy does it, my boy," Dick said, leaning across the seat. "Just help slowly."

By the time he got out and walked around the vehicle, Christine was standing. Holding Allen's hand, she took Dick's arm and walked, slowly but steadily, across flagstones on the narrow lawn to the house. Barbara, who had been in the kitchen, was standing at the door. She was smiling.

"Welcome home, darling," she said. "Isn't this great. I've got the bed all made for you."

"I was hoping I could sit while you have lunch," Christine said with a tone of disappointment.

"Sure. We'll prop you up in the easy chair in the living room and eat there." Dick said. "But once we get you up the stairs, I don't think you should be going up and down very much."

"I'll run my own life," Christine responded tartly, the old fire still there.

Nevertheless, once she had gone upstairs, Christine stayed on the second floor of the house. It took several days before she felt strong enough to come downstairs at noontime for lunch on the porch. The gauze packing shrank in size, and eventually the drain was removed. By this time, Dick had seen the ravage to other parts of her body: the red scars across her chest, the wrinkled, white graft of skin on her shoulder, and the discolored, rectangular patch on her thigh from which skin for the graft had been taken. Another scar ran down one side of her neck which was shrunken in, accentuating her gullet. The lymph nodes had been taken from this site.

No artificial jawbone had been inserted to replace the one she had lost. That operation, Dr. McNaught had explained, would not be performed for several months. As he put it, they were waiting so as not to "stir things up." It was a cautionary remark, a reminder that the final outcome was still in doubt.

The indications, however, were favorable. Christine lost the pain she had endured, albeit along with half her jawbone and the teeth that had been rooted in it. Nevertheless, aside from her appearance, still partially disguised by bandages, she seemed the same. And her strength returned, so that the day came when mother and daughter fussed with each other in the kitchen about who should prepare Christine's food. A couple of days later, Barbara announced that she would be returning to Scarsdale and Bob, who was weary of being alone. She and Christine made plans that, in a couple of months, after all the bandages were removed, Christine would drive to Scarsdale with Alice for a few days. In the meantime, Christine and Dick planned to take the children to Cape Cod for a brief vacation.

* * * * *

They left in late July to stay in a beach house in Wellfleet on the outer arm of the Cape. The Haskins had offered to pay the exorbitant rent, and their generous gift was readily accepted. The house was not far, perhaps a mile, from the high dune where Christine and Dick had first tested their love. Not, as it turned out, that they were able to locate the exact spot, despite diligent searching during long walks on the beach. The shifting sand and the frailty of memory defeated them, although both agreed on the general location.

In any event, they would not have returned to make love. Desire for both was dampened by Christine's physical condition. Moreover, their sexual union had long since become a biweekly, routine coupling and had ceased without remonstrance several weeks before the operation. In the dark, they had held and caressed each other, but nothing more. Christine's hard and supple body was now irrevocably marred, and as they touched, Dick was grateful that he could not see, did not have to look down at her lopsided breast and pale, shriveled shoulder.

The house at the Cape was large, comfortably but plainly furnished, with weathered shingles and, on the seaward side, a rambling porch that half encircled it. It was a summer place. Inside, the studs in the walls and the beams in the ceilings were exposed, and prior occupants had lined the window sills and porch railings with shells and pieces of green and blue glass worn smooth by the restless sea. Christine and Dick spent many hours on the porch, reading, and from there they could watch Molly and Allen at play on the beach. On hot, clear mornings, sometimes before breakfast, the children whooped down the low dune before the house, dragging rubber inner tubes and rafts behind them, and plunged into the ocean. They alternately fought and rode the curling waves that foamed across the brown, wet sand.

So Christine's recuperation continued. Twice, Dick drove her to the hospital in Hyannis where her dressing was changed. During their walks on the beach, people remarked her appearance, but in the way of north Europeans and Americans, they did not stare. Only children seemed to notice. One afternoon, while they sat on towels alternately reading and looking out to sea, a young girl walked over. She was with her mother, who had shaken out and laid down a blanket and then unfurled an umbrella on a spot on the broad beach not far away. The girl had seen them and, her natural curiosity aroused, had toddled to a place about fifteen feet from where Christine was sitting. There she stood, thumb in mouth and small belly protruding under her tight, blue bathing suit, and stared. Christine tried to entice her to come closer, but she would not, and after about five minutes the child turned and ran back to her mother.

For ten days the weather was clear. The sky was an arching vault of blue. They were experiencing a Bermuda

High, a persistent ridge of high pressure stalled off the north-eastern Atlantic seaboard. In the mornings, setting a table for breakfast on the porch, Christine invariably said to Dick: "I'm from Bermuda. Hi!" The play on words amused her, and the 'good' side of her mouth tilted upward in pleasure each time.

Eventually, near the end of their two-week stay, there was a cloudy day. And the next day, rain. It drummed on the roof and coursed down the gutters. A sullen sheet of gray, the sea was flattened by intermittent squalls. Molly and Allen were confined to damp games on the porch, and they began to quarrel. The vacation had been an idyllic interlude in their fractured lives, a healing period, but without regret they packed the car to leave. On a Saturday morning, bags in hand, Dick ran amidst the falling drops to place the luggage haphazardly in the open trunk. He lashed a suitcase under a tarpaulin on the car's roof, then stamped, dripping, into the kitchen.

"Okay," he shouted through the living area to the porch, "We're all packed. Let's go."

Christine was the first to enter the room. "Look at your sandy shoes! I just swept in here. Why are you always so inconsiderate? Now I'm going to have to do it all over again."

"What the hell do you want me to do? Stand outside in the rain?"

"Just be a little considerate, that's all."

"Just be…? I didn't notice you outside packing the car."

"With this on?" She pointed to her bandage. "How could you even say such a thing? You're impossible."

Molly, struggling into a rain slicker, tiptoed around her mother and ran to the car. "Make sure you lock the door," Dick yelled crossly over his shoulder as he followed their daughter.

They drove away in frozen silence.

* * * * *

Not long thereafter, the remaining gauze dressing and bandage were removed.

Christine, her strength renewed, had driven herself to the doctor's office. The procedure took only a few minutes. Dick saw her when he returned home. She was working in the kitchen, and her back was turned to him as he entered.

"I'm home," he said. "Well, turn around, and let's take a look."

"I don't want to." She continued cutting vegetables on a chopping board on a counter next to the refrigerator.

Dick took a step forward, stopped, uncertain what to do. "C'mon, honey. I've got to see it sometime. It's… it's not going to matter."

"I hate it," she said despairingly. "I just hate it."

Dick walked over to her and placed his hands on her shoulders. "Now turn around," he said gently, "and let me see. I'm sure it's much better than you think."

"No, it's not! It's not! It's not!" She hunched forward. He tried carefully to turn her, and as he did, she put down the knife and covered her lower face with her hands. Her eyes beseeched him. Slowly, Dick moved his hands from her shoulders and wrapped his fingers around her wrists.

She did not resist. He pulled her hands downward and gazed at her.

"Actually, it looks much better than I thought it would."

"No, it doesn't." She tried to pull her hands up again, but he stopped her.

"It's fascinating how they did it. Will that skin," he pointed to the graft beside her mouth, "turn the same color as your… you know, the rest of your face?"

"I don't think so." The tone of despair returned to her voice. "It will always be noticeable, except maybe," she grimaced, "if I put a lot of powder on it. I asked Dr. McNaught. He said the skin on my shoulder didn't get as much sun as my face, and by this time they're just different."

"But not that different, really."

"Yes, they are." She was defiantly dejected. "It looks horrible."

"No, really. It doesn't. And once the new jawbone is back in place, it'll be almost as good as new. That's what's really bothering you, I'll bet. It's the lack of symmetry."

"Oh, Dick." She buried her face into his chest beneath his shoulder. "Do you really think it isn't so bad? Can you still love me?"

"Absolutely. And you've gotten rid of those bandages. I'll tell you, I'm glad to see them go."

Christine stepped back. Her lips, on the good side of her face, curled bravely upward. "I hope you get used to it… I hope I do, too," she added ruefully.

The graft was a different color, lighter in complexion than the remainder of her face. It covered an area approximately the size of a silver dollar next to her abbreviated mouth. Dick was right. It was the lack of symmetry that was far more noticeable. That, and the scars. As careful and as skilled as Dr. McNaught had been, the lines in her chin, her lower lip and her cheek where new tissue had been joined to old were lumpy and uneven. The transition was not smooth. And her face, where the jawbone had been removed, caved inward to her equally indented neck. Christine had become a woman with three quarters of a mouth and eighty per cent of a face.

Yet she lives, Dick reminded himself, as he lay in bed that night. Molly and Allen still have a mother. He rolled over and put his arm around his wife. I thought modern medicine was supposed to make you as good as new. What happened to all those miracles of plastic surgery? It's a lie. He lay there, holding on to her tightly. It's a lie. For the rest of my life, I've got to live with it, get used to it. But she's right. She looks… His mind would not, could not, finish the thought. And finally, in mixed gratitude and despair, he drifted into a confused and troubled sleep.

Chapter 15

A Frozen Tableau

1975

A few weeks later, on a Wednesday in mid-September, Christine drove with Alice to Scarsdale to visit her mother and father. Alice had a sister in Darien and planned to spend a few days with her before bringing Christine back. On Friday Allen left to spend the weekend hiking near Mount Washington as part of a school environmental program, and Molly departed to spend the weekend with a school chum and her family at their summer house on Lake Winnipesaukee.

* * * * *

"Can I have some more?"

"Of what? The squash is all gone," Carol said. "There's plenty of spaghetti."

"I meant the spaghetti." Dick pointed at the bowl on the table. "Sure is good."

He passed his plate to Carol, who ladled a generous portion of spaghetti and sauce onto it.

"Hey, whoa! Save some for leftovers."

"There's plenty. Anyway, you're not fat."

Dick was sitting on the long side of the dining room table, facing Carol and Walter's two sons. Carol was at one end, Walter at the other. The room, though not large, was elegantly furnished with an antique mahogany wood table and sideboard with matching chairs. Over the table hung a modest chandelier, and over a fireplace at one side hung an oil painting of woods and a pond after a new fallen snow.

"Here, Tommy, let me put some more on your plate," Carol said. She took the plate of the boy sitting next to her. "You didn't get enough to begin with."

Walter, his portly stomach brushing the table before him, did not ask for a second helping. "If anything, Dick, I think you've lost weight." He patted his stomach genially. "Wish I could do the same."

Carol raised an eyebrow and stared at him.

"Can Christine prepare dinner," she asked Dick, "or are you still doing it?"

"Well," Dick hesitated, "we both do it. Her more than me now. I'd say Christine prepares our dinners, and I just fix them."

"Pretty well, according to her," said Walter.

"I've gotten better at it. And, you know, Barbara helped… I didn't lose any weight."

"I guess Christine's okay enough to drive to New York," Carol ventured. "It's probably good for her to get away."

"And good for me," laughed Dick, "to have you invite me to dinner, so I don't have to eat my hamburgers or chicken."

"We wanted to. It's been a long time."

"Hope you don't mind me coming over on a Friday night. That's probably your time to relax."

"No, no. Walter's been pestering me to have you both over for a long time. I'm sorry we couldn't have Christine, but this seemed like a good time, and we're busy tomorrow night."

"You said Christine will be staying with her folks for a while?" Walter asked.

"Yeah. It'll be good for her. She'll be spoiled rotten and waited on hand and foot. And her parents are really anxious to see her."

Walter said, "They'll be surprised, I think, at how well she's doing."

"There's been a real change since Barbara was here," Dick replied. "No more bandages for one thing. She's going in and out of stores and did some grocery shopping a few days ago."

"How do you think she really is, Dick?" Walter inquired earnestly. "How's she taking it?"

"Walter!" Carol spoke sharply from her end of the table. "I don't think that's an appropriate question, particularly in front of the children."

"It's all right," Dick said. "I don't mind. I might keep secrets if I had any, but I don't. She seems fine, and she's gotten most of her energy back."

"What I meant, mostly," said Walter, "is how she's adjusting to the change in her appearance."

"She's no different. She goes ahead as if nothing's happened."

"That's Christine for you."

"Yeah, she says I have to look at it. She doesn't."

"And how do you...?" Carol checked herself. "There's not much for dessert. Some ice cream and cookies."

The two boys were immediately interested, and each clamored for a plate.

"Not me," said Walter.

"Me either," Dick echoed him. "After that second helping, I'm stuffed."

"Let's walk it off," Walter said. "It's a nice night. Whadda you say?"

"I say great idea. I could use it."

Only Carol demurred, then relented. "Let's get this table cleared," she said. "The boys can eat dessert in the kitchen. You two go sit in the living room and wait for me. I just want to wash a few things first."

"Need some help?"

"Nope. I'll be faster alone."

Walter had returned home late, and as a result supper had not been served until nearly eight o'clock. It was dark outside, but a dark broken by the gray shadows of trees with leaves that, in their waning days, rustled in brittle dryness against each other. Yet it was nevertheless a summer night, a close, warm evening on the forward cusp of autumn.

Within a few minutes Walter, Carol and Dick quit the house and walked along the side of the street that passed in front of it. A couple of cars sped by them, headlights beaming. After a quarter mile, they turned onto a narrow road that dipped down to a stone bridge across a meandering creek. There they stood in the middle, peering over the side at the inky snake of water coiling beneath them. The moon's reflection, streaked by wisps of cloud, hung, suspended, undulating on its rippling surface.

"Let's take the old Indian trail around the hill," said Dick, gesturing vaguely in the direction of a low rise of trees not far in the distance.

"Or we could walk into the meadow," countered Carol. "It should be pretty in the moonlight." On the other side of the bridge, flanking the creek, stretched a broad meadow, its grassy expanse broken by scattered clumps of bushes and trees. The meadow usually flooded in autumn, after the ground had frozen, and was a favorite place for ice-skating in winter. But in the spring, after the ice and snow had melted, the water receded, leaving rich, fertile land. The ground was still soft, but the meadow was dry to walk upon, covered with tall grass that had yellowed in the summer heat.

"Why don't you two go ahead," Walter said. "I'm really tired. I think I'll go back."

"You sure?" Carol asked. "It's such a nice night."

"Yeah, I'm bushed. I'll see you back at the house." Walter began to retrace his steps on the bridge, then trudge up the narrow rise of road whence they had come.

"We'll be there in a few minutes," Dick shouted after him. They watched as his heavy figure disappeared in the gloom.

"So what'll it be?" Dick asked. "The hill or the meadow?"

"Let's walk on the meadow."

They clambered down a bank from the road on the far side of the bridge. "I'm glad I'm wearing long pants," Dick grunted as he pushed a bush aside.

"So am I."

Carol led the way. Dick was aware of the crunching sound made by his shoes against the stubble beneath the grass. The ground was uneven, disguised by the grass, and in a couple of places he stumbled. Night noises surrounded him: the burp of a frog from the creek, the swishing of the grass as they pushed through it, but overwhelmingly the incessant whir, almost din, of cicadas in the black border of bushes and trees that encircled the meadow. And over them hung a pallid, gibbous moon, bathing their visible landscape in pale light, so that they seemed to be walking on a surreal chessboard between dark pieces that loomed on either side.

It was toward one of these, a copse of four gnarled trees about a hundred yards from the road, that Carol walked. When she reached the shadow, she turned.

"Isn't it beautiful?"

"Yes," he replied in a whisper, unwilling to break the spell of the place.

"Oh, Dick." She placed her hands on his shoulders. Swiftly, he placed his on her hips. The first kiss was brief, almost chaste. His hands moved across her back, pulling her toward him, while hers clung to his neck. The second kiss was long, lingering. And so was the third.

Carol stepped back, panting slightly. She fumbled at the front of her blouse, awkwardly unbuttoning it in the muted light. She dropped it on the grass, then undid buttons at the side of her slacks. They slid to her ankles where, with her shoes, she kicked them off. For a brief moment, she stood before him in her undergarments, then removed them also.

"When I'm old and gray and sitting in a rocking chair

on my front porch," Carol murmured, "this will be nice to remember."

But Dick stepped back, gaping at her. Motionless, he moved neither forward nor backward but stood, transfixed. He saw the hair falling over her shoulder, the darkness of her nipples against her pale flesh. Through the interlaced branches of the trees, speckled shafts of moonlight played upon the soft contours of her body and accentuated her beckoning smile. Engulfed by desire, still he did not move. Nearby crickets sawed on in unbroken rapture to the night, and the whirring sound of the cicadas in the surrounding bushes and trees seemed to grow louder and louder, a cacophonous accompaniment to a frozen tableau.

Chapter 16

Things Seen and Unseen

1975

Dick paced the confines of his office, stopping occasionally by the telephone but then moving on. He hesitated by the window, his fingers fidgeting in his moist palms. It had been three days since he had enjoyed dinner with Carol and Walter and then, afterward, had ventured into the meadow in the moonlight with Carol. The evening had ended in bitter recriminations on her part and in embarrassment and confusion on his. He needed to talk with her and to somehow explain his inexplicable behavior.

After several minutes he walked to his door to make sure it was shut and locked, then retreated to his desk and sat down in his wooden swivel chair. Reaching for the telephone, he took a deep breath and dialed Carol's number.

After a couple of rings he heard her familiar, cheerful greeting. There was a pause, then with feigned casualness, Dick spoke, "Hi, Carol, it's Dick. Are you free to talk?"

There was a second, even longer pause. For a moment Dick thought that she might have hung up on him.

"I was wondering if you'd call," she said slowly. "Yes, I'm free, if you mean that nobody else is here." Again there was silence.

"I need to explain," Dick said, his words rushed. "I need to make clear what happened. It had nothing to do with you. It was me."

Carol's response was icy cold, her words clipped in barely concealed anger. "It was humiliating. You… you humiliated me, led me on. I was just left to stand there, to put my clothes back on, while you backed away."

Dick winced at the recollection. "I wanted you. Carol, you have no idea how badly. I just couldn't. Not then, anyway. You have to believe me."

"Of course I believe you," she snorted. "Look what happened!"

"We need to talk, and not like this over the telephone."

"What's there to talk about?"

"There's plenty. It's… it's not over. It just took me by surprise. I guess I hadn't gone as far as you in my thinking."

"Well, you certainly put on a good act. It fooled me. And made a fool out of me."

"I didn't mean to, and I'm sorry. Look," Dick fumbled for a solution, "let's go for lunch and talk this over. I know a place where we can meet. My treat."

"How generous."

There was silence again. Carol added quietly: "It would probably be better – and wiser – if we stopped right here."

"And we can, we can. But I just want to explain and make it up to you, if possible."

Dick heard Carol inhale deeply, then exhale slowly in resignation. "All right. I don't see the point. But all right. I don't suppose it can hurt."

"I know a place in Framingham. It's a little, out-of-the-way restaurant, very cozy, really, and we can have lunch there."

"When?"

Dick looked at his calendar. "Next week would be best for me. On Tuesday. At noon. Will that work for you?"

"Any day next week would be fine."

"Excellent. It will make things better if we meet, I promise you. Let me tell you how to get there."

* * * * *

A week later Carol and Dick met at the appointed time. As Dick had said, the restaurant was a cozy place. Small and dark, it had booths along the outside walls, and the tables were covered by checkered tablecloths. A small jukebox hung on the wall by each table.

Dick arrived first and sat in a booth by a window. Outside it was drizzling, and he could hear a rhythmic drip from a downspout near the window. The leaves on a nearby tree were glistening wet, and the tires of occasional passing cars made swishing noises on the slick pavement. He was facing the door and saw Carol enter, her head covered by a broad-brimmed hat. Without smiling, she approached him, hung her tan raincoat on a hook on the outside of the booth and squirmed onto the seat opposite him.

They looked at each other, and Dick managed a wan smile. It was not returned. "Would you like some wine?" he asked. Carol nodded in assent. Dick summoned a plump, harried, middle-aged waitress and placed the order. The waitress, after announcing that her name was

Cynthia, unceremoniously dropped two menus on the table and retreated through a curtain into the kitchen.

"Well, I'm glad you came," Dick said. "I was worried you might not." He took a deep breath. "You're looking very beautiful today. I mean, like every day. Nothing unusual about that."

For the first time, Carol smiled. "Oh, Dick, you can't help yourself. Come on, let's talk. This doesn't have to be a funeral." Dick had folded his hands on the table, and Carol reached over and patted the left one.

The waitress returned with two glasses of house Chardonnay. Smiling broadly when she saw two apparent lovers, she placed the glasses on the table. They both ordered a sandwich. Thereafter, using his right, free hand, Dick sipped his wine while continuing to look directly into Carol's eyes. She reciprocated his actions and gaze.

"I'm not sure what to say. I don't have a prepared speech." Dick laughed nervously, and his Adam's apple jerked involuntarily up and down. "I've done a lot of thinking about that situation. I feel very badly about what happened, but i'm relieved that no one got hurt."

"Only you, probably, with your conscience."

Dick fiddled with his glass. "My image of myself is changing."

"Dick, for goodness sake, I hope so. Learn to accept yourself for who you are – a human being in a difficult situation."

Dick broke off their mutual gaze and again fiddled with his glass. "This is really hard," he mumbled, "but I might as well admit it – to you and to myself. I really wanted to make love to you."

"Then why didn't you?" Carol challenged him.

"I couldn't. I just couldn't."

"It's all right, Dick. I understand. Lots of men have that problem."

For a moment Dick appeared perplexed. Then he smiled. "That's not it. I was ready all right. But I kept thinking of Christine, of her sad face in all those bandages. And how much she needs me, and how hurt she'd be if she ever found out. I don't know. Maybe I'm a prude after all."

"You're no prude. Old school, maybe, and honorable in a strange sort of way. It was awfully embarrassing for me, though."

"I'm sorry, really sorry. I couldn't… I was caught… caught between what I wanted to do and what I ought to do. I'm a real mess."

"A mess? No, Dick, you're not a mess. You've been a tremendous support to your family." Carol spoke gently. "You've got a problem most of us are awfully happy not to share."

"You're so beautiful," Dick blurted. "And I wanted to make love. Terribly. Sex between Christine and me has never been that great, and now I'm afraid I'll never have it again. It's been weeks. Actually, months. I just can't do it anymore. I love her, I really do, but that part of our life is dead. I look at her and I… and I can't."

Dick dropped his eyes again, his mouth folded down in a tight frown.

Carol said nothing, but she continued to pat his hand. "And she gets so mad at me," Dick resumed. "She says I'm withholding myself on purpose, and I'm not. If she ever found out about you and me, she'd kill me."

"Kill you? She has nowhere else to go. Of course she'd be very angry, but she doesn't have to find out. It's our secret."

"I hope what I just told you is secret too. I've never mentioned it to anyone else." Looking forlorn, Dick sipped his wine. "Can we try some other time? Can you forgive me?"

"I'm not sure I need to. But, yes, I forgive you. When you're ready, if you ever are, tell me. It might never happen. I don't know. I might change my mind. But we can leave that for the future."

"And in the meantime, I'm sort of like a priest with involuntary vows of chastity." Dick exhaled softly and bitterly.

Carol shook her head slowly from side to side. "Dick, we can remain friends and you can talk to me whenever you want. I'm glad we had this chat. You made things much more understandable for me."

"Then I'm glad too."

"Let's let the future take care of itself." Carol was about to say more, but the waitress arrived with their sandwiches, and the topic of conversation changed. For about an hour they chatted animatedly about the quotidian details of their lives until Dick realized that he had to return to work. Leaving a generous tip, he paid the bill and helped Carol on with her coat. After grasping his umbrella that had been dampening the seat next to him, Dick walked behind Carol to the door.

* * * * *

Mary, the wife of Bob in Woodbury and a friend of Christine and Carol, had been shopping that morning in Framingham with a friend. It had taken longer than planned, and both were famished. The friend suggested a small, out-of-the-way restaurant where they could enjoy a good, inexpensive lunch. Mary agreed, and they drove to a side street where the restaurant was located and parked at one end of the short block. The drizzle of morning had turned to a light rain. Mary was fumbling for a collapsible umbrella in her purse when she saw two figures emerge from the restaurant. Her friend was about to exit the car when Mary grasped her arm.

"Wait a minute," she said. "I think I recognize those people." Her grip on her friend's arm tightened. "Oh my God, it's my neighbors. I know them. Don't get out yet."

Mary watched as Carol and Dick walked to Carol's car that was parked across the street from the restaurant. Carol was holding tightly to Dick, her arm looped through his. When they reached the car, she turned and placed her arms around Dick's neck. They embraced, and their lips touched in a lingering kiss. Dick held the door for her and then watched as she drove away. Hunched over, his umbrella raised and his collar turned up, he walked up the street past the car in which Mary was sitting and around the corner. She was certain it was Dick Blodgett. He never glanced in her direction.

Chapter 17

Shattering Revelations

1975

Not long thereafter, Dick called Dr. Bader's office to arrange a meeting. He wanted to find out, to the extent possible, the true nature of Christine's prognosis. To his surprise, Dr. Bader agreed to see him the next day.

When he arrived, Dr. Bader invited him into his small office that was cluttered with books and stacks of papers, and he asked Dick to take a seat in a comfortable armchair in one corner. After removing some books and medical texts, Dick did so. An elderly man of average build with thinning white hair, Dr. Bader had been an invaluable source of support to Christine, and both she and Dick had come to admire and appreciate his skill as a surgeon and his compassion as a human being.

"I think I know why you're here, Dick," Dr. Bader said. "This is as good a time as any to discuss Christine's case."

"I'm sure you can understand," Dick replied, "that I… we… have got planning to do, and I need a frank assessment of our situation."

Dr. Bader ran a hand through his thinning hair and down past his ear to his neck. He then tugged at his chin. "I have to be a bit careful here," he said. "These cases are always difficult, and no one can say with one hundred per cent certainty what the outcome will be. Still," he paused, looking directly at Dick, "I'm optimistic about Christine's prospects. We didn't detect any cancer cells in her lymph nodes which is a good sign. On the other hand, Dick, I must caution you that it is possible a few cells escaped and have traveled up a nerve pathway to her ear and brain."

"Can radiation take care of that?" Dick asked.

"To be honest, no. Radiating her brain would kill her, and we wouldn't be able to operate, so we simply have to wait and see."

" You mean if that happens she'll die." Dick had heard the note of optimism, but that pronouncement was obliterated by Dr. Bader's cautionary remarks.

Dr. Bader pulled at his chin again. "I'm afraid so," he said, "but don't focus on that. She may live to ninety. Yes, it's possible her life will be much shorter, but how much shorter we can't say. If cells have escaped, they may lie there in remission for years."

"Or she may only live for another couple of years?"

Dr. Bader nodded in assent. There was a long interlude of silence. Then Dick said, "How will it happen? I kinda don't want to know, but I think I ought to… I ought to be prepared for it."

"I don't believe you should contemplate that at this point," Dr. Bader said. "I'll just say, because the base of her brain might be affected, she will probably die in the dark without hearing, but she'll know you're present by the touch of your hand. My advice, Dick, is to try not to think about that right now."

Dick sighed. "I'm sure this wasn't easy for you," he said finally.

Dr. Bader smiled wryly. “I’ve had better moments.” He rose, walked around his desk and placed his hand on Dick’s shoulder. “I want to emphasize that her operation went very well – as well as could be expected, and I’m pleased with the result. If somehow we haven’t caught all of it, I won’t be the physician in charge of Christine’s treatment, but I’ll stay in touch. And you can call on me anytime for advice. For now, I suggest you go and lead a normal life. None of us can predict the future, and there’s no point borrowing trouble into the present that may never happen.”

Dick was composed as he left the office, but once he reached his car in the hospital parking lot he pounded its roof with his fist. How, he raged bitterly in a convulsion of grief and remorse, could a loving God permit such suffering? I’m back to where I was when this all began, he thought. I’ve got to see this through, to be a loving, caring husband and father. This nightmare won’t end.

* * * * *

After an extended stay with her parents, Christine returned home. Dick was glad she had finally returned to him and the children, and they all shared a delightful dinner by candlelight that he prepared. Christine, too, was happy to be back with her family in her own house in Woodbury, although her mood turned sour after a few days. Once again, she accused Dick angrily about his failure to initiate sex, and he was speechless in return. One evening, looking beleaguered, he rose from their bed and went downstairs where he sat alone in the dark until after midnight. When he returned, Christine was asleep.

He had not called Carol or seen her since their rendezvous in the restaurant in Framingham. He had thought about her, about how delightful it would be to meet her in a hotel or motel room, or in a field, or anywhere. Once, in his office, he reached for the telephone, but he drew back. Was it moral compunction, fear of being caught, or the recollection of his conversation with Dr. Bader and his love for Christine? He did not know, and in his indecision, he let the opportunity, if it was one, slip slowly away.

One beautiful day not long after her return, Christine suggested that they take a walk. It was early afternoon and warm in the sun, the weather now clearly alternating between the last, lingering days of summer and the florid, wistful gaiety of autumn. Leaves tagged about on the ground. The sky was crystal blue, and the tops of the swamp maples and saplings were bright red and yellow. Beneath that fringe of color, the trees still wore a mantle of brittle, weathered green. Christine and Dick had decided on a picnic, and they were seated on a blanket near a pond ringed with bushes and ocher-colored grass, not far from Carol and Walter's house. They had been for a quiet, contemplative walk by the pond, through woods and a stubbly pasture flanked by a stone wall, before selecting a place to sit down.

Christine had prepared cucumber sandwiches and hard-boiled eggs, and they ate in silence. Dick opened a bottle of white wine and poured the tawny liquid into two plastic cups. It was as if a spell had been cast upon the field, and neither wished to break it.

But finally Christine spoke. She turned to Dick and wiped away some wine that had dribbled from her mouth onto her now scarred and insensate chin. "I've got a question to ask you, Dick. I've waited a while and thought about it a lot. Please hear me out, and then I'd like your answer."

"Well, sure," Dick said, suddenly and uncomfortably aware of her somber mood. "Say what you have to say."

"Dick, a couple of weeks ago Mary stopped by our house. You were at work. At first I couldn't believe what she was saying. I dismissed it as malicious gossip – you know how she is – and frankly cruel. She didn't need to say it."

"Say what?" Dick interrupted, puzzled.

"Let me finish. She said that she saw you and Carol leave a restaurant in Framingham together not long ago. She was in a parked car and saw you. She said you were walking arm in arm and that you kissed each other goodbye at Carol's car. Not just kissed. It was a passionate kiss, she said." Christine stopped speaking for a moment. She had been looking down at her hands, tears welling in her eyes, and now she looked directly at Dick. "Is it true? Are you and Carol having an affair?"

Stunned, Dick picked his ear while silently staring out at the surrounding trees and the tumbled end of a stone wall, his face a blank mask. His Adam's apple rose and fell. When he eventually replied, he said hoarsely, "The answer is yes and no. I won't deny that it was me, but Carol and I are not having an affair."

Christine flinched. "I can't… I can't believe this. People don't meet secretly and kiss passionately if they're not involved with each other. Now I know why you won't make love to me. What were you doing, setting up some kind of tryst?" Her voice began to rise, and she drew away from him. "What happened to the sacred vows we spoke to each other at our wedding? What happened to 'for better or for worse' or 'in sickness and in health'?" She paused. "You know, Dick, my parents adore you. What will they think now when I tell them about your behavior? What will our neighbors think?"

"Please don't do that," he begged, bowing his head. "Why must you tell everyone? You know I still love you, and it's not that I won't make love to you, it's that I can't… I just can't… at least right now. Why can't we work this out between us, go to counseling if that would help?" He looked at her and saw a face drawn up in sorrow or rage, he could not tell. "Christine, I'm telling the truth, so calm down." He reached for her arm. "Carol and I are not having an affair, I swear it."

"Swear all you want. The facts speak for themselves. Don't come near me, don't touch me." Pulling her arm close to her body, she stood up, leaving Dick with the blanket and the luncheon supplies, and walked away toward their home. An hour later he found her there, staring out the living room window and unresponsive to his entreaties to talk further.

They did not, however, part company. And two weeks later, Christine followed through on her threat. At the conclusion of an elegant dinner at the home of neighbors, a question arose about Carol and Walter. No one had seen them lately. Christine had had too much to drink, and she blurted to the guests seated around the table: "I'll tell you why you haven't seen them! I'll tell you why. My darling husband has been having an affair with Carol. He's been fucking her all over town. That's why."

The conversation at the table ceased, and Dick felt himself reddening. He opened his mouth but could not speak.

The hostess, who was having her own marital difficulties, glared at him. "That's disgusting," she said. "Absolutely disgusting."

There were ten people – five couples – at the table, and two couples averred that it was time to go home and departed. Along with Christine, the others drifted into the living room, and Dick sat at the table alone.

A variant of that scene was replicated elsewhere, and Dick began to suspect that Christine was drinking excessively. He found a near-empty bottle of bourbon in the kitchen with no explanation offered. Her drinking began to mimic that of her father, and after cocktails and dinner, their evenings were punctuated by bitter arguments. Trivial matters would set them off: a utility bill, vacation plans, a relative's visit, anything that could be used as an excuse for anger, and then the arguments escalated without respite. Usually at some point Dick would leave the room or house, Molly's strained face haunting him as he stomped away. On returning, he would sometimes find the bedroom door locked.

Finally, Dick left their home permanently. Christine, who had despised his presence, begged him not to go. He rented an apartment in a neighboring town and mended relations with his friends, most of whom were understanding and supportive. Dick's life revolved around work and long, lonely walks. In a welcome interval, as he had done several times during the worst episodes of Christine's illness, David drove north to be with his brother for a few days. Dick told him everything that had happened. David heard him and said nothing. He joined Dick on his walks or for evenings sipping beer in the apartment. "You're in a tight spot," he said, shaking his head. "Hang in there, if you can."

David related the latest news of his children and fretted about taking a new job dealing with the sale of novel financial instruments. But mostly it was Dick who talked, repeating himself over and over without a resolution of his predicament. Patiently, David listened. Dick cherished his presence and urged him to stay longer, but eventually David had to resume work and reunite with his wife and young family. He left, promising to return and inviting Dick to visit whenever it would be convenient.

Chapter 18

Another Fresh Start

1975–1976

The next time they communicated, it was Carol who called Dick at his office. She asked if they could meet, and he suggested lunch again in the same restaurant in Framingham. She sounded flat – the gaiety and sparkle were gone – and she asked, with a flinty edge in her voice, "Aren't you afraid someone will see us there?"

"What if they do?" Dick replied. "Would it change anything?"

"No, I don't suppose so," Carol answered wearily. "Name the time, and I'll be there."

They met a few days later. As before, Dick was seated in a booth by a window facing the door. The tree outside the window was bare of its leaves that, in brittle fragments, scuttled about the sidewalk in miniature whirlwinds. As Carol walked through the door, he noted with a tinge of disappointment that she was wearing a heavy wool sweater that disguised her curvaceous figure. Grim faced, she sat in the booth.

After a few awkward moments, Carol held out her hand and grasped Dick's while she eyed him with a pensive frown.

"Haven't you told Christine that we're not having an affair?" Her tone was accusatory, exasperated.

"Of course I have. Many times. But she says the facts speak for themselves."

"I suppose they do," Carol said in a voice of resignation. She looked at Dick, frowning, then added, "Do you remember that time, long ago, when we had that conversation on your porch about how attitudes about sex were changing?"

"You mean about Bud Klein?"

"Yes. And one of us said, maybe Christine, that someone always gets hurt. At least that's how I remember it."

"I remember Christine was pretty moralistic and inflexible."

"Nothing's changed there," Carol interrupted bitterly. "Well, someone has gotten hurt – me. There's gossip all over town, so I'm told, and I'm the lady with the scarlet letter."

The plump waitress came to the table, and Dick ordered two glasses of wine. With a knowing smile, she hurried away.

"Not just you," Dick said. "Christine's been hurt, and so have I."

"Not in the same way. That damn Mary, that busybody, goody-goody little snitch. She could have come to me first for an explanation." Carol paused. "Anyway, Dick darling, with the news all over town, I told Walter that part of the gossip was true, that we'd had an intimate lunch."

"Oh, my God," Dick exclaimed in alarm. "Is he going to come after me?"

"No, for goodness sake. I didn't tell him everything,

and I denied having an affair. He was very understanding. But a few days later he said that he'd found a nice house in Marblehead, right on the water, and if we can get the price down a little bit we should think seriously about buying it and moving. Not immediately. Not yet. But Walter says our lives in Woodbury are finished. We've moved once before, Dick, and it's probably going to happen."

"Wh… when do you plan to do this?"

"I don't know. It will probably be sometime soon. It's the end of our beautiful friendships in Woodbury."

Dick stared blankly at her. "Marblehead! That's maybe forty, fifty miles away. This is terrible news."

* * * * *

Dick and Carol stayed in touch, usually by infrequent telephone conversations but occasionally through inadvertent meetings when both were doing errands in the town. Those contacts ended after Carol and Walter sold their house, and the day came when they moved away. Walter purchased the new home that he had found for them in Marblehead. There was no fond farewell, no tearful leave-taking. One day they were in Woodbury, and the next day they were gone.

Dick saw Christine frequently during this time, often when he returned home to be with his children. For both, their days were filled with distracting activities. Dick taught and did research. Christine tended to Molly, the house and the garden. She had lunch often with friends and volunteered at local charities that seemingly had a bottomless need for help. At night, however, there was no one with whom to cuddle, no one with whom to discuss the day's events. Throwing her arm out to one side as the clock ticked toward midnight, Christine would find only a cold, empty space. Thoughts tumbled in her mind, bringing no rest. Sometimes she beat the pillow with her fist in anger and frustration, but in calmer moments she wondered whether she had been too precipitous and harsh in her reaction to his transgression.

Over time Christine's feelings toward Dick softened, and her anger waned. And Dick in turn began to consider returning home, a reconciliation and a concerted effort to mend their marriage. Christine begged him to consider marriage counseling, and they located a therapist, Dr. Bernard Katz. He was a portly man of medium height with a bushy, black beard and horn-rimmed glasses. His second-floor walk-up office was a block from Harvard Square in Cambridge. Christine had made inquiries, and Dr. Tomlinson and a friend had recommended him.

Dr. Katz interviewed Christine and Dick separately and then together. Impassively, with a world-weary smile, he heard about the reputed affair and Dick's denial of it. Until almost the last session, he never mentioned it again except once, when he remarked that, if there had been an affair, it was a symptom, not the cause of their difficulties. And it was the cause that he sought.

After several sessions in which he sat, sphinx-like, listening to them talk, he opined that healthy couples act like and treat each other as two adults. In their marriage, however, at an unconscious level, Dick had often treated Christine, so sure of her opinions, as a mother surrogate.

But Dick was growing and changing, and Christine's cancer accelerated the process. In her new state, Christine had become more dependent and vulnerable, and Dick had of necessity been required to take charge. In a sense, he had become the father. The dynamic between them had been totally reversed. But it was still a child to parent relationship. To it, Dr. Katz suggested, Christine had brought her latent hostility to Bob, her real, often distant, father.

Neither Dick nor Christine could have pointed to one 'Aha!' moment that clarified their relationship. It may have been Dr. Katz's insight combined with ample evidence of Dick's contrition. Over time they drew closer together, although the basic problem of Christine's cancer and their altered sex life loomed in the background, unresolved. Dr. Katz suggested further therapy, but Dick balked, citing the expense, and so they agreed that the therapy should end.

"Well, where do we go from here?" Dr. Katz said during their last session as their hour with him drew to a close.

Christine and Dick looked at each other, then at Dr. Katz. "I'm not sure," Christine said.

Dick looked back at Christine. "Me neither," he said. "I could, I suppose… you know… come home… that is, if Christine would want me to."

"Not if you're going to continue being a cheat. Everyone knows about you, about your behavior."

"Let's remember why you're both here," Dr. Katz interjected soothingly. "You can have strong feelings, Christine, but no marriage will work if there is constant blaming. I think we should hear what Dick has to say."

Christine and Dr. Katz both looked in Dick's direction. He gazed bleakly around the room and took a deep breath. "Well, according to my own moral code, I don't think that what I did was so terribly wrong. I was flirting with danger, I admit that, and particularly dangerous given Christine's condition."

"Oh, come on," Christine said crossly. "It was a lot more than flirting, and you have a real problem if you can't figure that out."

Dick's face scrunched into a frown. "I've stated repeatedly that I did not have a sexual affair with Carol. I admit that I was attracted to her, but that was all. People can control their actions – or so we assume – but can they control their wandering thoughts or emotions?"

"Dick, grown-ups don't put themselves in situations where their thoughts and feelings can get out of control. And anyway, you had more than wandering thoughts. You kissed and, according to Mary, you kissed passionately."

"I'm not denying it, but how can a kiss by itself be so wrong? Isn't it much worse if a man hates his wife but never strays, or if he abandons his wife to spend his time gambling, or drinking, or... or working at the office until late at night, every night, even if it's to support his wife and children."

"That's not infidelity," Christine retorted with conviction, "and you know it."

"No, I do not. Is there some kind of objective standard written in gold letters up in the sky, or does it depend on the expectations of the people involved and the circumstances they find themselves in?"

"Dick, there is a standard, or have you conveniently forgotten your wedding vows?"

"No, I haven't. But our circumstances have changed."

For several moments, Dick stopped speaking. Christine, who had been staring at him, looked away, and her distorted, lower lip quivered.

Hastily, Dick resumed. "My point is that nowadays we think of infidelity more as a breach of trust in a loving relationship, not as behavior resulting in a breach of property rights. And if love remains, or, for that matter, if it wanders without conscious intention, how can there be infidelity?"

Christine again stared at Dick. "You've lost me. Your point – it's something you've obviously thought about – is what?"

"Oh for God's sake," Dick sputtered in exasperation. "Is what? Don't you understand? I never lost my love for you, even though our relationship has changed. That much I've learned from all these sessions."

"But your feelings can't excuse your behavior."

Dr. Katz broke in, speaking softly, "Christine, I don't know whether there was an affair or not. Adultery in a legal sense probably didn't happen." He hesitated for a moment. "And, Dick, you have to admit that there are degrees of infidelity, and you implied as much yourself. There was smoke here, and where's there's smoke, there's at least the beginning of a fire."

"All right, I'll admit that much, and I'll try hard to never let it happen again."

"That's not good enough, Dick. Trying hard isn't the same as saying your behavior won't be repeated."

"Okay. It won't happen again. That's a promise with respect to my behavior. As for my thoughts and feelings..." His voice trailed away. He riveted his gaze at the floor, then glanced up at Christine. "This much I can say. I'm committed to you, Christine, and to our marriage. I'll cherish and support you 'till death us do part."

"I guess, then, Christine, it's up to you," Dr. Katz said.

* * * * *

A couple of weeks later, Dick moved back into their comfortable house in Woodbury to resume their lives together.

Chapter 19

A Promise Broken?

1976

But it was not the same. A major surgical procedure had been performed, and the patient – their marriage – would take a long time to heal. The wound was still tender, and the first halting steps to recovery were slow and occasionally painful. There were episodes of remission. And like a bandage being ripped away, there were moments of trauma, often sudden and unexpected.

At first, at home once more, Dick felt awkward, like a visitor in a country he had once known but that had changed in his absence. The children were older with slightly altered habits and expectations. The shift was subtle, but noticeable to him. Allen spent more time away with his friends; he was less willing to devote a weekend to his family and forego the opportunity to engage in sports. Molly bickered more with her mother, as girls are wont to do as they grope toward independence.

The major difference, though, was in the relationship between Christine and Dick. Outwardly civil, even demonstrably loving to each other in the presence of friends, they circled each other like two prize fighters in a ring. Their friends quickly accepted them again as a couple, but the internal dynamic between them, now forever changed, was less easy and more prolonged to rebuild. A subtle wall had been constructed, and their task was to tear it down brick by stubborn brick.

In moments of stress, Christine would too often forget Dr. Katz's admonition that constant blaming eroded a happy marriage. She would greet some inadvertent misjudgment on Dick's part with sarcasm, not rage, but the effect was the same. Or she would demand a chat that soon became a monologue about his past errant behavior or his inability to perform sexually.

Reluctantly, Dick concluded that the operation on their marriage, while more than partially successful, would leave a condition of permanent disability. He recognized a deep bond of affection for his wife, but he slowly began to question whether the marriage was viable. And his doubts were reinforced by his behavior – behavior that would have been unthinkable in his previous life. As Allen had remarked, "There were our lives before the cancer and our lives after the cancer, and nothing has been the same again."

Several months after his return, Dick had an opportunity to attend a conference in New York City. He decided to go. On the first day a reception was scheduled in the late afternoon. The next day consisted of lectures and the third of 'break out' sessions in which small groups were given an opportunity to discuss and explore the material presented the preceding day. Attendance required staying for two nights in a New York hotel. None of his faculty colleagues were interested in the subject matter – the interaction between psychopathy and the criminal law – and Christine, still shy about her appearance in public gatherings, opted to stay home with the children instead of accompanying him.

Inside a side drawer of Dick's desk at work was a postcard. He had saved it as a memento, not an invitation, but a few days before his departure he rummaged in the drawer and found it. The postcard was from Cathy, his former secretary. It contained an address and telephone number.

It's probably long out of date and useless, Dick thought. Temptation was balanced unevenly against a near certain expectation of failure, and so he concluded that there could be no harm in a futile telephone call. With a rising sense of nervousness that surprised him, he dialed the number on the card.

A familiar voice, never forgotten, answered.

With a sharp intake of breath, Dick hesitated momentarily. "Oh, ah, Cathy, it's me, Dick Blodgett. I really didn't think I'd reach you."

"Well, you have, and I knew right away who it was. How wonderful to hear from you! I thought you'd forgotten me."

"Forgotten?" The timbre of her voice calmed his unease, and Dick continued to speak with more self-assurance. "I called to find out if there might be a chance to see you some evening next weekend, like Friday or Saturday."

"I'm not free either night, but," Cathy answered hurriedly, "I'm pretty sure I can cancel Friday. Sure, let's get together then."

Delighted, Dick proposed dinner, and Cathy accepted. He put down the phone, pleased that he had made the call while at the same time reminding his conscience that it was only a reunion of old friends, only a dinner to relieve an otherwise lonely evening in a big city.

Cathy knew Dick's telephone number at work from her days as his secretary, and she called a day later to say that she had reserved a table at a moderately priced, albeit charming restaurant where they could dine in relative privacy.

And so they met again, this time under the clock at the Biltmore. As before when she first became his secretary, Dick was struck immediately by her fresh-faced appearance, attractive but not classically beautiful, her long legs and the vitality that animated her voice and gestures. It gave him a quickened sense of surprise and pleasure, much like viewing an arresting painting once seen long ago. During drinks and dinner at the restaurant, they chatted animatedly, as if it were old times in his office. A candle on the table cast a muted, flickering glow on their features. Dick told poor jokes, and Cathy laughed. She described her job and the antics of her fellow employees, and Dick brought her up to date on gossip at the law school.

They lingered at the table, despite reproachful glances from the maître d', who wanted it for other customers. When, finally, it was time to leave, Dick helped Cathy into a jacket she had draped over the back of her chair. "This was a grand evening," he said. "It was everything I knew it would be."

"For me, too," Cathy replied. "I'm so glad you called."

"Are you up for a walk?"

"Great idea." She grinned. "Let's do it."

While they had been eating dinner it had showered, and the glistening pavement was slick from fresh rain. They strolled along the street, talking and bantering as they passed restaurants and store fronts, time slipping by unheeded. When they arrived at Park Avenue, hurrying taxis honked and maneuvered as they sped past, their red tail lights casting shimmering patterns in puddles at the intersection where they were standing. The light turned, and they jostled their way across. Dick took Cathy's hand and did not relinquish it on the other side. A few steps farther on by a loading dock at the base of a tall building, she pulled him gently aside.

"Let's go to your hotel room," she whispered. "We could, you know, hug and kiss there."

Scratching the back of his head, Dick did not answer for several moments. He took a step forward, a smoldering, molten stirring in his loin, then stepped back with a questioning expression on his face. "No, Cathy," he said quietly. "It's not that I'm not tempted, because I am. But you know as well as I do that hugging and kissing will lead to making love."

Cathy sighed. "I shouldn't have asked. I knew I'd kick myself if I did… and also if I didn't."

Dick's features were strained in the muted light. "I'm married… I took wedding vows. But…"

She did not allow him to finish. "I hope you don't think less of me for asking. Perhaps I shouldn't say this," she confessed, exhaling. "I'm half in love with you."

Their voices had dropped, as if they were two

conspirators. Looking down at her earnest, upturned face, Dick said, "To be honest, I'm flattered to be asked by such a lovely woman. But, Cathy, it's infatuation, that's all. And, I admit, it is for me also." He took her hand again. "I'm in love with Christine. I have a life with a wife and children. I think the world of you, I really do, and I don't want you to become the reason for breaking up my marriage and messing up my life more than it already is. And frankly, if we made love, it would probably mess up your life, too."

An elderly woman walked by with her Pomeranian dog. They stopped talking until she passed.

"Is there any chance I can see you tomorrow, maybe for dinner again?"

"I'd love to, Dick, but I'm going to have a very busy day. In fact, I should be going home to get some rest." She looked away, then wiped the tip of her nose. "It's starting to drizzle." In the light cast from a street light at the corner, Dick could see tiny beads of moisture on her hair. He held out his hands, palms up, and soon they too became damp.

"Let's walk to Madison Avenue," Cathy said.

Dick put his arm around her shoulders, and she put hers around his waist, snuggling closer. Slowly, they walked up the street, quiet now, each listening to a beating heart. When they reached Madison Avenue, Dick stood at the curb trying to hail a taxi, and one eventually swerved to a stop in front of him. Cathy grasped his arm. Reaching up, she kissed him lightly on the cheek.

"I hope," Dick said, holding the door open for her, "that we can do this again."

"I'm just a telephone call away. Please do call

whenever you come to New York." Laughing, Cathy tossed her hair as she entered the cab. "Alone, of course."

His hands thrust deep into his trouser pockets, Dick watched as the taxi sped away. He felt his cheek, recalling the touch of her kiss, then trudged back to his hotel, head down, hands still deep in his pockets.

On Sunday afternoon, slightly depressed, Dick returned home. If he felt guilt, it was attenuated. He and Cathy had not made love, yet he had come close to a forbidden line. Christine asked, and he answered, perfunctory questions about the conference and his stay in New York. He did not have to fake ardor when they retired to bed. Their sexual coupling had ended, at least for the time being.

For three nights after dinner he retired to a den that had become his home office and sat, alone, in the dark.

He did not go to New York again.

* * * * *

Only a few weeks after his trip to New York City, sitting in his office one summer afternoon, Dick received an unexpected visit from two men from northern Nigeria. One, tall and dignified, was Dr. Ibrahim Kubura, Director of the Institute for Interdisciplinary Studies in Zaria in northern Nigeria. He was dressed impeccably in a dark western suit with white shirt and tie. His companion, immense in girth, was Bashir Shagari, then head of the Public Law Division and later Dean of the Faculty of Law, a component of the institute. A singular and striking figure, Bashir Shagari was wearing a flowing white robe that fell to his ankles and a round, richly embroidered hat. Both men were a deep, licorice-black, and the teeth and eyes of the latter gleamed white against his cheerful, rounded features.

Major events in a person's life, hinges of fate that turn that person from one plane of existence to another, often arrive in simple, unheralded ways. A man walks down a path and comes to a fork in the way. It seems of little moment to choose one destination or another, and so he chooses one of them. But soon he realizes that he is in a distant country, and the way back is forever barred.

These gentlemen were looking for American professors to come to their law school at their expense and teach for a year or two. Dick did not hesitate; he leaped at the opportunity. Africa! The Dark Continent! It was a chance to put Woodbury behind him, to escape the contradictions of his life, to be of service to others and to have a glorious adventure.

PART TWO

ZARIA

Chapter 20

Arrival in Africa

1977

In late June, nearly a year after Dick's meeting with Dr. Kubura and Bashir Shagari, an explicit offer arrived. He wrote back accepting the offer but adding some questions. An answer did not arrive for almost a month, and it was largely unresponsive to his inquiries. However, he was informed that, after a transatlantic flight from Boston to London, he would fly on Nigerian Airways from London to Kano, a city in the north. As Kano is approximately 100 kilometers (over 60 miles) from Zaria, he would be met at the airport by some functionary from the institute and driven to his final destination. An unspecified residence would be made available. Christine agreed that she, Allen and Molly would join Dick at the start of the new year – Allen for a couple of months as part of his mid-trimester in college as a 'term abroad', and Molly for the second semester of her freshman year in high school.

Tickets arrived shortly before Dick's scheduled departure. By this time he was getting somewhat used to sketchy information and last-minute arrangements, although not without anxiety. He got the required vaccination shots and secured a supply of malaria pills. He also inquired of colleagues who had taught in Africa what his destination might be like. "Oh boy," one of them had said. "You're in for an experience. Northern Nigeria is one of the least Europeanized parts of Africa."

Christine packed a small trunk with household supplies, being unaware what might be available at his final destination. The day following a small farewell party, she and Molly drove Dick to the airport. After fond farewells, he bundled himself into a BOAC aircraft for a nighttime, transatlantic flight to Heathrow Airport, London, armed with naïveté, enthusiasm, unfounded trust, a modicum of courage and boundless ignorance.

It was at Heathrow Airport, for the first time, that Dick experienced culture shock and doubts about the enterprise upon which he had embarked. Nearly everyone in the lounge, piled with boxes and items of luggage, was black. With one or two others, he was the sole Caucasian. Many of his fellow passengers were speaking a language, or languages, that he could not understand. With mounting trepidation, he boarded the plane, took his assigned seat and composed himself to the extent possible. Intermittently, he dozed. In the dark of night, the airplane sped across the Mediterranean, across the bleak expanse of the Sahara, and finally, about four in the morning, it skimmed to a landing in Kano, a southern terminus of the trans-Saharan trade route.

Weary and bleary-eyed, Dick exited the plane and walked across the tarmac to a low building. His first impression was of heat, which struck him like a torrid wave. After being interviewed by a customs agent and collecting his checked baggage, he proceeded into the main room of the terminal. It was not what he expected. The Kano International Airport was about the size of a dingy county airport in the United States. It was crowded with people. There were no booths for exchanging money. The restrooms were locked, and if a call of nature was urgent, the unlucky passenger or guest had to relieve himself or herself in a surrounding field. People were sprawled on benches and asleep on the floor. An unsmiling porter in a ragged brown shift carted his luggage and trunk out the front door. And there Dick stood in the dark, without any money, in a strange country miles from his destination, and looked about for the promised person who was to greet him and drive him to Zaria.

There was no one. Dick searched the small parking area with his eyes, not daring to leave his possessions. No one. Then he spied another former passenger, an elderly agricultural economist and Scotsman, who was loading luggage into a van. Dick walked over and inquired if, by any chance, his fellow passenger was going to Zaria and, if so, whether he could hitch a ride. The man assented, and then with some dismay watched as Dick hauled over his bags and trunk. After some maneuvering, they and the driver managed to stow everything on board. Dick nestled into the cramped back seat with the Scotsman, and the trip to Zaria began.

The road, empty at first, consisted of two rutted and uneven lanes that traversed a flat landscape. The passengers spoke very little. In the dark, a large bird wheeled in front of the car and then crashed into the window next to Dick. As dawn brightened the sky, he observed that they were passing men on bicycles and pushing carts. By the sides of the road in the distance, he could see smoke rising from small villages composed of mud huts with thatched roofs. And then, as they entered Zaria, he spied an old, deranged woman seated by the road. Bare from the waist up, with drooping, withered breasts, she was idly tossing bits of straw into the air.

The Scotsman dropped off Dick and his accouterments at a conference center. Dick was simultaneously excited and exhausted. Leaving his luggage momentarily, he checked in with school authorities in an adjacent building. A very pleasant, middle-aged man – an administrative assistant of some sort dressed in a blue robe with an embroidered hat – arranged for his room at the conference center and then asked if Dick would care to ride with him to Kaduna. Like many Nigerians, the man spoke fluent but heavily accented English.

Kaduna is a city larger than Zaria and about fifty miles to the south. Tired and bleary-eyed as Dick was, he accepted the invitation. Horn blaring, they pulled out of their lane on a two-lane road and passed other cars, barely avoiding automobiles and trucks approaching from the opposite direction. Dick was alternately fascinated by the scenery and terrified. They passed on curves and uphill, blind to what might be coming. Pedestrians scattered like chickens before them.

After his companion completed his errand, they returned to Zaria: the same harrowing ride. Relieved that their journey had ended without injury or fatality, Dick napped afterward in his assigned room. He had an adequate dinner at the conference center. Then, in the dusk of early evening, he explored his new surroundings, strolling under leafy trees on streets near to his new quarters. He found a bench and sat down. He was in a strange sea of people wearing unfamiliar attire who spoke English with a different accent, who ate different kinds of food, who drove with careless abandon and who, for the most part, lived in dwellings far different from his own. For the first time in his life he was totally cut off from the people and places he had known. There was no way out: no money, no telephone or other means to communicate with his known world, no exit visa, no honorable way to break his contract of employment. He missed Christine terribly, needing her confidence and comfort and realizing that he would have to find confidence and comfort within himself. His thoughts wandered to Carol and Walter, now gone from his life. Sweat trickled from his brow, and he shook his head in bewildered contemplation of his new life.

Chapter 21

Zaria Described

1977

Dick was in northern Nigeria in a dusty little city called Zaria, actually more a collection of villages than a cohesive city. At the start he roomed in a visitors' center called a conference center that was like a seedy 1950s motel in some arid, forgotten place in the American southwest. It was not by appearance the sort of facility in the United States where one would pull over late in the afternoon expecting a clean room, a well-appointed dining facility and, in summer, a lovely, kidney-shaped pool. It had most of these amenities but with the air of a run-down truck stop or hot pillow joint. There were motel rooms, each with its own bathroom, around a U-shaped courtyard, and a dining hall with waiters where guests sat at long tables. But all looked shabby and worn, better days long gone.

The place where Dick lived and taught was called the Institute for Interdisciplinary Studies which included a business school, a law school and an accounting department; it was about ten miles from a much larger main campus that had buildings one could associate with similar structures at an American university. In-between the main campus and the institute where Dick was located were a smattering of buildings, including a motel and a restaurant/cinema, but for the most part the scenery consisted of flat fields interspersed with occasional, stunted trees and mud-walled native compounds.

Dick's room at the conference center was a reasonable size, albeit sparsely furnished, with a bare, hanging light bulb and an open, unscreened space just beneath the ceiling for ventilation at the top of the stucco walls. Screens were an unnecessary luxury. Behind the center was an oval track, little used and indifferently maintained, and every other morning Dick went there to jog for two or three miles while it was still relatively cool. The kitchen help often came out to observe the odd, crazy baturi (foreigner), and they stood, cheerful, laughing and friendly, as he labored by. Vultures with wingspans of three or four feet congregated in or near the track, attracted by kitchen scraps. Dick grew so used to their presence that he ran, unfazed, as they flapped upward in their ungainly fashion only a few feet in front of him.

Slowly, he met people and was less lonely. They were an odd assortment, mostly Europeans, and he came to think of himself as having been thrust into a play without knowing his part or lines. People walked on stage, said outrageous things, and walked off. One was a Polish woman, a radiologist, who had an Egyptian boyfriend. The three of them often played scrabble in the evenings. There was a young American couple, Dot and Ned, he an assistant professor at the University of Pittsburgh and she a librarian from Arizona. There was also a young English couple, Penelope and Peter. A slim Oxford graduate, Peter was a young doctor working at the local hospital on an idealistic adventure, and his beautiful, ebullient wife,

Penelope, was a nurse. Through them he met Simon, another young doctor, who was a B'hai of Iranian descent who had been educated in England.

* * * * *

Because of his age, or possibly because he was bringing family with him, Dick was assigned a house. Even at his relatively young age, his years commanded respect. His younger friends were assigned to apartment blocks or chose to live in the Old City. And thus all of them left the conference center after about a month and settled into their new quarters. By then Dick had acquired a white, Volkswagen Beetle on the basis of a loan from his new employer. Thereafter he was free of the conference center and its surroundings, and then his house, and could travel much farther afield.

Dick's house had probably been the colonial residence of a British civil servant or district officer many years before. It was situated on perhaps a half acre of ground adjacent to the residence of Dr. Kubura. Set back from the road amidst trees and tropical, flowering bushes behind a driveway that circled a massive flame tree, the house was a modest but attractive dwelling on one level with two bedrooms and a bathroom, a living room with an adjacent dining area, a kitchen and, out back, a shed that had once served as the kitchen (and became the 'boys quarters'). In the rear there were an orange tree, a grapefruit tree, several papaya trees and two banana trees, plus room for a vegetable garden. Compared to most, Dick and his family were very fortunate.

The walls of the house were probably constructed of cinder blocks or mud bricks covered inside by a kind of thick plaster and outside by stucco. They were about a foot thick and painted white inside and out. Above them was a thick, thatched roof that gave the premises an authentic, tropical flavor. All the windows had ornate, lattice grilles over them, giving them a Moorish appearance, but their purpose was more to discourage entry than to provide ornamentation. Outside lights in the front and back discouraged prowlers, and triple padlocks on the front door also provided security. Every evening Dick also locked the door from the living room leading to the bedrooms before retiring to bed.

In the living room a couch and four wooden chairs were covered with yellow, green and pink cloth. Straw scatter rugs and pillows with an African tie-dye design gave the room a bright and sunny appearance. There were overhead fans in the living room and bedrooms, and on one wall Dick hung a Fulani sword in an ornate scabbard and an antique string instrument.

Dick's house was not far from the conference center, perhaps a block away. Both it and the conference center, and the academic buildings and dormitories, were in a gated compound, or enclosed area, of approximately 200 to 300 acres. It was a green island in the midst of dun colored squalor. Inside there were airy, spacious houses on flowered grounds set back from tree-shaded streets. Tall poinsettia bushes formed hedges that flanked the roads. There were modern academic buildings, built, to be sure, for a tropical climate, concrete tennis courts with the lines improperly drawn, and apartment houses and dormitories. All was clean and reasonably well maintained.

However, once through one of the gates guarded by old men in fading gray uniforms, Dick was confronted by a different world, a near medieval pageant. Only the main roads were paved. One ran by the large compound containing the institute, then through a small cluster of stores with a bank; this area, including the institute, was basically a village or small town called Tudun Wada. It was a section of Zaria. From there the road ran on to Congo, another section and the locale of the main campus. Between Tudun Wada and Congo stretched fields with rows of mounded earth for irrigation purposes. Dotting the otherwise level terrain were occasional twisted trees and tall mounds of huge rocks called inselbergs, some of imposing size. They looked as if a giant had idly sprinkled a few boulders here and there to lend variety to the otherwise flat, semi-arid landscape.

Cars, motor scooters, old trucks and men walking or peddling bicycles clogged the roads accompanied by a continuous, discordant beeping of horns. Dick's senses were assaulted by abject poverty far beyond his prior imagining. The mud side-streets of the town were lined with run-down, adobe like buildings, some with tin roofs. Rickety stalls, lit by kerosene lamps at night, offered cloth, food and implements of every kind for sale. Mounds of trash and fluttering scraps of paper were everywhere. The stores were simply caves in mud walls, some reached on crude planks over drainage ditches, but with a surprising assortment of modern goods inside.

Just beyond the stores, cattle with long, curving horns

could be seen ambling across the street. On the sides of the road, or on paths crossing fields, one might see four, five or six women walking in a line and balancing bowls or large bundles on the their heads. Sometimes these items were stacked two or three high, yet still the women kept them in perfect balance. Riding bicycles, the men similarly balanced trays with piles of meat, vegetables, or bundles of sticks, anything, on their heads as they rounded corners with carefree abandon. Many had different patterns of scars on their faces to denote their tribe of origin.

Then there might be, amidst the Hausa men and women in their colorful long robes, an occasional Tuareg, one of the fierce warriors of the desert, with head and face swathed in black cloth and a long, curving sword jingling at his side. Lepers riding donkeys clopped by with only stumps for hands and feet. So also one could see children crawling by the sides of the roads, paralyzed from the waist down and using rough wooden clogs on their hands to pull themselves forward. The blind, adults and too often children, stricken by an evil worm after swimming innocently in the muddy river that ran through town, hobbled by the sides of the roads. A babble of noise rose everywhere and goats, sheep, donkeys, chickens and an occasional emaciated dog roamed among the colorful procession.

Proper sanitation and hygiene were clearly lacking in the baked, mud-brick hovels that constituted the dwellings of a large number of the local inhabitants. In the year before Dick arrived, thousands had died of cholera, and malaria was endemic to the area. Every morning Dick dutifully took an anti-malaria pill to ward off the disease. Manifestly, there were disability and illness for all to see, yet the populace, at least in individual dealings with Dick, were to all outward appearances content and cheerful.

The old, traditional area for shopping, the Sabon Gari, still existed on the outskirts and did a thriving business. It consisted of a maze of alleys, many covered by brightly colored cloth and no more than a yard wide, lined with stalls only a few feet wide. Everything was for sale: cloth, thread, buttons, food in neatly arranged piles, cutlery and even hubcaps. One long shed contained the meat market. Carcasses of sheep and goats hung from the ceiling on hooks, testicles hanging limply, and as the animals' heads were severed, they were thrown casually onto a large heap outside the door. One bargained for everything, but there was no hard sell. If business was slow, shopkeepers could be seen lying on the floor or on tables fast asleep.

Woodbury was far away.

Chapter 22

A Chance Encounter

1977

At the beginning, when he was not in a classroom, Dick spent most of his time reading. Often he perused American textbooks on the law or novels that he had brought with him. Nigerian source materials were scant. For his class on criminal law he had been handed a copy of the Northern Nigeria Penal Code, nothing more, the outer fringe of its pages badly chewed by cockroaches.

On weekends, when all was quiet, he retreated to the old law school, a one-story colonial quadrangle enclosing a large courtyard of flowering trees and bushes. There he sat propped against a post of the portico that ran around the interior. Large spiders, a hand breadth in width with yard wide webs, kept him company.

A new law school building, three stories tall and modern in design, was in the last stages of construction, and classes were moved there not long after his arrival. Faculty members were assigned offices. Dick's was on the first floor with a desk, chairs and a telephone that never seemed to be connected to anybody or anyplace – in short, it was purely ornamental. Once he had his own place of retreat, he did his daytime reading there.

He was not lonely. In the evenings he sat by himself under a cone of light in his living room, again reading contentedly. When he thought of Woodbury, it seemed a place with its own pleasures and discontents that he had left far behind. Increasingly he felt untethered to its social mores, although habits of thought and action still identified him as an American in a foreign land.

Once he had a car and his own house, his other principal activity was shopping, mostly for food but also for household implements and mementoes to bring home. Purchasing food was truly different from what he had known. He had to contend constantly with the vagaries of a capricious work ethic and a different conception of time, measured sometimes by European and at other times by Nigerian standards. If a shopkeeper was not present, not 'on seat', he was usually told by an assistant that the person would be back 'latah'. No time was ever given.

Moreover, there was no guarantee of quality and no shopping center where groceries and household goods could be purchased in one place. Finding supplies was never predictable, and he had to go to one store for soup, another for salt, another for bread, and so on. One source, Dick soon learned, was men on bicycles balancing trays on their heads, who arrived without warning at his front door and attempted to sell carrots, cucumbers or other vegetables. Often these wares were stunted and of inferior quality. Dick always bargained for a fair price, although invariably he paid too much. Vegetables could also be purchased after bargaining from the piles laid out on the ground in the Sabon Gari, and staples, often at fixed price, could be obtained from the few small stores or the one crude supermarket in town.

* * * * *

Late on a Saturday morning, Dick drove in his new Volkswagen to Tudun Wada, the small collection of stores near the center. As usual he had to visit several stores in search of the items he wanted. He kept loose change in his pocket because he was confronted at each stop by a different cast of a dozen or more laughing children ranging in age from about six to twelve. All were shouting, "Me guardee, me guardee," meaning, "I will guard your car." It was not clear to Dick why the car needed guarding, but it was clear that the children needed the small pittance he gave them. Usually he chose one of the younger ones who, beaming in triumph, then stood watch while Dick was in a store.

Dick's next-to-last errand was at the small, local bank in the center of the one paved road that ran through town. The usual throng of children besieged him, and he gave one delighted small girl the task of guarding his car that was parked in a perfectly safe place along the street. The bank consisted of one large room with a teller's window in the wall opposite the entrance. A large crowd was milling about, jostling and elbowing their way toward the window. Dick stood at the back, mulling whether to enter the scrum or return another day. He did not see a woman enter behind him and then stand, perplexed, near to him at the back of the crowd. After several minutes, she plucked at Dick's arm.

Would he tell her, she asked, how long it would take to reach the teller, because she wanted to get on to the post office. Dick advised her to be patient, that he was going to the post office himself, and that he would be glad to give her a ride in his car. They chatted as strangers in a foreign country often will, and he soon noted that she was an attractive English woman, fair with even features, a trim figure, blue eyes and straight, dark hair.

She was also a delightful conversationalist, and they had a merry time discussing the travails of living in Nigeria. Her name, he quickly discovered, was Daphne. She mentioned, as if in passing, that she had only recently arrived, did not have transportation and had walked to the stores, a knapsack on her back.

"Where are you staying?" Dick asked.

"In the compound where the Institute for Interdisciplinary Studies is located," she answered.

"Really? I live there too. Are you, by any chance, connected to the law school?"

"I told them I'm a graduate student, and maybe it counts that I'd like to be. Anyway, they let me have a couple of rooms."

"Well," Dick said, "it's going to be a long, sweaty trudge to get back there. I'll take you in my car." After leaving the post office, Dick held the passenger-side door open for her and gaped as he observed her climb with slow, languid movements into his car.

Dropping her off at one of the apartment blocks for graduate students not far from his new house, Dick leaned out the window. "It's been great fun talking with you."

"Yes, it has been, and it would be nice to meet again." To that suggestion Dick was noncommittal, and he departed, but not without an imperceptible catch in his breathing.

Chapter 23

A Fateful Decision

1977

In the days following his encounter with Daphne, various chores, primarily preparing notes for class, consumed Dick's time and energy, but, returning from a shopping expedition or reading alone in his office or at home, the memory of her recurred insistently. Her image remained with him as he ate supper and retired to bed. Dick reminded himself that he had promised to be faithful in his marriage, but surely, he thought, all he sought was companionship, that he was merely seeking a friend. He was aware, but tucked deeply into the recesses of consciousness, that there was no one to monitor his activities, that his evenings were free of commitments, and that friends, family and the social strictures of community were far away.

As he had done with Cathy long before, Dick convinced himself that there could be no harm in simply asking someone to join him to observe a Moslem festival. His conscience thereby satisfied, or at least kept at bay, after a lapse of several days he drove to Daphne's apartment building. Weeds grew through cracks in the pavement of the parking lot in front. The building, one of several at odd angles to each other, was constructed of cinder blocks covered by white stucco streaked with dark stains. After a couple of inquiries about the location of a young English woman, he finally obtained her apartment number from another resident, who pointed helpfully to her door. He trudged up stairs to the second floor, his confidence draining with every step, then navigated his way down a gallery choked with laundry flapping haphazardly on makeshift lines and an assortment of household items such as battered tricycles and discarded, plastic chairs.

After a moment's hesitation he knocked on her door, his heart pounding and his palms moist. Daphne peeked through a curtain, then opened the door. Dick immediately noted her fair skin contrasted with her dark, lustrous hair.

"Hi," he said, stammering slightly. "We met the other day, and I was wondering..."

She interrupted him with laughter. "Do come in, please. And yes, I'd love to."

"But I haven't asked you."

"Dick. It is Dick, isn't it? I'm sure you didn't drive here just to chat about the weather."

"Yes... I mean, no, you're right," he confessed, then blurted, "How'd you like to go with me to see some kind of festival or parade on Friday? It's in the morning, and I'll have to go to work afterwards. But I'll have the morning free."

"That would be simply lovely," she said in her lilting English accent.

Chapter 24

No One Will Know
1977

The guttural singsong chant of a muezzin's call to prayer, amplified by modern technology, resounded throughout the area where Dick lived and frequently woke him in the mornings. He often observed men at a nearby, outdoor mosque kneeling in prayer during the day, and when a bull was slaughtered there, he inquired and was informed of a festival to take place in the Old City. It was to this festival that Dick had invited Daphne.

It was early November. The Friday celebration, a popular part of longer festivities, was to take place in the Old City about a mile from Dick's house. He had not yet been there, and so the outing was also an exploratory adventure. The original Zaria had been a walled city, and high, mud-brick walls remained. Inside was a warren of twisting alleys and streets that wandered among mud compounds. All the dwellings, with their guardian walls surrounding courtyards, were constructed of baked mud, giving the place, including the streets, a uniform tan appearance. Penelope and Peter had recently moved there, but Dick had not yet had a chance to visit them.

On the appointed day, Dick picked up Daphne in mid-morning and drove to the Old City where he parked by the main gate outside the wall. Slightly late, they walked quickly up a broad, dirt road to a central square crowded with people. Daphne gripped Dick's arm to keep pace, and he responded with excitement to her clinging touch. Breathless, amidst a large, packed throng of onlookers, they found a place to stand before the Emir's palace at one end of a dusty square about the size of the village common in Woodbury. Across from them was a many-turreted mosque.

At eleven o'clock the babbling crowd, hitherto alive with conversation and excited greetings, suddenly grew quiet. Down the road toward the square from the main gate galloped a solitary horseman, richly robed on a horse bedizened with tassels and ribbons on its reins and saddle. He wheeled about before a reviewing stand and then returned at a gallop up the road.

Daphne was standing on tiptoes to see over the woman in front of her. Standing behind her, Dick grasped her shoulders and whispered, "Look! Look!" There was movement of some sort far down the road, and it soon materialized into a loosely organized parade, even down to crude wooden signs indicating town of origin. Bodies of men on horseback came trotting toward them, all with flowing robes and turban cloth about their heads and necks. Many carried spears, and not a few had swords jangling from their sides. Before them came wild, half-naked, frenzied dancers, some hurling objects high into the air and then catching them, one leaping to and fro with a sword. A few were blowing six-foot long, thin horns with bell-shaped ends pointed skyward. Other foot walkers were interspersed among the riders, shambling along in Arab clothes and carrying long-muzzled, ancient rifles that they occasionally fired into the air.

Next, the Emir – fat, impassive and seated on a palanquin – rode by preceded by a band of trumpeters. Over him servants were holding a large, tasseled beach umbrella. Occasionally he waved genially to the gawking onlookers. His stately progress appeared to be the parade's culminating event, and Dick, thinking the ceremony had ended, nudged Daphne. But the respectful, silent crowd did not move, and after a breathless pause, a tumultuous mass of Hausa horsemen, robes flowing out behind them, galloped up the road in a swirl of dust and through the square. Some were half standing in their ornate, high-pommeled saddles without holding the reins, while others were holding the reins in their teeth.

Their departure signaled the end. It was an impressive spectacle, and for several minutes Dick and Daphne stood in place and watched as the crowd slowly dispersed. A man walked by with a monkey and a muzzled hyena on a leash. Another, a leper, rode by on a donkey, smiling under a broad-brimmed hat, and yet another old man attracted a crowd by uncoiling a six-foot cobra that was wrapped around his arm.

Dick and Daphne were entranced. "That was just lovely," she burbled when they were seated in his car and driving back to her apartment. "Every bit of it."

Dick said nothing. When they arrived at the parking lot before her building, however, he cut the engine and swiveled to look at her. "I'm glad you liked it," he said. Then, in a rush of words, he added, "How would you like to go to the movies with me next Wednesday night?"

"I'd love to," Daphne responded eagerly. She patted Dick's arm, and he flinched slightly.

"Around six? We can have a drink there too."

Daphne's eyes danced with amusement. "Yes, Dick, around six o'clock, and you don't need to look so solemn about it. I'm not going to bite you." She exited the car, and Dick watched her trim figure mount the stairs. When she reached her balcony, she turned and waved.

Chapter 25

Infidelity

1977

On the appointed evening, again with difficulty, Dick located her second-floor apartment. He had on his usual slacks and polo shirt. Daphne had chosen a light, cream-colored dress with a low neckline that emphasized the contours of her body. Because of harmattan – the season when dust filters down from the Sahara, blocking the rays of the sun – she had a blue, cotton sweater draped over her shoulders. Dick swallowed involuntarily when he saw her, and he kept casting admiring, sidelong glances at her as they descended the stairs to his car and set off for the movies.

Dick drove along the two-lane highway between Tudun Wada and the main campus in Congo for a half dozen miles before turning onto a short, rutted dirt road. Their destination was the Lebanon Club, a sprawling establishment that featured a restaurant, a bar and an outdoor movie theater. After purchasing tickets, they seated themselves in adjoining, rickety chairs in an open enclosure flanked by rustling palm trees. The sky was pearl-gray with the undersides of clouds painted a pink tinged with orange; it slowly faded into dusk, and a few stars winked in the sky as the film began. It was an old American import with stilted language from a previous era. When the reel snapped for the second time, plunging the scattered, bored audience into darkness, Daphne suggested that they repair to the bar.

They took seats at a small table, and Daphne ordered a Scotch and soda. Prudently, Dick ordered a beer. Daphne laughed easily at his attempts at humor. Dick readily described where he was from and where he had gone to school. More guarded, Daphne volunteered that she had grown up and gone to school in Buxton, England, with two brothers and a sister. Each had another drink, only, this time more relaxed, Dick switched to a gin and tonic. In a lull in the conversation their eyes met and held, so that Dick's stomach began to flutter with excitement.

"Why don't we, you know, return to the car," he suggested, putting down his drink.

Daphne gazed at him for several moments. Her blue eyes searched his face. "All right," she said softly, her tone even but equivocal.

And there, in the dark of an African night, they kissed, a chaste brushing of lips, then a second time long and drawn out. With one arm clutching her tightly, his free hand groped for, then found her breasts. Squirming, their bodies rubbing against each other, they kissed again more passionately. Dick pulled his face away, his eyes riveted on hers. Panting, he said, "Let's go back to your place."

Again, Daphne hesitated. She too was panting. "I'm not sure. I don't want…"

She never finished. "Not sure?" he queried "Why? Why not?"

"Because… well, it's been a long time, and I'm not

sure I'm ready." In private panic, she wondered if she could ever unite emotional attachment with the physical act. Yet she had enjoyed his company, had enjoyed his warmth and humor, had enjoyed the touch of his body, and his wounded, beseeching look convinced her. "All right," she said, "let's go."

In his ardor, Dick easily brushed aside her apparent doubt. They drove in silence, then, after parking, mounted the stairs at the end of her building to the second floor. A neighbor smiled as they walked by.

Once inside a plain room with whitewashed walls and a modicum of wood-framed furniture, they kissed again, still standing. Daphne took Dick's hand and led him into her bedroom where each disrobed the other. The first thing Dick saw was her lovely nakedness; the second was an intricate tattoo of a serpent coiling and uncoiling around her waist and across her abdomen. Daphne noticed him staring at it.

"You like it?" she asked defensively.

"No... well, sure. I mean, I've never seen anything like that before."

"I hope you get used to it, my dear. It was a stupid mistake, but it comes with the territory."

Still gaping, Dick lay down on the bed with her and pulled Daphne to him. Their kisses grew more ardent, and his hands explored her breasts and fondled the moist cleft between her thighs. Teasing, slowly, she began to stroke him.

Half draped across her body, Dick suddenly sat up, as if waking from a spell. "Daphne," he said urgently, "I can't do this."

She raised herself on one elbow. "What are you talking about? You're hard as a rock."

"Not that. Not that. It's just… for Chrissake, Daphne, I'm a married man, I promised, and my wife and children are arriving here in a couple of months."

Daphne drew back, surprise on her face. "You didn't tell me," she said accusingly. With an unwavering gaze, she studied him, then shrugged. "Well, we've come this far, and bloody hell, you're not the first married man I've gone out with."

Pinioned on the tremulous lip between duty and desire, Dick lay back, confused, and Daphne snuggled closer. He could feel her body and smell her hair. "I've turned this down before," he mumbled, "and I'm not going to do it again."

"Do what?"

"Never mind."

The rest of the evening had a curious, dream-like quality. They made love, Dick on top, and then made love again in the middle of the night with her straddling him. There was more lovemaking on a living room chair as dawn was breaking, and then they slept for three hours.

Daphne made breakfast for him in the late morning. Afterward, as he was about to leave, she said, "It would be marvelous if we could meet again. How about next Saturday? Why don't you come here for dinner?"

"Sure, I'd love to," he said. "I'll come at six."

But his unease grew in the next couple of days. He wanted to put his life back together with Christine, or at least at a conscious level he thought that was something he ought to do. On Friday he finally decided to decline the invitation. The phone in his office did not seem to be connected to anything, and in any event, he could not recall seeing a telephone in her apartment. A personal meeting was unavoidable, therefore, and so late that morning he drove to her building. He knocked, then knocked again. There was no answer.

Defeated, Dick let fate decree, despite the protests from his conscience, that he was meant to come to her apartment for a home-cooked meal. He refused to let his mind drift beyond that point, and he did not, indeed could not, know of Daphne's fears and reservations. After pre-prandial drinks and ample helpings of wine during dinner, they made love again, and again he spent the night. And the next morning, he stopped deluding himself. He readily agreed to see her again.

Chapter 26

Reality Dawns

1977

Dick padded across the hall from the bathroom, naked except for a towel wrapped around his waist. Water still dripped from him, and his wet feet left footprints on the tile floor. Daphne was sitting up in her rumpled double bed, a pillow propped behind her, watching him.

"Are you looking at me?" Dick asked, laughing.

"Why would anyone want to?" She paused, a mischievous grin on her face. "Actually, I know why. I was wondering if I would need binoculars to see your willie."

Dick started to unravel the towel.

"No, stop! Or maybe don't stop. I love your body, and anyway, you look at me, so why shouldn't I look at you?"

"Because men are supposed to look at women, not the other way around."

"Well, we do, but we're not so obvious about it… like now. But it's you I'm in love with, sweetheart, not some image of you." Daphne tilted her head and smiled. "You're the best man I've ever met. In fact, I'm not sure I've ever met anyone quite like you."

"Or me either. Like me, I mean." Dick laughed again.

"Can't you do better than 'me either'?"

"Okay, I love you passionately."

"You're a slow learner, Dick Blodgett, but you're getting there."

He sat down on the bed beside her and stroked her hair. "Why don't we…?" he started to ask, but Daphne interrupted him, pushing him away with mock exasperation. She swung her legs over the side and then, after standing, smoothed the nightie she was wearing with both hands. "Coffee?" she asked, "Or tea?"

Dick made a face.

"I forget with you Americans. It's always coffee in the morning, isn't it."

"Coffee and cold cereal, and in my case orange juice. Not that you can get any around here."

Daphne turned as she reached the door to the bedroom, an edge to her voice. "Will we ever have breakfast at your house? It would be lovely to stay there, so much more room. And I'm sure you've fixed it up so that it looks beautiful."

"I have," Dick sighed, "but you know the reason."

Daphne pouted. "You don't want your steward to see us together. Why do you care what some African servant thinks of you? What is he going to do, report you to Mommy and Daddy in America, even assuming, of course, that he can write."

It was already a familiar subject, never resolved. Dick had seen Daphne again shortly after their first night together, then again and yet again. Each time he had spent the night at her apartment, and the nights had begun to merge together. Initially, he had been infatuated by the toss of her dark hair and her crystal blue eyes that seemed to sparkle in serious conversation. But those had been the bait on the hook. Now he was captivated by her mischievous vivacity, her intelligence, her teasing laughter and her love-making. And it was the last that ensnared him, that made him dream of her in his idle moments – when dressing in the morning, when eating lunch or when reading notes before class. She was clearly the teacher and he the willing pupil, and there seemed little that she had not explored and mastered. Costumes, bindings, different positions and techniques, all were familiar to her and an unexplored continent of delight to him.

And yet he was puzzled, increasingly puzzled. Beneath the laughter, the easy charm, lurked something hard to discern. It coiled and uncoiled, appeared and disappeared, like the rippling snake tattooed across her abdomen.

He had first been aware of it two weeks before when they had decided to enjoy a swim on a Saturday afternoon. Their destination: a pool – and as far as Dick knew, the only pool in Zaria – located behind a tan, two-story motel not far from the Lebanon Club and half way on the road to the main campus. They drove there in Daphne's newly-purchased Subaru station wagon. Upon parking and stepping out of the automobile, a crowd of a half dozen small, ragged children surrounded them, begging for the chance to 'guard' it.

Dick groped in his side pocket for a coin, but Daphne placed her hand on his arm. "Let me," she said. After fumbling in her purse and eventually extracting several coins, she gave one to each of the children and then, looking about, designated a diminutive, shy boy, who was standing in the rear, to be the 'guard'. Thereafter, as she and Dick made their way to the front door, the children pressed and frolicked about her, shouting and laughing, and one kept repeating, "Thank you, Sah!" in fractured English.

Traversing a gleaming reception area, obviously designed to attract foreign visitors, Dick and Daphne made their way out a rear door and changed into bathing suits in a low building containing toilet facilities, showers and locker rooms at one end of a large courtyard. A pool, Olympic in size, occupied most of the area. It was encompassed by lounge chairs, a grassy verge and high walls topped by crimson bougainvillea. Small boys, hazarding a climb on the outside walls, peeked occasionally over the top. Their eyes fixed quickly on Daphne, the only woman present. Forbidden to reveal their bodies in public because they were in the Moslem north, no other women were there. Daphne, who was wearing a two-piece bathing suit, was also the focal point of surreptitious glances from a pool attendant and a couple of male guests at the motel. She enjoyed the attention conferred by her unique status, particularly when, rising to swim, she stretched languidly, flaunting her feminine figure as if unaware of her provocative behavior.

Dick was embarrassed by the attention she attracted. At one point in the afternoon, while they were lying next to each other on lounge chairs beside the pool, he quietly suggested that perhaps she should be more modest and aware of the cultural norms of the place they were visiting. Daphne cut him off. "I'll behave exactly as I please," she retorted. "If the bloody Moslems don't like it, they don't have to look."

Later, looking dreamily up at the vault of blue sky above him, Dick said, "You certainly were generous with those children. Now they'll expect money every time they see you."

"So what?" was the answer.

"It could be expensive, well, probably not, but do you have that much?"

Again he received a terse reply. "I have enough."

Dick stared at her, his brow furrowing. "Well, I guess… I mean, are you independently wealthy?"

Daphne cut him off again. "Dick, I told you. I have enough. If you've ever gone without, you'd know what it means to those children. Just from the look of them they must be orphans, or their families are very poor."

"I don't know." He rolled on his side to look at her. "Not orphans probably, but some of them may live with their fathers."

"Not their mothers?"

"In this part of the world, if a man decides to divorce his wife, all he has to do – at least this is what I've been told – is say 'I divorce you.' Maybe three times, I'm not sure. The wife and mother go back to her family, and the children stay with him."

Daphne looked shocked. "How awful!" she exclaimed.

"Awful? I mean, why so awful? He's probably better able to feed them than she is."

Daphne stared at Dick, a hard glint in her eyes. "Remember the day we met? You do remember, don't you?" Dick nodded. "I was sending a note to my sister.

She's the only one in my family I communicate with, although I think she talks to my mother. I heard from her several months ago."

"Okay, so what has that got to do with..."

Daphne kept talking. "She told me my father was now an old, sloppy drunk, that he was probably dying, and I thought... Do you know what I thought? I thought good. The world will be much better off without him." She spat out the last words. "I despised him. Him? Raise children on his own?" Daphne hunched her shoulders and scrunched her face in a visible expression of disgust.

"I'm sorry to hear that. I'd no idea." Dick thought of his own loving parents and also of Christine. She had been in awe of her father, had thought him often too distant, but she respected and admired him.

"Don't waste pity, Dick. Don't waste it on me, and certainly don't waste it on my father."

* * * * *

When they first met, Daphne had told Dick the truth. She had indeed been raised in Buxton, England, in a family of modest means. She had a sister and two brothers. This much he had been told. But beyond that she had not elaborated, had not added details or sketched the emotional life within her family. Nor did she intend to.

Her family had moved often when she was very young. Her father was from Lancashire, and his quarrelsome nature too often led to brief stints of employment. Along the way, he had married her mother, a native of Ulster, and they had four children. Daphne was the oldest. Her birth had been a premarital mistake, but the small family made do and added more. A job in a local bakery in Buxton had ended her father's restless wandering in search of a permanent job. The family settled into a red-brick council house on a street cluttered with similar houses but few trees.

"You'll do as you're told, lass," her father scolded his older daughter. His puffy face was red from either anger, too many nights at a local pub, or both.

"But why, Dad, why do I have to sit by myself in the kitchen?"

"Because you're not fit for decent company, that's why. She isn't, is she, Alice?" he shouted into the next room where the family was gathered to eat their evening meal at a plain, wooden table. Daphne's sister and two brothers stared down at their plates. Her mother answered wearily, "Henry, come and eat. Leave the child alone."

"I'll teach you," her father said, "if it's the last thing I do. You've been nothing but trouble since the day you were born."

Daphne's large, blue eyes were rimming with tears. Her dark hair contrasted with her pale skin. "She's a beauty, all right," her mother had said when she was a toddler. "She's a Celt for sure. You can see the Irish in her."

To that comment her father had responded, "Aye, and was I the father? I'd still like to know."

Her mother had sat, hands clasped in her lap, and had said nothing. She shook her head in silent rejection of his accusation. And Henry had melted at sight of her evident distress. He had sat down beside her. "What's done's done," he had said in his broad Lancashire accent, "and can't be undone. We'll make the best of it." But his suspicions lingered, and Daphne had never been a favorite.

"I didn't do anything," she wailed again.

Her father wheeled about on his way to the table. He wagged a pudgy, accusing finger. "You were twenty minutes late, twenty minutes with that William. And you can get in a lot of trouble in twenty minutes."

"Nothing happened," was the stubborn reply.

"We'll know the answer to that now, won't we, long before nine months are up. You sit there, and you'll continue to sit there, until I tell you this family is ready to receive you back. And no more going out with that young man. You're staying at home."

Daphne slumped in her chair and poked at her food. Her shoulders shook. It was true, she had been out with William. She liked him. They had toyed and petted each other, and the joy of their mutual fondling had been exciting for a seventeen year old girl. Heedless in their shared excitement, the petting had indeed taken time – at least twenty minutes too much time.

The punishment lasted a week. No meal was excepted, and she was the last to be served at suppertime. Often most of the food had been eaten, although her mother tried to save enough for her. Her father avoided her sorrowful glances, and she retired – alone, rejected and often hungry – to her bedroom after dinner.

"Dad," she implored him, "why are you doing this to me?" He did not answer, not on that occasion, simply waved her to the dinner table when he decided her punishment was enough.

It was not long thereafter, a few days at most, when she saw William again. "I've missed you," he said. "I guess your old man was really angry."

"He was, and I'm angry too. I'm not a child anymore, and I should be able to do what I want without starving in the kitchen. He's no right, no right, to treat me that way." Her words were defiant, but she was careful to be in the house at the appointed time. She was not careful, however, about being seen in public with William, and one late afternoon, returning from school, her younger brother saw them talking and laughing together outside a corner shop. He related what he had seen to his mother, and she in turn told Daphne's father after he had returned home from work.

"Come down here," Henry shouted upstairs to his daughter. Daphne, alert to the sound of his voice, descended with trepidation. She had not reached the bottom step when her father, a beefy man, reached out and grabbed her throat.

"What's this I hear? What's this? You've been seeing that boy again? Is that it?" His eyes bulged as he spoke.

"No… well, a little. Just as friends."

"By God, I'll take a strap to you."

"Dad, please, nothing's wrong. You must believe me."

"You'll be eating in the kitchen again, my girl, and for a long time." Henry's cheeks puffed out. "I'll not rear another bastard in this house. Do you hear me?"

"Another…?"

"Henry, stop it! The girl has done no wrong." Her mother intervened. "For goodness sake, why are you so angry?"

"Because we made a mistake… you made a mistake… and I'll not have another."

"I hate you," Daphne mumbled, her voice barely audible.

"What did you say?" Her father's eyes bulged again, and he raised his hand to slap her.

Daphne's mother, plucking up her courage, placed herself in front of Daphne and glared at her husband. "Enough!" she said. "Enough of your bullying and accusations. You are as much to blame as I, and it's about time you admitted it."

Henry's open hand slowly dropped to his side. He stared at his wife. "She eats in the kitchen," he growled. For a few moments, panting, he looked about like a wounded bear, then turned slowly and labored up the stairs to change his clothes.

A few days later in the early afternoon, Daphne's sister discovered Daphne in their shared bedroom packing her clothes in a large cardboard box. She was about to secure it with a length of rope cut from the tag end of a clothesline in the rear of the house.

Her sister was aghast. "Daphne… what… what are you doing?"

"I'm leaving, that's what I'm doing."

"Leaving? You can't. Where will you go?"

"Manchester, maybe London. Any place but here."

"Why? Don't you like it here? Why are you going?"

"Because I'm not wanted here. Didn't you hear him? He said I'm not his child, and he's so mean to me."

Daphne's sister laid her hands on the box. "Don't leave us. It'll be my turn next, I know it."

"I'll find you," Daphne said, choking slightly, "and you can join me. I loved Dad, and I thought he loved me, but he doesn't."

"Of course he loves you," her sister replied. "He just doesn't know how to show it. You should stay. You must. How will you live? You don't have any money."

"Yes, I do," Daphne said. She cleared her throat, a fierce conviction now in her voice. "I've saved some, and I took some from the top drawer of Dad's dresser. It will serve him right. All he does with that money is buy beer at the pub to drink with his friends. I'll make better use of it. Probably make him happy that I'm gone."

She hugged her sister, then dragged her makeshift suitcase down the stairs. Grabbing the rope in her hand as if it were a handle, she looked wistfully into the sitting room as she walked by. Her sister trailed behind, still pleading with her to stay. After glancing back once on the front walk, Daphne turned resolutely forward and trudged toward the railroad station. Her sister, in tears, watched her go from the front stoop. She waved, but Daphne did not look back.

"She'll return," her father had said bravely to console her mother, but the weeks and months went by, and she never did.

Chapter 27

Further Revelations

1977

Dick drove to Chelleram's, a large warehouse containing an incongruous assortment of items for sale: appliances, canned goods, hardware of various types and, in the rear, stacks of Star beer. He rattled in his Volkswagen down a dirt road that branched from the only paved street in Tudun Wada. Once inside, he purchased a large can for gasoline, a medium-sized plastic container of purified water and a couple of cans of food safe from contamination. Chelleram's did not sell a can opener, but he found one in a small hardware store – more a hole in the wall than a store – down a side street from the bank.

His preparations completed, Dick announced his plans to Daphne. It was several days after they had ventured to the pool. Excited, Dick told her of his preparations and said that on a day when he was not teaching they could go sight-seeing by driving to Jibiya, a small market town 325 kilometers away – about 200 miles – on the border with Niger, northwest of Katsina, the last city in Nigeria directly to the north.

"It'll be great," he added, flinging his arm in a wide arc. "An adventure! I've got all the supplies, so all we need to do is stop for a picnic somewhere. I've got extra gasoline, and we'll be back by suppertime."

"I wish you'd asked me first." Daphne did not smile. She stood, unmoving, without any sign of eager anticipation. "To the north, you say? How far away is it?"

"About a half day," Dick answered, slightly deflated. "We'll leave early and have plenty of time."

"Aren't the roads dangerous? Is it safe to drive with gasoline in the car?"

"I'll be careful, don't worry." Dick was surprised by her dubious reaction. A trip, he had thought, would be precisely the thing to pique her interest and elicit enthusiasm.

Daphne shook her head slowly from side to side. Her mouth was drawn down in a frown. "All right," she said finally. "You've gone to all this trouble. You say it's only a day of driving? You're sure?"

"Absolutely."

They set off in the early morning, and the landscape slowly changed as they drove farther north into the Sahel. In Zaria the land was flat but covered with long grass and dotted with trees and, occasionally, clumps of boulders. Near Jibiya it was burned scrub brush, rock and sand stretching to the horizon. The occasional trees were black and twisted and the stream beds dry. Near the town, as they approached, they saw a vulture sitting on the blackened body of a steer.

The town itself and its market were very similar to the villages close by Zaria, i.e. crude and undeveloped. The presence of numerous camels and donkeys, however, gave it a different flavor. There was a large pen or enclosure near the town's center where camels were ambling about waiting to be sold or traded at the market. As Daphne and

Dick approached this place, they had to walk down a broad path perhaps a hundred feet long. On either side were women – it seemed fifty or more – sitting on their haunches holding out their hands in supplication. They were all lepers. Their hands were mere stumps of fingers, and several women had covered their faces to hide the ravages of the disease.

Daphne opened her purse and felt about inside. She did not have enough coins for them all, and she was reluctant to give money to some and not to others. With a look of dismay, she clutched Dick's arm. "We've got to get out of here." Her voice was low and urgent. "This is a dreadful place."

"But we've only just arrived."

"I don't care. Please, let's go." Nervously, she looked around, peering down an alleyway as if she were an escaped prisoner avoiding detection.

"What's wrong?" Dick asked. "Why are you… you know, so agitated?"

It seemed Daphne did not hear him. She began to pull him back to the car. "How far north are we?" she queried, almost breathlessly.

"I told you. We're in Jibiya. It's on one of the caravan routes from the Mediterranean that pass through here to Katsina and on to Kano."

"A caravan route?" Daphne trembled. What if the Americans had returned to Tunis? What if they had met Jory? What if he was on his way, even now? What if… what if…?

"How far away is Sokoto?"

"I don't know." Dick was baffled. "Maybe a day's drive,

maybe half a day. It probably depends on the quality of the roads."

"Dick, we're going home, and we're going home now. I knew this was a bad idea."

For most of the trip back to Zaria, they journeyed in silence. It was hot, but because of harmattan and the dust it carried, they drove most of the way with the windows only partially open. About half way back on a vacant stretch of road, Dick pulled over to pour gasoline into the tank. Daphne sat huddled in the passenger seat, her head down and her arms between her knees. Dusty and tired, they arrived in Zaria as a pink glow brushed the western horizon and deep shadows were etched under the trees.

Dick stayed at Daphne's apartment, but they did not make love that night. She prepared a light supper and afterward, indifferently, told Dick he could leave or stay. He chose the latter, but he slept fitfully. It was not that he could not answer questions swirling in his mind. He did not even know the questions.

In the morning, following a light breakfast that he prepared for himself, Dick left for work. He spent most of the day teaching or reading in his office, assiduously taking notes from a reference book open at the side of his desk. From time to time he put down his pencil and sat, staring out the window, lost in thought. He imagined driving to Daphne's apartment, but he decided to leave her alone. There was no way to reach her by telephone.

Uncertain and baffled by her withdrawn behavior, he drove to her apartment in the late afternoon and hesitantly mounted the stairs to the second floor. When he knocked on her door, Daphne greeted him warmly.

She was cheerful and impish as usual and had already mixed a gin and tonic for him to enjoy before dinner. An aroma of cooked chicken, rice and beans filled the apartment. Talking animatedly as they ate, they discussed their recent trip. Dick remarked on the heat and the blasted landscape, so different from the rolling, verdant hills of New England with its swiftly running rivers and its people free of disfiguring disease.

At bedtime, after flinging off their clothes, they made love. But it was not the same as it had been. To Dick, at one point, Daphne seemed there but not there, an automaton, a woman with all the right, practiced physical moves, but with no emotional affect. Her kisses were compulsory, and there were no murmured words of endearment. The act completed, she did not lie next to him, cuddled in his arms. Instead, she rolled over and was soon asleep.

In the early morning Dick slipped out of bed alone. Daphne was snoring softly, shrugging a light blanket draped over her. Fruit bats emitted their call, a pure sound like a small bell, and in the silence he could hear a truck coughing to life somewhere in the distance. It was slightly cool unlike the enervating heat when he first arrived in Zaria, and he pulled on a sweater. Carefully, he opened, then quietly shut, the bedroom door and tiptoed to the small kitchen to prepare coffee. Despite his best efforts, he rattled two cups that he withdrew from a cupboard. Before long, the coffee pot steamed as boiling water filtered through the ground coffee to a decanter below. Dick poured the brown, aromatic liquid into the cups and then, carrying them carefully, pushed open the bedroom door with his foot and entered.

Daphne was lying, curled, at the foot of the bed.

"Surprise!" Dick said. There was no response. "Here, honey, I've made you a cup of coffee."

Daphne did not look up. She stayed coiled in a fetal position. After placing the cups on a bedside table and brushing aside the mosquito netting, Dick sat down beside her. "Is something wrong?" he inquired anxiously. Tenderly and gently he began to stroke her shoulder.

"Don't touch me!"

Dick withdrew his hand rapidly. "What… what's wrong?"

For several moments there was no response. "Just stay away from me."

Frowning, his brow furrowing, Dick moved farther away. He studied her, head tilted. "Would you mind telling me what's wrong? Was it something I did? Or said?"

"No," was the muffled response.

"Then would you please tell me what in God's name is going on."

Daphne unwound her body from the tight position it had been in, but she continued to lie on her side, tears streaking her face. "It won't work, Dick. It will never work. I can't get my mind, my feelings, to act together with my body. I can fake it. Oh, I'm good at that. But I'll never, ever, ever put the two together." She reached over and patted Dick's face. "And please don't look so hurt. It's not about you, it really isn't."

"Then what is it?"

Daphne cast her eyes downward, appearing to examine the crumpled sheet just beneath her. "It's of no concern to you, Dick. Or… or maybe it is, but I don't want to talk about it. That bastard did this to me. It happened a long time ago."

"That bastard? Who? There must be something… let me help you," he said with mounting conviction.

"You can't help. There is nothing, nothing you or anyone can do." Daphne wiped her cheek and smiled ruefully. "Please go," she said. "And don't come back… not for a while, anyway."

"Go?"

"Yes, Dick, go!" Her expression hardened and her voice became emphatic. "Drink your coffee, collect your things, and get out… get out while you can."

* * * * *

Traveling via Manchester, where she changed trains, a beautiful, seventeen year old girl with a large cardboard box arrived at Euston Station in London. The conductor on the train had noticed her. She was staring at the gray, drizzly scene that flashed by outside the window, tears rolling down her cheeks, and he had asked if everything was all right. "No," Daphne had answered, "it isn't," and she had turned away to gaze again out the window.

Daphne dragged herself and her box off the train, a little excited, a little frightened, and was walking along the platform when a slight, middle-aged man began to walk beside her. He was wearing a wool cap and a dark suit with a carefully knotted red tie. Daphne noted that he also had what appeared to be small diamonds between the gaps in his upper front teeth.

"Excuse me, Miss," the man said, "but are you looking for a taxi? Or a nice place to stay for a well-brought-up young lady? I represent some of the finest establishments in London for respectable young men and women."

"I don't need your help," Daphne replied emphatically.

"Let me carry that box for you," the man continued cheerfully. Daphne clutched it tighter to herself, but she stopped, bewildered by the rushing crowds of people and her total lack of knowledge about her destination.

"What kind of establishments?" she asked the man. "Are they safe and," she hesitated, "not too expensive?"

"Just right for a fine young person like yourself looking for a place to stay – your own room, clean bathroom down the hall, other women your age to keep you company."

Daphne had resumed walking toward an exit, the man tagging along beside her. She stopped again. She had nowhere to go. "Can you take me there?" she asked. "I need a place to stay."

A half hour later they arrived in a taxi paid for by the man at a large townhouse in Soho. Its double front doors beckoned at the top of a short flight of stairs. The man escorted Daphne inside, spoke briefly to a formidable-looking woman behind a desk in the foyer and then, with a hearty, "Cheerio," departed. From time to time, Daphne saw him again, always bringing young women to the premises.

The woman behind the desk was middle-aged, tall, blond with a prominent nose. "So, you want a place to stay?" she said almost accusingly. "We have a room on the third floor. It should do."

“What do I pay?” Daphne looked nervously at the expensive furnishings in an adjacent room, a kind of library or reception area.

“We’ll discuss that later. You can eat at a pub at the corner, and we’re having a social hour down here at eight o’clock. You are, of course, invited.”

Shortly after eight o’clock, Daphne entered the room off the foyer that she had seen before. Two young men and four young women were there, and all hastened to greet her. Daphne noted that they offered only their first names. The women were attractive, although their attire – high boots, low-cut blouses – was unfamiliar to her. One of the young men introduced himself as Durell. He was tall, muscular and ruggedly attractive despite a broken nose and a gold tooth that gleamed when he smiled. The other, Jory, was of medium height and whipcord thin. He had almost effeminate features topped by rumpled, blond hair.

Except for Durell, the others drifted away after introductions. Not long thereafter, two of the women left the room. Durell offered Daphne a drink of Scotch whiskey.

“I’m not sure I should,” Daphne said.

Durell laughed, an easy chortle. “Go ahead. It won’t kill you.”

“It’s just that… um, I’ve never had it before. I’m not sure it would be good for me.”

“There’s always a first time,” he urged. “Try it. You may find you like it.” He held out a partially filled glass.

Daphne took a sip and made a wry face. Durell laughed again, and she took another sip. An hour later, slightly tipsy and delighted that she had made a new friend, Daphne retired to bed. The next day she explored her new neighborhood and again went to the room off the foyer in the evening to enjoy the company of others. This time she drank too much, vomited in the bathroom down the hall from her bedroom, and went to bed with the ceiling spinning above her. She had a headache in the morning and stayed in her room for much of the day. In the evening, however, she ventured downstairs, resolving not to drink again.

Durell was across the room when she arrived, talking privately with Jory. He approached her, smiling, and asked if he could speak with her. He led her to the hall outside the room and then to a doorway that, upon being opened, led to a stairway downstairs.

"Follow me," he said.

"Why? Where are we going?" Daphne wondered if some pleasant surprise awaited her. She was troubled, though, when the forbidding female at the front desk and then Jory followed her.

"Just stay with me," Durell commanded. He flicked on a light, descended the stairs and entered a room with gray, concrete walls that was bare except for a couple of wooden chairs. Daphne followed him, still thinking that perhaps Durell had some hidden treat in store but puzzled why she had been summoned to a basement room.

When the foursome reached the middle of the room, Durell turned to the receptionist. "How much does she owe?" he inquired, as usual in an easy, conversational tone.

The woman was holding a sheet of paper in a hand that shook slightly. "Let me see," she said, peering at the sheet in the dim light. "It comes to 297 pounds. That's for three nights lodging, including tonight, and several drinks."

"Pay when we get back upstairs," Durell said.

"Pay?" Daphne began to tremble. "I… I don't have that much money. I thought… I had no idea…" Her voice trailed away as she looked anxiously from one person to another in the room.

"You thought it was all for free?" Durell's voice had become harsh. "You'll pay money now or you'll pay later by selling drugs or yourself." He paused. "I think yourself. You're quite beautiful, and we have all the necessary connections."

"No… I won't. This is all a mistake. I'll find the money, get a job. You can't make me…"

Daphne never finished. Durell punched her just below her rib cage. It was a boxer's blow, delivered hard and fast. Daphne doubled over in agony. "No," she gasped. "Please, no. I can't…"

Jory moved forward, fast as a striking pit viper, grabbing her hair and yanking her partially upright. Durell landed another blow, this time with his clenched fist to Daphne's left jaw. For a moment she lost consciousness. Blood trickled into her mouth and down her chin as she tumbled backward into the wall. Jory sprang forward and began to kick her with his heavy boots as she curled away from him, holding her hands over her head for protection.

"Well?" she heard Durell say.

"Stop," she moaned. "Please, stop. I'll do what you want."

"Jory!" Durell barked. "Come back here." He crossed the room and picked Daphne up. She was groaning in pain as he placed her gently on one of the chairs. "Now," he said, again in a conversational tone of voice, "we'll discuss the terms of your employment. To start, let me be clear. Everything you earn you will give to me. I shall give you an allowance." He took a handkerchief from his pocket and wiped away the blood drooling from her mouth. "You're working for me, and I hope this will never have to happen again."

"What if I run away?" Daphne managed to spit out, a hint of defiance still there.

Durell's tone of voice hardened again. He shoved her head back. "Then I shall find you, beat you much worse than tonight, and probably kill you. That may depend," he said in a low, grating voice, "on how much use you'll continue to be to me."

The next day, her cheek bruised and her lip swollen, Daphne went shopping with Durell. He bought her a pair of high boots and revealing blouses. She had not worn lipstick before. He purchased some and added mascara. With a warning, he gave her five pounds and instructed her to see him in a few days when her injuries had subsided. No payment would be required for her room.

A couple of days later, seeing Durell and Jory chatting in the foyer, Daphne shrank away from them in terror. A new life for her had begun. She became an escort, a bauble on the arms of powerful men at private assignations and often debauched parties. Gradually coarsened by the nature of her work, she remained a charming and vivacious companion, and her allowances grew, although never enough to repay her mounting, manipulated debt. And always, always in the background lurked the threat of physical violence, usually administered by Jory, Durell's vicious henchman and enforcer.

Durell lived on the floor beneath Daphne, and occasionally he demanded that she spend the night with him. No other women in the house were awarded this dubious privilege. Durell explained that he did not mix business with pleasure, but Daphne's obvious beauty entranced him.

And then, four and a half years after Daphne's arrival, the alarmed receptionist discovered Durell dead in his room. The stench had alerted others that something was wrong. He died of a massive overdose of heroin, either because he had been careless in diluting it, unlikely but possible, or because someone else had negligently or intentionally not cut it before handing him the needle to inject into his arm.

The Metropolitan Police wanted to speak with Daphne. She was a prime suspect if there had been foul play. But she had vanished, as had also an enormous amount of ill-gotten cash that Durell had kept hidden in his room. The other women in the house were not very helpful. They offered the police a physical description of Daphne, but they knew her only by her first name and knew nothing of her prior life or present whereabouts.

A day after Durell's death and two days before his body was discovered, a blond-haired woman wearing thick eyeglasses boarded a flight to Tunis. Her passport stated that she was Susannah Watkins, a florist who worked not far from the house where Daphne had lived. Ostensibly, the purpose of her journey was tourism. After arriving and finding a place to stay, this woman removed her eyeglasses, rinsed her hair and, not long thereafter, obtained a job in a Tunisian travel agency. Her fluency with English was helpful and, being intelligent, she soon learned basic Arabic.

The woman calling herself Susannah Watkins lived alone, not far from the souk. One day, a few years after relocating in Tunisia, she came home by chance at lunchtime, and a neighbor informed her that someone had called for her that morning and was apparently looking for her.

Suspicious, Daphne asked, "What did the person look like?"

"He was an Englishman, not too tall, thin. He had blond hair."

It could have been an innocent caller. But Daphne took no chances. Almost half the money taken from Durell's room had belonged to Jory. She never returned to work. Hurriedly, she threw clothes into a suitcase and packed her still sizable, unspent stash of British pounds into a small bag. Shortly afterward she arrived by taxi at the residence of an American couple she had met only days before at the tourist agency. They had told her of their plans to drive across the Sahara, following an old caravan route in a refitted Land Rover.

"Would you take me with you?" she had pleaded, her suitcase at her feet.

"I'm not sure we'll have room," the woman had

responded. “George,” she had added, addressing her husband, “can we take another person? We’ll need more supplies.”

“Please, please,” Daphne had begged.

In the end, the couple relented. George decided an extra helping hand might be useful. Daphne took her turn driving, then trying to sleep, as they jolted across the Sahara and the porous border into northern Nigeria. Fatigued, dusty and joyful, they arrived after several days in the mud-brick city of Sokoto, a half day’s drive from Zaria.

Chapter 28

Farewell

1977–1978

One week passed. Two weeks. In the middle of the second, restless, Dick walked late at night from his house to Daphne's apartment. Alone, he stood in the parking lot, gazing at her window. A soft glow filtered through her curtains and illuminated the railing on the balcony. Then the light winked out. Wearily, with a sigh, he trudged home.

Did he want her? He did, and he did not. He wanted the sex, her laughter, her mischievous frivolity, but he had glimpsed enough, just enough, to make him wary. She was exciting, but she was not steady, predictable Christine, who was due to arrive in another month. It was not that something was missing from his awareness, although it was, hidden from view. It was rather that something was there that he had not seen before, a distemper perhaps, a mercurial shift of mood, an annealed vulnerability and hardness, like the sides of the same coin.

The fall term had ended, and he had composed and administered his examinations. The students were drifting home, some far to the south, for at least a month. Never bustling with activity late in the day, the law school was now quiet, a secretary or teacher a fleeting ghost in the hallways. He had little to do but sit in his office and grade papers, many of inferior quality so that he wondered if the fault was the students' or a deficiency in his teaching.

Despite being a Moslem section of the country, there was scattered evidence – in addition to the scheduling of classes in fall and spring terms – that the Christmas season was at hand in Zaria. The only limited supermarket in Tudun Wada featured a Styrofoam Santa and some tinsel on a shelf near a cash register, and there was a string of lights outside another tiny shop, a mud hovel reached by a board that teetered across a drainage ditch, probably owned by Christians.

These small, pathetic attempts at holiday cheer only darkened Dick's mood. He had his solitary work to distract him, but that was all. From time to time friends like Peter and Penelope invited him to dinner, and on these occasions he tended to drink too much and wake with a headache in the morning. A barren Christmas without presents and the shouts and laughter of children, and then a New Year celebration devoid of family and old friends, awaited him.

Depressed and lonely, during the third week he walked again at night to Daphne's apartment. A full moon glittered through the tops of trees and cast a spectral glow on her white building. For long minutes he stood again in the parking lot, scuffing the pavement with his sandals, looking at the muted shaft of light shining from her window. With an audible sigh, Dick turned to go, then stopped and turned again. More minutes passed before he moved forward, slowly mounting the stairs and edging along the balcony toward her door. He raised his hand, hesitated, then knocked, and he heard a rustling within.

Daphne pulled the curtain of her window back, searched outside, then flung the door wide open. "Dick!" she exclaimed eagerly, "Dick, you've come back." Without thought or reserve, she embraced him. His arms had been hanging limp at his side, and slowly he raised them and embraced her in return, first tentatively, then fiercely. They did not kiss but stood hugging each other before, almost breathless, Daphne invited him to come inside.

She sat on a low couch, covered with cheerful pink cloth, at one side of the sitting area. The seat next to her was vacant, but Dick chose to sit in a yellow, cloth-covered chair facing her. Daphne raised an eyebrow, that was all, and asked if he would like a refreshing drink of soda or beer.

"No thanks," Dick said, settling back. For several moments he gazed at her, then surveyed the room as if it contained something important he might find. "So," he cleared his throat and pursed his lips. "So," another try, "how are you? Is everything okay? You're safe and sound?"

"Yes, Dick, safe and sound." Daphne smiled, a saucy curl to her lips that he well remembered. There was another awkward moment of silence. "Are we starting all over?" she said softly, this time with a look of serious concentration.

" I don't think so. But," he added hastily, "it's so good to see you. I won't deny I missed you. I missed you a lot. I was lonely."

"And so was I. Come! Sit next to me! I promise I won't

molest you. Sit here," she patted the cushion next to her, "and let's talk."

And talk they did, but by unspoken consensus he did not touch her for the longest time, nor did she invite it. It was late in the evening when Daphne grasped his arm and draped it over her shoulders. He let it hang there, a useless pillow for her head. But in response to her questioning glance, his hand drifted down and clutched her about the waist. Cuddled together, her head resting on his chest, they sat quietly, their aimless conversation no longer a necessary proof against awkward silence.

There were footsteps outside, a door unlocked and opened. Daphne struggled to sit up, partially disengaging herself and looking at her wristwatch. Leaning forward, she kissed his cheek. "Dick, darling," she said, "it's time for you to go. Will I see you again?"

"Yes," he blurted, carefully extracting his arm and standing up. "When?"

"Tomorrow, in the early afternoon. You can pick me up."

They went shopping together, as much shopping as was possible given the limited supplies available. Dick paid a tailor in a shop with a rough plank floor and a goat tethered outside the door to sew a multi-colored, tie-dye blouse for Daphne. It had small, square buttons down the front fashioned from wood cut from a baobab tree. Smiling broadly with gaps in his teeth, the tailor had risen from his foot-powered sewing machine to perform the measurements. Dick also ordered two more for Christine and Molly to be fitted after they arrived while Daphne, listening intently to his instructions, busied herself examining fabric piled in a corner. In addition, Dick ordered a safari jacket for himself and another for Allen, guessing their size would be the same. This time Daphne joined in selecting the material and advising on the right cut. They strolled afterward, hand in hand, to the small and only supermarket in town. Daphne needed kitchen supplies. Dick purchased a can opener for her, and they laughed at the unromantic nature of the gift and the lack of fancy paper and ribbon to wrap it in.

In the following days, Dick and Daphne went often to the swimming pool. Her flirtatious behavior did not change and attracted a bevy of small boys peering over the top of the enclosing wall. Usually only one or two other men were present - visiting Nigerians or expatriates. On one occasion another Caucasian woman joined them, but she was French, and as Daphne did not know the language and Dick spoke it poorly, they quickly abandoned the attempt to communicate. The woman had a large, Gallic nose and a pudgy body that bulged out of and over a too skimpy bathing suit, and her presence did nothing to detract from Daphne.

Sometimes Daphne proposed dinner at her apartment for the two of them, sometimes not, and in any event Dick always left for home late in the afternoon or early in the evening. She would often ask him to leave early, saying that she could not be with a man that night. No explanation was ever offered. Yet on other occasions she would prolong leave-taking, clinging to him like a lost child. On Christmas Eve they attended an Anglican service at a small, white-clapboard chapel situated on a low knoll in the middle of what had once been the

European quarter, mostly occupied by British civil servants. Daphne knew most of the hymns; Dick knew the words, but the tunes were often unfamiliar. A wreath with small, colored ornaments acquired somewhere decorated the altar, and that minor reminder of the season brought a lump to his throat. Afterward, leaving the chapel, they encountered Penelope and Peter. Dick had seen them sitting in a pew near the front. He introduced them to Daphne, and they greeted her warmly, apparently unfazed by the knowledge that Dick's family was soon to arrive. They easily understood from Daphne's accent that she was from England. The usual inquiries and pleasantries ensued – Where are you from (they guessed from the north)? How long have you been in Nigeria? And, you simply must join us sometime for dinner. Daphne seemed very pleased to meet them, and she volunteered that actually she had lived for many years in London.

Dick did not know that, and on the way home he asked her about it. "You never told me you lived in London."

"I must have… well, I did, for several years."

"What were you doing there?"

"This and that. Nothing important. It's really too boring to talk about."

The next day was Christmas, and Daphne asked Dick to join her for dinner. They ate at the small table adjacent to her kitchen. Daphne had bought lamb that was sold at an agricultural field station a few miles outside town. Dick had tried it already once he had a car, and the experience had given him lockjaw for several minutes. He gamely expressed delight and tried it again. She also served Yorkshire pudding from a tin purchased from the supermarket, and for dessert she had contrived an African version of English trifle. They ate with gusto and consumed a bottle of red table wine that Dick had found on a shelf in the back of a hardware store.

Making love afterward, the first time in weeks, was a different experience for both. Instead of frantic grappling or energetic experimentation with different positions, their love-making was slow and gentle, preceded by caresses and kisses. Panting, the act completed, they lay in each other's arms face to face.

"You are the most wonderful man I've ever met," Daphne murmured.

"And you're the most beautiful woman."

After a long interval, in a gesture he had experienced before, Daphne tapped his nose with her forefinger to gain his attention. The gesture was playful but her face was solemn.

"I wanted it to end this way."

"End?" Dick propped himself up on an elbow to look at her. He had known the moment was coming, had even rehearsed a few words. "End?" he repeated.

"Yes, Dick." Tears were forming in Daphne's eyes. "You're wife and children will be here soon. Between us, it can't work. It was a lovely evening, a good ending. We should say goodbye tonight."

"Daphne, I don't want…"

She placed a finger on his lips. "Neither of us wants this. Let's hug and say goodbye."

A tender kiss, almost chaste. The door closed behind

him. Dick slouched home, disconsolate. When he arrived, he padlocked the front door, checked the other doors, turned on the outside floodlights and entered his bedroom after locking the door to the sleeping quarters. Almost ripping the mosquito netting as he yanked it aside, he flung himself on the bed. He thought: She was right. It will never, ever, ever work. It won't. He lay in the dark, bereft and resigned to a fitful, sleepless night.

* * * * *

But it was not the end.

Peter and Penelope asked Dick to join them at their compound in the Old City to celebrate New Year's Eve. He drove there, unenthusiastic but reluctant to spend the evening alone. Other doctors and their wives had also been invited. It was a convivial gathering, but for Dick it was a glum affair.

"That was a very nice woman you were with at church," Peter remarked, almost, but not quite, casually. He had sidled to where Dick was seated by himself outside under a canopy, and, after putting his drink down on a nearby table, had sat beside him. "We invited her to join us this evening, but she declined. Said she was busy, and I'm not surprised. How did you get to meet such a lovely creature?"

"She's a friend, a colleague at the law school," Dick answered, his Adam's apple rising slightly. It was a lie, a transparent one easily unmasked by an inquiry to anyone at the school, but he was too disconsolate to care.

"Ah, I see," was Peter's only response.

And then three days before Christine, Allen and Molly were to arrive, Dick was sitting in his office in the afternoon, the fan overhead chunking in a fruitless effort to dry the film of sweat on his brow. The building at that hour was, as usual, nearly deserted, although students had begun to return for the spring term. His door opened a crack, and he thought at first it was a returning student. When it was pushed open farther, however, Daphne walked in.

Dick jerked back abruptly in his chair, although he attempted to disguise his consternation. "How did you find me?" he said, quickly recovering his composure.

"A nice young man who was leaving the building directed me to your office. And it's very nice, I must say." She looked around, then took a seat in one of the two available chairs in front of Dick's desk. He noticed that she was wearing shorts and the blouse he had given her for Christmas.

"Well, ah, what brings you here?"

There was an interval of strained silence.

"We need to talk." Again silence, so that only the sound of the whirring and clattering fan filled the room. "Dick," she said finally, "we love each other, and I was wondering if, maybe, we could still see each other… you know…from time to time after your family arrives. Just a little," she faltered. "I really miss you."

Dick dropped his head into his hands. Looking up finally, a pained expression on his face, he said, "Daphne, please. It's over. You said it yourself."

"But we love each other. You do… you do love me, don't you?"

"I did. But there are things about you I don't

understand. It's a long word, but contumacious comes to mind, or willful, or soft and gentle and then hard as… as, I don't know… as obsidian. It bothered… it bothers me."

"What does that mean? What did you call it? Ob…?"

"I'm not sure. A really hard rock, I think."

"So you're saying you don't love me?"

"No… no, I'm not. You're the most unusual and interesting woman I've ever met. I was mesmerized by you, fell in love with you. I guess I still am… but I also love Christine."

"How can you love two people at the same time?"

"I don't know. But you can. In different ways and for different reasons." His mouth turned down, Dick wiped one of his eyes. "I should be with my family. I ought to be, and I can't do that and sneak around to see you."

"Ought?" Daphne bristled, rising from her chair. "Should? Why can't you do what you want?"

Dick leaned back. "Please. This is so painful." For a few moments he raised his right hand, made a fist and wiped his mouth with the back of it. In a low voice, he said, "I guess I want to do what I ought to do. It's as simple as that."

Daphne rose and walked behind her chair, resting her hands on the back. She tossed her dark hair and stared at him, eyes flashing with anger. "You really mean it?" she sputtered.

"Yes, darling, I do. This hurts me as much as it hurts you, but I can't go on with this anymore. The last time I saw you was the end… you said so yourself."

Daphne walked to the door and grabbed the handle.

Turning, she spat, "You're a fool, a real fool, Dick Blodgett, but if that's what you want, you can have it." Her chest heaved. "We really loved each other, damn it." She slammed the door behind her.

Chapter 29

Reunion and Arrival

1978

Christine's last letter to Dick was postmarked three weeks before her scheduled arrival. It gave the flight number on Nigerian Airways, the date and the time. Dick had replied, but it had taken ten days for her letter to reach him and another ten days for his response, saying that he would meet her, to be delivered in Woodbury. He could not be certain his letter had arrived in time.

Thus all parties acted on blind faith. Dick had no way to verify that their flight from London would depart and arrive as scheduled, or even if it would depart at all. With hope and a prayer, leaving his house after midnight, he sped through the stillness of the night with hardly another car in view on a new, straight, two-lane highway that had just opened between Zaria and Kano. It was an enormous improvement over the curving, rutted road that he had traveled only four months before. He covered the distance to Kano in about an hour and a half. The airport was as he remembered it, small and provincial, yet he saw it through different eyes. Dick went inside. Along the walls and on benches people were sleeping, some with blankets pulled over them, and, as before, there were no facilities for guests or travelers.

The plane arrived a half hour late and disgorged its

passengers, most of them disoriented from lack of sleep. Dick paced anxiously, relieved finally when his family cleared customs and stepped into the terminal. With hugs and kisses, they had a jolly, if tired, reunion. By the time they were half way to Zaria, the sun had risen, an orange disc over a flat savannah dotted with plane trees. Smoke was drifting from compounds along the route. On entering Tudun Wada, they passed the low, mud-brick hovels of the inhabitants with chickens and goats wandering about, sticks of firewood stacked against walls, piles of trash heaped in front of low doorways and fragments of paper, iron implements, boxes, anything, scattered on the bare, treeless ground. There was silence from the weary travelers, a muted holding of breath. And then Dick drove through the gates of the compound surrounding the institute into a green world. Adamu, his steward, greeted them on the circular driveway before their charming, thatch roofed cottage and hefted their luggage inside. With relief, the new arrivals made their way indoors and inspected the premises. They shed their winter clothes and donned summer attire. Dick served them a large, English breakfast with eggs, bread – toasted in the oven – jam and coffee, and shortly thereafter, all lay down for naps and knew no more until late afternoon.

Dick soon introduced Christine and his children to his new friends – Penelope and Peter, and Dot and Ned. And, of course, they met Adamu. In the following days, Dick took them on tours to acclimate them to their new surroundings. They were as shocked as he had been by the pervasive poverty and prevalence of disease – the lepers, the blind and the children with paralyzed lower limbs. He also showed them the location of stores, the institute's classrooms and the offices of maintenance personnel. Early on Dick drove them to the Sabon Gari so that they could experience the old market with its crowded alleyways and incessant haggling over price for all manner of goods. Children and an occasional adult trailed behind Molly, fascinated by her blond hair and blue eyes, and Christine, delighted by the colorful apparel of the women, stopped at every booth with cloth fabric to examine the material.

Absent during the mornings and early afternoons, either teaching or preparing for class, Dick had to leave his family to their own devices. Allen and Molly had school work to absorb their time and energy. Christine became a favorite of Adamu, who often accompanied her on shopping excursions. He showed her the best places to buy fabric, and she purchased light green, diaphanous curtains for the windows and saw that they were properly tailored to fit each one. Fascinated by her new surroundings, she used the car to venture to the Sabon Gari to shop for food and to the main campus to hear lectures. Through Penelope, she met a young English woman who was engaged in an archeological dig. On several days each week she joined her in a cave at the top of an inselberg to laboriously scrape and sift the dirt there in a search for prior, human habitation.

It was hot, ceaselessly hot. With the coming of harmattan in the late fall, the wind descended from the north blowing up fine particles of dust from the Sahara that covered everything with a fine film, obscuring objects at a distance and occasionally blotting out the sun.

The temperature dropped markedly, particularly at night and in the early morning, so that Dick had worn a sweater to keep warm on the trip to Kano to pick up his family. By early February, however, the wind shifted, harmattan ended, and the heat intensified, most notably at midday when the sun was directly overhead. For most of the night it was still too hot to lie under covers. Dick and his family began weeks of longing for rain, but it would be two months at least until the wind shifted again, blowing up from the Bight of Benin in the south with its welcome moisture from the sea. Until then, their days were dry and hot, the sky a seamless vault of blue, and they looked in vain for dark clouds on the southern horizon.

During the hottest part of the day in mid-afternoon, the family's main respite was the pool, and Dick and his family went there often to escape the heat. Dick fretted about the possibility that Daphne might be there, or come there, but she never appeared. Often Allen stayed home, working at the dining room table. As a sophomore in college, he had a paper to write and only limited time in Nigeria to complete the task from scattered notes he had brought with him. Molly, six years his junior, was less encumbered. Her mother had undertaken home-schooling with the permission of her junior high school, and so her time was more flexible in the afternoon. Her presence at the pool drew the same curious attention that Daphne's had from the boys who climbed the perimeter wall to peek at her, but Molly either failed to notice or ignored them.

On many of these occasions they were joined by Matt Jameson, a young professor from a law school in Indiana, who had arrived in Kano two days after Christine and the children. Bright, tall and blond, with open, raw-boned features, Matt was in his mid-thirties and a bachelor. He had been recruited to teach in Africa in much the same way as Dick, and because he and Dick were the only Americans at the law school, they had quickly come to know each other.

Otherwise lonely, as Dick had been at the outset, Matt attached himself to Dick and his family. In addition to forays to the pool, he came frequently to the house for drinks and dinner. He had a relaxed, conversational manner, but there was more.

"Anyone who doesn't vote my way hasn't got his head screwed on right," he said one evening, smiling broadly.

That was too much for Christine. "Really, Matt, does mine look loose to you?"

"I guess you're the exception that proves the rule."

"No," Christine answered tartly, "you're proof that you people have your heads screwed on so tight there's no room left for brains."

The trade of insults was barbed but friendly. Matt laughed easily, deflecting animosity. Sometimes, however, he exhibited a blustery overconfidence that rattled Christine.

"She was the one who got away," he announced one evening when asked about his social life at home.

"Oh?" Christine parried. "There were a lot who didn't? Like what? The ones with poor eyesight?" A smile curled up on the undamaged portion of her face.

"I'll take them anyway I can." Matt rolled back his head and laughed.

Christine merely shook her head, and Dick sat back in his chair, often reluctant to interfere in the verbal parrying between his wife and colleague. They both liked Matt, it was hard not to given his easy charm, but Christine increasingly had reservations. "I don't like the way he talks in front of the children," she chided Dick.

He agreed, but added, "Look, he's good company and our only American friend at the law school."

Invariably, if he stayed for supper, Matt left shortly thereafter, claiming that he had studying to do. Adamu washed the dishes, carting hot water from a heater in the bathroom across the living room to the kitchen. That is, if the electricity was on, because often it was not so that flickering candles and a portable gas lamp had to illuminate the room. After five to six months of nearly total drought the reservoirs were down, and as a consequence there was less water to drive the turbines that generated electricity at the large dam near Kaduna. This problem, in turn, meant the water pumps shut down for lack of power, and the result was that, until the rains came in earnest, they were sometimes without electricity and water for hours at a time and had to keep the bathtub full in case of emergency.

Assuming there was adequate lighting and water, Adamu could wash the dishes and the family usually read for a while after Matt's departure, although Allen frequently wrote and rewrote sections of his paper. At bedtime, after the children had retired – Molly slept in a small bedroom adjacent to the master bedroom and Allen slept on a mattress in a utility room opposite the bathroom, a jury-rigged mosquito netting over him –

Dick and Christine had no distractions to avoid their lack of intimacy. To Dick, being with his wife was like trying on an old glove; it was warm, comfortable and fit perfectly. He knew her moods, could predict her often humorous, deft retorts to Matt, and loved their easy camaraderie.

To Christine, it was not the same. Within a few weeks of her arrival, she pointed out, as she had numerous times before, that she and Dick were living together more as affectionate siblings than as an intimate husband and wife.

"Why are you withholding yourself from me?" she complained bitterly.

"I'm not," he protested. "I'm really not." How could he tell her that he had experienced unrestrained passion with Daphne, that he could not generate that passion looking at her discolored, scarred face and shrunken mouth? He could not, would not, add a critique of her appearance to the physical insults she had already endured. "The problem is me," he said, vainly attempting to deflect part of the problem to himself. "Maybe I'm impotent. It's not that I won't, it's that I can't. And there's nothing unique about our situation. Lots of married couples don't have sex."

"Sure, if they're old and fat. But that's not us." Christine stared at him, then snorted angrily, "You're not impotent, Dick, never have been, so don't try to kid me." Creeping onto the bed, she turned her back to him and prepared for sleep.

Chapter 30

The Polo Club

1978

In the beginning of March Allen left for home and the remainder of his college year.

* * * * *

The scorching days of March drifted into April, and it was in that latter month when Dick and Christine discovered a new recreational activity. Driving north to the main campus about half way between Tudun Wada and the Lebanon Club, Dick had often seen a large thatch roof rising above the surrounding foliage and had wondered what it might be. But it was not until the first week of April, when he accepted an invitation from Penelope and Peter to join them, that he found out it was the Zaria Polo Club. Thereafter, Christine, Molly, Matt and Dick went there often.

During the week before Easter, the club sponsored matches between teams from cities all over northern Nigeria: Kaduna, Jos, Sokoto, Katsina, Maiduguri, Zaria and others were represented. Neither Christine, Molly nor Dick had seen polo matches before. Matt claimed that he had, but when questioned about the rules, he evaded an answer.

The polo club was set back and shielded from the road by dense bushes and trees. A curving, dirt driveway meandered to it and an adjacent parking area. There was a spacious, raised terrace covered with flagstones between the clubhouse and the playing field. It was dotted with folding chairs and tables shielded by large, colorful umbrellas. After ordering drinks – always beer, even for Molly – the four visitors sat together on the terrace to watch the play on the field.

Because of the absence of rain, the field was a dusty rectangle rather than the grassy turf that one might find in northern climes. The players were a mixture of white expatriates and Nigerians. They wheeled and turned on their horses in clouds of dust, which made it difficult to see the action on the field. Every now and then, however, one would break free, others in frantic pursuit, and thunder up the field.

Once, when this happened, Molly jumped up from her seat. "Wow!" she exclaimed, "That was really exciting."

"Nothing to it." Dick affected a Southwestern drawl. "I was born on horseback, used to ride the range in my younger years."

Christine cocked her head to one side. "Which range was that, Sweetheart? The one in your parents' kitchen?"

"Yeah, Dad," Molly added, giggling, "and you'd fall off that."

From under the brim of his floppy hat, Dick looked at his wife and daughter, suppressing a grin. "Okay, okay," he said, hanging his head in mock resignation. "I guess I exaggerated a little."

Matt enjoyed the playful banter, sometimes joining in, but he wearied of horses galloping to and fro in swirling dust. After an hour he suggested that the party go inside. Christine and Molly declined, but Dick agreed, and he and Matt rose and walked through a doorway at one side of the terrace into the building. Inside was a cavernous, semi-circular room with a high, vaulted ceiling of thatch and supporting beams. The walls were thick, whitewashed stucco with occasional, narrow windows – almost arrow slits – cut into them. A sweeping, semi-circular bar covered an entire side of the room, and a scattering of men and women were seated at it or at adjoining tables.

Seated at the bar, both men ordered a beer, and, after an interval when they sat and stared silently ahead, they began to talk. Their conversation covered the demands of work and, to the extent it was known, events in the United States. Dehydrated from the hour spent in the heat outside, they quaffed their beers quickly and ordered seconds.

Dick noticed that his companion was becoming slightly inebriated. Whereas Dick's legs were dangling down the sides of his bar stool, Matt was sitting up straight, his feet on the bar rail, craning his neck to peer around the room.

He turned to Dick. "Where is the, you know, pussy around here? There must be plenty of whores in this God-forsaken dump. You were alone for several months, so you must have met some."

Dick pulled his head back and blinked. "No," he said, "I didn't, and I've no idea."

"Aw, c'mon, Dick. Really, you've got to have some idea."

Dick frowned and shook his head. "Be careful, Matt. Aren't you afraid of catching some disease?"

"What are you, some kind of missionary?" Matt laughed. "I'm not going to pass up the chance for a piece of African ass."

"I'm sorry, Matt. I can't help you."

Matt sighed. "I guess I'm going to have to do some hunting on my own… Hey, Dick, if she has a sister, would you, y'know, like me to cut you in on the deal?"

Smiling, Dick shook his head again. "Count me out, Matt. Not while I'm here with Christine and Molly… actually, not ever… but don't think I'm passing judgment. I'm not." He thought of Daphne. "I'm really not."

Outside, the match ended. Christine and Molly entered the building and walked over to where they were seated. Asked if she would like a drink, Christine declined and said that she and Molly wanted to go home. On the way, they dropped Matt off at the conference center. Christine asked Dick what he and Matt had talked about, but Dick did not relate the conversation about women.

Chapter 31

Jihad and Yankari

1978

The rains finally came, not in daily downpours but in a couple of thunderstorms preceded by large, billowing cumulonimbus that loomed over the trees. Bringing temporary coolness from the stifling heat, they increased in frequency and intensity as the days drifted by. Enormous, towering gray clouds filled the sky every afternoon. The lightening was continuous; the thunder a constant crackle and occasional deep boom, and the sky, interlaced with lightening, was like cracked pottery or broken shards of glass.

From a dusty brown, the landscape rapidly reverted to a verdant green. Sitting inside at the dining room table, enclosed by whitewashed walls, Dick looked through the grille work on the windows at a transformed world. The vegetation noticeably thickened, and the leaves, ferns and bushes outside became resplendent in various shades of rich green, punctuated by bright spots of red and yellow.

Within three weeks of the first sprinkling, the spring term neared its end. Classes ceased and were followed by a two-week reading period. At this time, a final moot court competition was held at the law school in a large lecture theater. The decorum of these proceedings and the elegant lunch that followed were in stark contrast to events on the main campus. Ultra-conservative Moslem students began assaulting other students from the south. They objected to the southern female students, who often came to class in knee-length skirts and without head coverings, and to their male counterparts who were members of a palm wine drinking society. Serious injuries were reported.

The following Friday a student rose in a mosque near the main campus and claimed that Christians were planning on burning down the mosque. Hours later a small group of students and villagers from outside the main gate burned down the large, attractive staff club on the main campus. They also burned the office of the vice-Chancellor, a southern Christian, ransacked his residence and attacked his guards. One of them was badly wounded; another had his throat cut and died.

The next morning two girls from the south ran terrified into Dick's house at the approach of an open backed Mercedes truck filled with truculent, young men, and that night Dick was kept awake until three in the morning, anxious for the safety of his family, as he listened to the rising and falling shouts of a mob and the insistent, ominous beating of a bass drum. Deeply disturbed by these events and believing that violence might erupt on their own campus, Dick and Christine decided to make a long-delayed trip to the Yankari Game Reserve. Matt joined in their decision and elected to accompany them. There were no teaching duties to impede their departure.

It took many hours to drive from Zaria to Yankari. To get there, Dick first took the road southeast to Jos, a city situated on a plateau. As the travelers approached the city, they saw countless villages in among wooded hills, usually with several round, mud-brick buildings with conical straw roofs and cactus-like fences around them, in this respect quite different from the villages surrounding Zaria. Heading east after leaving Jos, they observed mountains in the distance, rising up gray on the horizon. They looked like images from a Chinese painting or, more fancifully, like inverted loaves of bread, steep on the sides with rounded tops.

They never reached the mountains but instead turned south on a road through scrub trees and tall termite mounds, some two to three times the height of a man. At the end was the Yankari Game Reserve, an extensive tract of forested hills. The focal point was a simple lodge, with chalets similar in design to the huts in the villages outside Jos, near a gorge called Wikli Spring. The weary travelers did not have reservations as it had been impossible to telephone in advance and reserve rooms. Arriving late in the day, they discovered that the Federal Health Service had booked all the chalets for a conference. Fortunately, rooms in the lodge were available, although they had not yet been cleaned for late arriving guests.

While waiting for their accommodations to be readied, they decided to swim in Wikli Spring. The receptionist warned them to be careful of baboons who enjoyed stealing unattended clothes left by visitors after they had changed into bathing suits. With this admonition in mind, they walked down a sloping path through scrub bush and trees to a broad, natural pool, perhaps fifty feet in length and thirty feet in width. Shaded by palm trees mixed in with tall ferns and other trees draped with vines, but with an open bank on the side from which they approached, the pool was fed by warm water gushing from the base of a fifty foot high sandstone cliff.

Dick thought that it was like being present at the dawn of creation. There was a small changing shed where they could secure their clothes. No one else was there. The water was a constant eighty-eight degrees, pure and clean so that their feet were perfectly, uninterruptedly visible above white sand at a depth of six to seven feet. Ignoring a couple of green snakes on the far side amidst interlaced roots and a troop of baboons, two or three of which watched intently as they swam, they splashed about for a long time, like luxuriating in a warm tub, before donning their clothes and trudging back up the steep trail in the late afternoon.

Their rooms, now cleaned, were waiting. Matt took one, Molly another and Christine and Dick a third. Christine and Molly elected to rest after their long journey. Dick arranged with Matt to meet him on the deck in half an hour, and he and Christine retired to their room. It was elegant in its simplicity; there were whitewashed walls, two single beds with brightly woven covers of African design, a dresser, and two comfortable chairs, also upholstered in a colorful African motif next to a rough-hewn, wooden table by the window.

Dick flung their single piece of shared luggage onto one of the beds. "Are you ready for a drink?" he said to Christine.

"I don't think so. I'd rather stay here and rest. But you go."

"What'll I tell Matt?"

"Just that I'm resting before dinner… and honestly, Dick, I don't want any more of his company right now."

"Oh?"

"You know what my mother says of some people: a little bit goes a long way. I hope that's not harsh, but he's more your friend than mine."

"You're okay?"

"Perfectly okay. And, darling, I do love you so much and the care you take of me. You'll enjoy yourself. Wake me if I'm sleeping when you return."

After kissing Christine affectionately on the forehead, Dick changed into a clean shirt and then ambled down the corridor to Matt's room. The two men walked through the lobby and out to a bar on a broad deck jutting out from the lodge. They chose two chairs next to a small table with a canting umbrella at one side. After sitting down, Matt carefully combed and patted his hair with his fingers. Dick explained Christine's absence. Several other people were on the deck, men and women, presumably Nigerians in casual western dress. They were seated across the deck with the exception of one couple enjoying tall drinks at a nearby table.

From the deck, Dick looked out for miles over undulating, unpopulated forest – not jungle with dense mangrove swamps, squawking parrots and an impenetrable canopy of vines and branches but rather a temperate zone forest with different kinds of bushes and trees than he remembered from home. It was a scene reminiscent of New England and totally different from Zaria and its surrounding countryside.

A slender young waitress, presumably Nigerian, in

muted, traditional dress – a colorful, long skirt and an equally colorful headdress – came to the table to take their orders. They each asked for a beer. As she turned to leave, Matt grasped her arm and said, "Thanks, honey, and make it snappy. We're really thirsty."

Offended, the waitress yanked her arm away. Retreating to a doorway, she reappeared a couple of minutes later with an elderly black man dressed in white slacks and a tan safari jacket. He seemed to be a person of authority. She pointed to Matt, and the man spoke with her and then re-entered the building. Seated sideways to the lodge, Dick could see them, but Matt, his back to the door, was gazing unaware at the forested hills bathed in late afternoon sunlight.

Dick pulled irritably at Matt's elbow. "The waitress was back there pointing at us and talking to a man who looked like he could be the manager."

"So what?"

"Oh, for God's sake, Matt, don't screw around. You grabbed that woman, and she obviously didn't like it. If we get kicked out of here, we've nowhere else to go."

"Okay, okay, it won't happen again."

The waitress brought them two large bottles of Star beer with glasses on a tray. Matt gave her a handsome tip, and she scurried away.

Dick poured beer into each glass. "Whew, I think we're safe, thank goodness. That was really fun today, the swim in that pool. It was spectacular."

"It sure was. I didn't much like those green snakes, but I guess if you leave them alone, they leave you alone."

"Same with the baboons."

"More or less. If we go back tomorrow, we've got to keep an eye on them. I don't trust them."

They sat in silence for a long while, sipping their beer and contemplating the scene before them.

Then Dick spoke. "Any luck finding women?" He regretted his question the moment it was uttered. For Christ's sake, he thought, why did I say that? But it was too late to snatch it back.

"No problem. No problem at all," Matt answered. "I met an Italian contractor who's here with his company doing road construction. He introduced me to a couple of young African women."

"Prostitutes?"

"I'd call them ladies of convenience. I don't pay them, but I give them presents. It's great fun."

"I hope you protect yourself. You never can tell."

"Most of the time. Well, half the time. That's the beauty of penicillin. I don't worry about it." Matt paused. "Anyway, why the lecture? I've found out, Dick, that you weren't entirely truthful with me." His tone was more teasing than accusatory. "I spoke with one of the Italians a few days ago, and he told me about a pretty English woman named Daphne… and that a doctor friend of yours said you had taken her out. Did you?"

"Well… ah, yes, kind of," Dick replied.

"What do you mean, 'kind of'? Either you did or you didn't. Did you get in her?"

"Ah… no," Dick said. "Actually, it's none of your business."

Matt chuckled. "So you did. Don't try to kid me. What was she like?"

Dick could feel his face flushing, reddening. "I don't know her at all well. Sometimes she seems a little depressed, maybe, but very friendly." He paused, then added, "If you've been having unprotected sex, you should leave her alone. It wouldn't be fair."

"Jesus, Dick, you really are a scout master. Be fair? The name of the game is to get laid, not be her escort to a tea party. If she's a big girl, she can look out for herself."

"I'd go slow, that's all."

"No," Matt said. "I think I'll ask her out and enjoy an English woman for a change."

Dick frowned and changed the subject. They chatted about other things, and both ordered a second beer. For the first time in days, Dick thought of Daphne. *Should I warn her not to go out with Matt?*

* * * * *

The next day the four travelers, hoping to see wildlife, boarded an open-backed Mercedes truck with large tires for traversing uneven terrain. They spent several hours bumping along rutted tracks, catching glimpses of warthogs, monkeys, antelope and a water buffalo in small clearings and along stream beds and, near the end, a herd of elephants in a lush, grass-covered meadow. Exhausted, they ate dinner heartily and retired early.

On the way home the next day, about twenty kilometers west of Bauchi on the way back to Jos, they spied a small sign by the side of the road advertising Neolithic rock paintings. They had time to spare and so decided to visit the site that was about ten kilometers from the highway. The road there was rutted in places so that pools of water had gathered, and occasionally they jolted over large rock outcroppings and over narrow bridges spanning streams. They were delayed by a herd of long-horned cattle being driven across the road by a boy carrying a long stick. Frequent villages along the way slowed their progress, and near them men were hand plowing in the fields, while young girls smiled shyly at them from doorways.

A crude sign at the end of the road, deep in the bush, indicated that the paintings were on an inselberg. And indeed, half way up, on the underside of a cliff canting outward, in a kind of red ocher paint, there were crude drawings of animals, most of which seemed to be leaping antelope with back-curving horns. The paintings appeared to be very old, but there was no plaque of any sort with a statement authenticating their age. There was also a shallow cave nearby, formed by a large slab of stone that had come to rest on other stones. Dick stood at the entrance, looking out over the landscape below, as if he were a Neolithic hunter surveying his domain. I'm just a speck on a continuum, he thought, the chance descendant of countless people who, in their own unique circumstances, must have experienced my joys and struggled with my doubts and fears.

"What are you doing?" Christine shouted to him. "We're about to leave."

"Just looking out over my lost kingdom," Dick shouted back, as he began to scramble over rocks to join her.

"I love that about you. What an imagination!"

"And I love you too." Dick jumped to her side, a final leap, and grabbed her around her waist. "Have you got the fire going? I'm ravenous for some – let's see, what will it be this time? – zebra soup. That's my favorite."

Christine grinned, raising one side of her face. "Coming up, chief, as soon as the children collect firewood."

When they arrived back in Zaria, Dick hugged Christine in an affectionate, homecoming embrace. This time she stiffened, reacting in silent distrust. For a moment they stood facing each other, a puzzled expression on Dick's face. "I do love you," he said. The response was a wan smile and a murmured, "I hope so." The moment passed. Dick turned and retraced his steps to the car to retrieve their luggage.

They soon discovered that the disruptions had ended, the police and army having taken control. Moreover, the students were drifting home to their villages. Three days after their return, Dick gave a final examination and began the tedium of grading.

But he took time during this interval to drive with considerable anxiety to Daphne's apartment. There was no answer to his knock on the door. He decided, therefore, to write her a note stating simply that he wanted to speak with her. More detail, he feared, might incriminate him if the reason for his desire to warn her was somehow revealed to Matt.

Chapter 32

Truth Revealed?

1978

Plans for their departure began in mid-May, almost two months before the actual event. The process was endless and endlessly exasperating, and inefficiencies had to be dealt with at every turn. Securing airline tickets required numerous visits to the main campus – driving back and forth, back and forth – and three trips to the airline office in Kaduna, fifty miles away. It was no use telephoning Kaduna for information, a simple matter in the western world. There were telephones, to be sure, but it might take three days before getting a connection to a neighboring city.

The process required a seemingly infinite number of forms, signatures and stamps, all of which had to be acquired from people who were too often not 'on seat'. There was an insistence on just the right number of copies, pictures, stamps, etc., and then it was never clear whether one had followed procedures accurately because the rules seemed to change capriciously and without notice. And even when that did not happen, almost always approvals in just the right order were required, and as mistakes were commonplace, one had to return to have the errors rectified – only when the frustrated, desperate supplicant returned, quite often the person being sought would have gone out for an indefinitely long period of time, and no one else in the office would be authorized to do the work.

The students, however, compensated for much of Dick's frustration. After exams were finished, a few of them came to his house to say goodbye. Their loving appreciation washed away his irritation. It was very hard to reconcile with the apparent rudeness in other situations. Dick recognized, however, that in many of his encounters with the bureaucracy there was no intention to be rude. The officials with whom Dick dealt were joining the modern world and adjusting haphazardly to governance by segmented minutes set forth on the round face of an impersonal, mechanical contrivance, and many made an overt distinction in their transactions between 'Nigerian time' and 'European time'. In the former, in a village where everyone lived for a lifetime, what difference did it make whether someone was seen at ten in the morning or at noon? And thus what difference did it make whether someone was 'on seat'? He or she would not be far away.

In the midst of these travails, Dick and Daphne met again. It was a few days before his departure with Christine and Molly. He was in the house alone. Christine was away enjoying an afternoon with her friend, the English archeologist, and Molly was visiting at a neighbor's house. Dick had just finished a late lunch and was drying a dish when he heard a knock at the front door. After putting down the dish, he walked into the living room and saw Daphne standing on the small front porch. She was wearing slacks, sandals and, just like the last time in his office, the blouse he had given her for Christmas.

Flabbergasted, Dick opened the door and invited her to come in. "It's nice to see you," he said unconvincingly. "You're looking even prettier than I remembered. But why? I thought… I thought, if you wanted to meet me that you'd come to my office, like before."

"Your note didn't say anything about location, and anyway, you weren't in your office. You do live here, don't you?"

"Yes, but…"

"But what?"

"But so do my wife and daughter, and I don't think…"

"You don't think it would be a good idea for them to meet me? What's the matter, Dick? Are you ashamed of me?" Daphne's voice quivered as she looked around. "I wished we'd shared times here. You did well."

"Yeah, I did." Dick's hands were moist with nervousness. "Why don't we go over to my office? That's your car I see in the driveway, isn't it? We could drive there right now. I've got something to tell you."

"So tell me right here." Daphne smiled wanly, and she marched farther into the room.

"No, I don't think… Okay… well,… it's about a guy named Matt Jameson. If he makes contact with you and asks you for a date, I don't think you should go out with him."

"Why not? I already have. He's not you, no one ever will be, but I like him."

"It's just that he's not right for you… and…"

"And?"

"Well, maybe I shouldn't say this but… but to be honest, he goes out with prostitutes."

"Is that what you wanted to tell me?" Daphne, stricken, dropped her eyes. In a quiet voice, almost a whisper, she said, "What do you think I was?"

"You were…? I don't believe…"

"It was a long time ago." She clutched his arm. "I didn't want… I was forced. You must… you must believe me."

Dick stepped back, staring, then quickly recalled his immediate peril. Drawing himself up to his full height, he said, "Now look, Daphne, why don't we finish this conversation in my office or over a beer somewhere."

Daphne's face puckered and she started to cry. Her voice faltering, she said, "I heard you were leaving. Matt told me it will be soon, and… and most likely that means we'll never see each other again. I… I came to say goodbye."

Daphne placed her arms around him and nestled her face, tears flowing, into his chest. For a moment Dick stood still, frozen, then he slowly embraced her. "It's over, darling, it's over. It has to be. I'm married, and we have to accept that." He heard the sound of a familiar car engine and glanced outside. It was Christine returning in their Volkswagen. Daphne heard it too, and she hugged him tighter.

"What are you doing?" Dick hissed. "You've got to get out of here. Go out the back door. Hurry!" But Daphne would not let go. He tried vainly to pry her arms loose. Dick heard Christine park their car behind Daphne's on the circular driveway, slam the car door and then mount the steps to the porch and front door. There she hesitated momentarily before entering.

"Who?… What is this?" she stammered.

"It's not what you think it is, it's really not."

"Not what I think it is?" Christine said icily. "It's exactly what I think it is." She turned to Daphne. "And who are? Get out! Get out of my house this instant!"

Daphne slowly relinquished her grip and, pulling Dick's arm, pleaded, "Stay in Zaria. Come with me. Please, Dick... please."

"Daphne, I... I can't." He did not move. The scene lapsed into slow motion, Daphne pulling, Dick resisting, Christine standing aghast at one side near the door. Finally, shivering, breathing heavily, Daphne looked up at Dick, who stared wild-eyed at her, his jaw clenched tightly, then to Christine and back to Dick. She let go of his arm and, hunching her shoulders in mute resignation, walked toward Christine and studied her face. "I understand. Yes... now I understand."

Stumbling, Daphne retreated out the door and down the front steps to her car. She wiped her eyes with the back of her hand. Dick heard gravel crunch as she drove slowly away. He was frantic. "You've got to believe me, Christine, nothing was going on. That's Matt's girlfriend. They had a fight, and I was trying to comfort..."

"Comfort?" Christine mimicked him, her voice laced with sarcasm. "By hugging? You have lipstick all over your shirt."

Dick looked down, saw the pink smudges. His face betrayed bewilderment and guilty confusion.

Standing near him, Christine glanced first at the departing car, then around the room. "And she had on my blouse – same buttons, same material, same color. What did you do, buy them both at a sale?" She took a step toward him. "You… you," she continued, sputtering. "You're not the man I married. You've turned into a cheat right here in our own home. Right here. What were you thinking? What if Molly had come home?"

"Christine, please. I love you. Really I do. And I wasn't doing anything wrong."

"Do you expect me to believe that?" Christine clenched and unclenched her hands at her sides. "She was in your arms. What were you going to do… make love with that… that creature on the couch or in our bedroom?"

"No, I was not. You must believe me."

"You bastard," she spat in quiet fury, emphasizing each word. "I forgave you once, but you can't keep your hands off women." Her face contorted in sorrow and pain. "You promised, Dick. Do you remember that you promised? Am I so ugly that you… with that…?" Turning abruptly, she walked to the door to their sleeping quarters. With tears now forming in her eyes, her voice trailing to a whisper, she looked back at her husband. "How could you do this when I need you so much?" He heard the door to their bedroom slam shut.

Dick tottered to a chair in the living room, sat down and held his head in his hands. How… how could this have happened? There's no explanation I can offer that won't make me look like a pathetic liar.

Through the open windows, the muezzin's call to prayer drifted into the room, an incongruous coda to the recent events of the afternoon.

Chapter 33

The Journey Home

1978

Molly returned late in the day, and she and Dick ate supper without Christine. She asked where her mother was, and Dick told her she was in their bedroom. He did not volunteer a further explanation. From her wide-eyed expression, he could tell that Molly wanted to know more but was afraid to ask. Later in the evening, Christine crept from the bedroom and made her way to the kitchen. She gave Molly a reassuring hug but said nothing to Dick. When he retired to bed, she was either sleeping or feigning sleep. Rolled onto her side, she had her back turned to him. He made a few soft noises to initiate conversation, but she did not stir.

Neither did she communicate the following day, but she did speak with him tersely the day after. Dick was leaving to run an errand when Christine entered the living room. She tugged at his sleeve.

"Why don't you stay here? That bitch wanted you to be with her."

"Christine, we're husband and wife. We're also a father and mother."

"Those are just labels, Dick. The reality is…" She never finished.

"The reality is that I want to protect you. I love you and always have."

"Do you?" Her eyes searched his. "I don't think so."

Later that day Dick did manage to convey the details of their journey home – first a stop of several days in Tunisia, then a trip through Europe to London and thence home to Boston. She stared at him without comment while he related the details, and he had to infer that the absence of a refusal implied consent. She apparently recognized that any attempt by her to make separate plans would be foolish. Christine knew how many visits to various offices her husband had made to get clearances for their combined departure.

Concurrent with the crisis at home, they had to continue preparations for departure and leave-taking. These tasks they performed separately. As the day to leave approached, it brought with it mixed feelings of joy and sadness – joy at the prospect of returning home but sadness at leaving much that they had come to cherish. They had all become very fond of their steward, Adamu. The little fellow was so upset by their impending departure that he started getting drunk every night, and one evening he stood outside the house engaged in a long conversation with a bush. Their devotion to him was reciprocated. Loyally, he had tended to the house and garden, daily swept the driveway, kept the premises neat and tidy, and sometimes came into the house in the evening for storytelling and laughter.

There was nothing they could do to remedy his distress; his home was Africa, just as theirs was the United States. But they tried to soften the pain by giving him gifts and extra money. Dick bought him a wristwatch, but the next morning he noticed that Adamu was not wearing it, and when he inquired the reason, Adamu was evasive. Dick guessed that the watch was meaningless to him and that he had traded it at the Mommy Depot for sex. Adamu could not read or write, so letter writing would be useless to find out what the future might hold for him. With helpless pangs of regret, Dick surmised that their steward would drift off into Zaria or back to his 'hometown', another scratched entry in the annals of the poor.

Dick hired a driver, and the family traveled in a university van to Kano on the day before their flight to Tunis on KLM. After securing lodging, he and Molly did some sightseeing, touring the old market in Kano. It was a veritable warren of small, overstuffed stalls with makeshift roofs interlaced with cramped, dirt paths and open sewers. The entire area had an air of dusky gloom, and they did not stay long.

Following a night in a fancy hotel, a luxury to which they treated themselves, they endured the usual jostling the next morning at the airport and, as they were among the first to reach the plane, easily found comfortable seats for their flight. Then they were airborne, back across the Sahara, this time visible from far above as an endless expanse of sand and black, rocky mountains. Christine and Molly slept.

As the plane droned on, Dick daydreamed about Zaria, about the line of African women, bowls balanced delicately on their heads, walking single file along a path through the bush; the dump trucks, or lorries, and long, open four-wheelers with men standing forward in the open backs or riding atop bales heaped high inside; the score or more of curious village children trailing behind Molly and gawking at her blue eyes and blond hair; the old men and women, in rags, many crippled or with limbs truncated by leprosy, seated on the ground by the sides of the roads; the cool greenness, like an underwater world, glimpsed through a window of the house in stark contrast to the white mud walls within; the laughing children surrounding the car and begging for a coin; the piles of gray clouds rising over the trees and checker-boarded fields; the filth and stench of the green water in the sewers running through the local market; an old man in flowing robes, anywhere, arm half raised and fist clenched with thumb up, saluting as he said, "Good morning, sah!"

He reflected that one simultaneously loves Africa and hates it. The one emotion that is not possible is indifference.

* * * * *

After landing in Tunis and being cleared through customs, they took a taxi to the Megara Beach Hotel, a beautiful resort recommended by older English friends in Zaria. It was located north of Tunis on a bluff overlooking the Mediterranean in the midst of manicured lawns, beds of neatly tended flowers and nodding palms. They left dirt and squalor in the morning to arrive in the afternoon at a green oasis by the sea. Their rooms had French doors that opened onto balconies from which they could see the manicured grounds, the turquoise sea and a large swimming pool, flanked by a small, outdoor kitchen.

Molly swam in the pool for the remainder of the day. Dick wandered down steep stairs to a broad beach, while Christine stayed in their room. That evening they enjoyed a quiet, elegant dinner on the verandah of the hotel. Christine spoke to Molly but only briefly to Dick. Exhausted from their day of travel, they retired early to bed.

Dick spent most of the next day on the beach. Christine chose to remain behind, reading – so he thought – a novel. She was seated on a folding deck chair on the balcony of their room, and he waved at the top of the stairs on his way to the beach. His gesture was not reciprocated. Molly joined Dick in the afternoon. She splashed about in the Mediterranean and also lay, absorbing the sun, on a gaudy beach towel next to him. She asked why her mother was so quiet, and he offered an evasive reply. They talked of other matters – their pending trip and her plans for school in the coming year.

Dick drank too much wine at dinner that night, a dinner of loud, forced jollity on his part. He went to bed shortly after leaving the table and fell into a deep sleep. When he woke bleary-eyed in the morning, sunlight dappling the garden beneath the balcony, Christine was gone. Her adjoining bed was empty; throwing his legs over the side of his bed, he reached for the closet that had contained her clothes. It too was empty, and her luggage was gone. Looking around wildly, uncomprehending but awake now, he rushed to Molly's nearby room and knocked. There was no answer. Slowly, he pushed open her unlocked door to discover that she also had vanished.

After returning to his room and dressing hurriedly,

Dick hastened along the white gravel path to the reception desk in the next building. The clerk, a short, oily man with a wispy mustache, recognized him. Dick demanded to know when 'Madame Blodgett' had last been there.

The clerk swiveled his head and peered at the clock on the whitewashed wall behind him. Obsequiously correct, he said that Madam had departed over three hours ago by taxi with a young woman… your daughter, he believed… and had left this note.

He handed a folded piece of yellow paper to Dick, who crossed the lobby and sat down heavily in a wicker chair by a tall, open window.

The note was brief. It said:

Dear Dick,

Our marriage isn't working. Or maybe it is for you, but it isn't for me. I feel too uncomfortable pretending and joining in a jolly family vacation. I'm taking Molly with me, and I'll have to explain why we're leaving.

Enjoy your vacation. You deserve it. Maybe you should go back. You're obviously wanted in Zaria.

Don't try to follow us. We'll be boarding a plane by the time you read this note. And don't return to our house in Woodbury. Let's not lead lives that are a pretense.

Christine

He returned to the front desk, his face betraying his dismay. His voice raised to near hysteria, he inquired, "Are there many flights in the morning that leave for Europe?"

The clerk, taken aback, replied, "Ah oui, Monsieur. They go to all major capitals… many airlines. It is very busy this time of day."

Standing by the desk in a state of agitation, Dick shook his head. "Are you sure?"

"Most assuredly, Monsieur." The clerk hesitated. "Does… does Monsieur require assistance of some sort?" Dick told him that he did not and trudged back to his room. He sat for a long time on the edge of his bed, trying to figure out what to do.

He decided to stay at the hotel for two more days and, after cancelling their previous plans, booked a flight directly to London for himself. The days passed quickly. On the second, tedious arrangements having been made, he once again went to the beach. Idly, he watched tall-masted sloops claw across the horizon. But he could not read. Thoughts of Molly, of Christine and of Daphne kept intruding, and he pondered whether the Moslem saying – it is written – applied to all that had happened.

PART THREE

WOODBURY and CALIFORNIA

Chapter 34

Dick and David

1978

The flights from Tunis to Heathrow and, a day later, from Heathrow to Logan Airport, Boston, were uneventful. Dick called Malcolm from London, and Malcolm invited him to stay for a few days until he found suitable accommodations.

Once on their way to Woodbury, Malcolm said, in his usual, direct way, "Okay, Dick, so tell me what happened. We've heard from Christine. Now I'd like to hear from you." Dick unburdened himself. He told Malcolm what had happened: of his trysts with Daphne, of Matt and of the final scene at his house.

Malcolm whistled. "I guess hell hath no fury like a woman scorned. You sure got blind-sided by that one."

Dick sighed. "I sure did. And the awful part is, Christine probably won't talk to me. And if she does, maybe I can explain why I already knew Daphne. But not why she felt at liberty to hug me. I tried to say that she was Matt's girlfriend, but she didn't believe me, and I don't blame her. Daphne was pulling on my arm, for Christ's sake, and begging me to come with her. Christine could see for herself."

Dick's explanation had been lengthy, and by the time he finished, they were nearing Woodbury. Malcolm drummed his fingers on the steering wheel. "Mind if I tell Alice?" he asked.

"No, go ahead. But I'd just as soon you kept it to yourselves. There's no way I come out of this looking good."

"I'm afraid," Malcolm said, "that you're right. If you tell Christine all the facts, assuming she'd talk to you, she'll be justifiably angry about your betrayal. Sorry to put it so bluntly, and if you just stay quiet, you have to admit that her interpretation of what happened is pretty reasonable."

When they arrived, Alice greeted Dick affectionately. "We want to hear all about Africa," she said, "but first you probably need to rest." She showed him to a guest room, and she was correct about his need for rest. He lay down and fell into a deep sleep.

When he awoke in the late afternoon, he called his house. As he suspected would happen, Molly answered the phone.

"Hi, Molly," Dick said tentatively. "It's your Dad. I just got in today. How are you?"

"Fine, I guess."

"I'm fine too. I'd love to see you."

"Okay… sometime."

"What's the matter? Why so guarded? Is your Mom there?"

"Yes." Dick could tell that she had placed her palm over the receiver. There was a muted conversation in the background, then, "Not right now. In a little while."

"I'll call again, sweetheart. I'm staying with Alice and Malcolm. Come over when you can."

"I will. Oh, Daddy, why… never mind. Sometime soon." She hung up.

Dick slumped in the chair as he put down the telephone. Alice had been watching and listening, and she quickly offered him a glass of wine. The dinner that followed was a quiet affair. They chatted at length about Africa before, tired and sad, Dick went to bed.

He saw Molly the next day. She rode her bicycle to Alice and Malcolm's house. Hesitantly at first, then tightly, she hugged her father. When they parted, he said, "I love you and your mother very much." He sensed that she was confused but wanted to believe. They agreed to meet again in a couple of days, and Molly cheerfully waved as she rode away on her bicycle.

Dick found a furnished apartment in the next town and returned to the law school. It was summertime, and few professors were there. His office had been vacant for a year and was hot and musty. He threw open the window, skipped up a flight of stairs to the dean's office to report in, and said hello to the secretarial staff. Everyone wanted to know what Nigeria had been like, and he did his best to inform them. He found out what his teaching assignments would be for the coming semester. All were courses he had taught before, and he had the books and materials on hand.

In the following weeks Dick spent a great deal of time in his office writing a report about his year abroad and preparing for his classes. The better part of most days was devoted to reading texts and law cases and taking notes. Classes were due to begin in late August. Christine did not call, or write, or send a message through Molly. There was only silence.

Busy during the week, Dick found the weekends

unbearable. He took walks, went alone to sporting events or art galleries and devoured novels and histories. He also discovered a new interest in writing poetry and, in his lonely hours, devoted himself to it. From time to time he asked women to join him for lunch or dinner, but these were antiseptic occasions, devoid of romance. He wrestled with the thought of calling Carol or Cathy, but, suspecting only further turmoil would come from it, he refrained.

He did speak often with his brother, David, and in mid-August, a week before the commencement of classes, Dick decided to drive south to visit him. In their telephone conversations, he had described briefly what had happened. David, who already knew about Carol, listened and commiserated. He was delighted when Dick said he would visit for a long weekend. David, his wife and their two sons had moved to Greenwich, Connecticut, during Dick's absence in Nigeria, and Dick was curious to see their new home. David had described it as 'rather grand' and 'just wait 'till you see it' which had peaked his interest.

In his old Plymouth, Dick drove first through the rolling, wooded hills of eastern Massachusetts, then southwest to Hartford. The highway was fringed by dense eastern forest so that he seemed to be driving in a cut, or trail, through pristine wilderness. A Mohawk village in a clearing would have seemed entirely in place and appropriate. The small city of Hartford gleamed on the banks of the Connecticut River; he drove through it, then through more verdant hills and valleys to his destination.

Dick was unfamiliar with Greenwich. It was difficult to make his way amidst a confusing tangle of winding roads flanked by large houses. With a pang he was reminded of his first trip to the Haskins' house in Scarsdale so many years before. He had just begun to conclude that he was lost when he saw a sign, his last name on it, beside a long, curving driveway leading to a courtyard in front of a huge, field stone house with latticed windows.

He parked and had just stepped out of the car when David burst out the front door and enveloped Dick in a massive hug. "Welcome! Welcome!" he said. "It's so good to have you here. Let me help you. Here, I'll carry that." He grabbed Dick's suitcase, saying, "Follow me. We have a really nice room set aside for you."

David's slender, dark-haired wife, Jill, entered the long front hall at one end as Dick and David entered at the other. Dick stopped, grinning, and Jill ran to him and gave him a gentle hug and kiss. "Dick, it's wonderful to see you. We're going to cook out. David's bought some corn and a really big steak, and of course you'll want a drink first."

"Or two… or three," Dick ventured.

"As many as you want, just so you tell us your adventures."

David led the way upstairs and down a corridor to the guest room which, Dick reflected, was almost as large as his apartment. "Wash up and then join us," David said, retreating out the door after depositing Dick's luggage on a stand by a window. "I'm sure you can find your way downstairs through this castle. We'll be in the kitchen, waiting."

About ten minutes later, having used the bathroom and combed his receding hair, Dick joined his brother and sister-in-law in their kitchen. It had a large, center island, a table with four chairs at one side and sufficient room for a couch and two easy chairs on the other side. Bottles of liquor were on a counter. Dick mixed himself a vodka martini, added a cocktail onion, and exited through French doors to a spacious, long terrace under a portico that ran the length of the rear of the house. Beyond it, down flagstone steps with lamps on either side, was a swimming pool that, David said, they could use later in the evening.

Although David was about ten pounds heavier and, to a careful observer, slightly fuller in the face, the brothers mirrored each other in appearance – in choice of clothing, in height, in hair, in tone of voice and laughter. With comfortable ease, they settled into lounge chairs with their drinks. Jill joined them, and she and David quizzed Dick about his time in Africa.

"I wish the boys were home to hear this," Jill said.

"Oh m'God, I forgot to bring something for them. Where are they?"

"At camp for the summer. It's given David and me a chance to be a young married couple again." Jill took David's hand and held it for a few moments. David leaned over and kissed her on the cheek. Shortly thereafter, he rose and put a thick steak on a grille built into a wall at the outer edge of the terrace.

They ate outdoors at a table protected by a mammoth, green, square umbrella. It was a simple meal accompanied by copious amounts of Spanish red table wine. Afterwards, Jill bustled about clearing plates. She said, "I'm sure you two have lots to talk about, and there's hardly anything to do. I don't need any help." Holding their half-empty glasses of wine, the two men settled into the reclining chairs they had occupied earlier. Jill had turned on a record player, and the music of Vivaldi wafted out the open windows to where they were seated. By this time it was dusk. The sun was setting behind tall oak trees at the edge of the property, and a dusty rose glow suffused the horizon and filtered through the dense foliage. Cicadas had begun their thrumming in the surrounding woods, and an occasional firefly flitted across the lawn.

David turned on the lights at the side of the steps leading to the pool and also in the pool itself. When he was seated, he said, "How's Bob, you know, Bob, your father-in-law? You were worried about him before you left."

"I'm not sure. The only news I get is through Molly. I think you know he had a stroke, and they've moved to a smaller house. Still in Scarsdale, though."

"Too bad. That big house of theirs sure was beautiful."

"No more than yours. These are pretty fine digs. You've obviously done well."

David frowned, waving his hand dismissively. "You know, Dick, when you don't have it, you want it. Or at any rate I wanted it. I'm not sure about you. You keep running after it, and when you finally catch it... well, you've caught a wisp of smoke."

"Not quite. This house is really grand."

"Sure it is, and don't get me wrong. Jill and I love it. But we could be just as happy in a cabin by a lake. You can only be one place at a time. You are what you are where you are – in bed, on the john, sitting in a chair, reading. Suppose there are twenty other chairs in a room.

So what? They're just for show. You can only sit in them one at a time."

Dick turned and looked at his brother. "This doesn't sound like you."

"That's because I've changed. Not some kind of metamorphosis, but I'm less interested in money, and I don't go out with women anymore." David chuckled. "Mind you, I didn't turn into a saint. I'm still me. My head still swivels around when I see a pretty skirt, but I've discovered that being rich can be boring."

"Boring?"

"Yeah, boring. The men at the club… all they talk about is golf or business or try to one-up each other, and the women talk with marbles in their mouths. You academic types at least think, which would be a refreshing change."

"I wouldn't overdo the thinking part," Dick said. He added, "It sounds like you're becoming more like me. And I've become more like you."

"More like me?" David scratched the side of his head. "Do you still lug around that load of guilt and worry about what other people think?"

Dick started to speak, then stopped. He sipped his wine, his eyes fastening on his brother over the brim of his glass. "You learned much earlier than I did that feelings of guilt are the flip side of high expectations – too high in my case. When you don't demand perfection, you don't beat yourself up when you don't achieve it. I can't say I don't give a damn what people think. But far less." He smiled ruefully, letting out his breath. "I know I'm not perfect – far from it – and for good reason."

Dick lowered his glass. "Let me tell you again what happened… and I don't mind if later on you repeat it to Jill." Hesitating at the beginning, he described his encounters with Daphne, much as he had done with Malcolm, and Christine's furious reaction. He did not omit any details. When he had finished, David rose and opened a bottle of Merlot. He poured some into Dick's glass and some into his own. Seating himself, he patted Dick on his knee.

"That's Christine for you," he said. "It sounds about what I would have expected."

For several minutes they were silent. Finally, Dick said, "What now? I can't get Christine to even talk with me, and I… I can't get her to understand that I still love her."

For a while David said nothing in response. The light from the lamps leading to the pool reflected off his concentrated features and shimmered on the curvature of his glass. When he spoke, he was blunt. "Do you still love her? I wonder sometimes if you aren't really in love with a sense of loyalty, of doing the right thing, and then your instincts betray you. Look, I've got two things to say. Let's test your proposition about your feelings of love in another context, a context I'm familiar with. Suppose a man gives away confidential information to a rival company, but he protests that he always had feelings of loyalty to the company that employed him."

"What has that got to do with…?"

"Just stay with me. Would that be infidelity?"

"Yes, but…"

"Why?"

Dick stared at his brother. "I hate it when you play law professor. Why? Well, because whatever he protests his feelings are, he violated the trust his employer had placed in him and that he had presumably encouraged."

"By parity of reasoning, then weren't you unfaithful no matter what your thoughts were – or are?"

"But…" Dick sputtered. "Look at the spot I was in… am still in. No sex for the rest of my life."

"Dick," David said gently, "people understand that. But you violated Christine's trust and broke your promise, and there's no way you can explain your way out of it. You might as well face yourself and what you did without flinching."

Dick started to interrupt, but David continued. "That brings me to my second point: accept responsibility, but go easy on yourself. I'm sure your friends are glad it was you with this problem and not them."

"All Christine understands is that I was with that… that woman," Dick lamented. "She doesn't – she won't – understand the context in which it happened."

"And maybe she never will. Your wife's tough and has pretty rigid expectations. Look, Dick, don't be so hard on yourself. With Carol… well, walking out in that field was as much her idea as yours, perhaps more. You hadn't had sex in weeks. Or was it months? And that might have gone on for years. But you're supposed to suck it up, go without, play the cards dealt you. Dammit, that's exactly what you were doing, but many women, and Christine's clearly in that camp, expect you to be faithful to the bitter end – easy enough, if you're not in the spot you were in. I love it when people preach a morality they don't have to struggle with themselves."

"That still doesn't explain Daphne."

"Aw, c'mon, Dick. So you screwed her way off in the boondocks all by yourself. Was that such a big deal? And then she falls in love with you and maybe you with her. What a mess! But you know something?" Stroking his chin, David looked directly at his brother. "Lots of men stray, and lots of women too. And often their marriages survive. You wrote once in one of your letters that your steward went to that place called the Mommy Depot. I'll bet no one called him a womanizer or philanderer. They would here."

"Maybe so. But there are good reasons for marriage and fidelity and stable families in which to raise children. They all go together. That's why adultery is a sin."

"Yes, but isn't it also a sin – a violation of yourself – to live a lie and pretend you're happy in an unhappy marriage?"

"What of the hurt you cause others?"

"What of the hurt you cause yourself? Aren't you just as valuable as they are? But it's not as if anyone will listen to my brilliant theories about male-female relationships. Except you. And you're my brother, so you have to."

Dick stifled a yawn. "You know, I appreciate that you always take my side. And I think it's great that you and Jill have gotten much closer together. If you don't mind my saying so, she must have wondered about you."

"No doubt… no doubt," David glanced inside to where Jill was putting dishes away in a cabinet. The light from the kitchen window played on the flagstones outside. He lowered his voice. "She suspected, that's for sure, but she didn't go blabbering all over the countryside the way Christine has done with you. And it paid off, because, like you, I had no excuse, but we're closer together now than ever."

Dick said, "It seems as though we've each found hidden parts of ourselves."

"Hidden, but always there. I'm proud to have you as a brother, but I'm not sure that was always reciprocated. You need to be more at peace with yourself."

"And I need to go to bed," Dick said, yawning openly. "It's been a long day, and with all this red wine, I'm going to have the worst headache in the morning and a mouth like the Gobi Desert."

David rose unsteadily to his feet. "When you go, just remember to turn the light off in the hall. And one more thing. If you ever need any financial help, Dick, I just want you to know that all you have to do is ask. I hope that doesn't sound patronizing, but within reason, what's mine is yours."

"I won't be asking… but thanks."

The next day it rained, and Dick and David went to the movies. The following day it was muggy and warm. They hiked in nearby woods, but the trail was rutted and muddy, and their progress was slow. Their conversation was about work and not their personal lives. That evening David took Jill and Dick out to dinner at a moderately priced restaurant. The topic of conversation was politics, and the brothers, agreeing completely, reinforced each other's opinions.

In the morning, promising to see each other soon, they said goodbye, and Dick commenced the four-hour drive back to his apartment outside Boston.

And the silence from Christine continued.

Chapter 35

Walter's Confession
1979

A few months later Dick spoke on the telephone with a former colleague in Indiana. They traded law school gossip, and near the end of their conversation Dick's friend said, "You know, I almost forgot. Your buddy, Matt Jamison, returned early from Nigeria."

"I wouldn't call him a buddy."

"Oh? Well, he's back, quit teaching and is practicing law in Bloomington. Already making more money than he did as a professor, or so I heard."

"That's sounds about right for Matt," Dick observed. "He'd be the first to tell you."

"He came back with some woman."

"Really?' Dick caught his breath. "Was she Nigerian?"

"Don't know. Probably just a student, maybe one of yours. Do you want me to find out?

There was no answer.

"… Hello?… Are you still there?"

"Yes… yes, I'm here. I was just curious. I was… it's not important. If you see Matt, say hello from me."

The conversation drifted elsewhere and soon ended. Dick sat back in his chair, rubbed his chin with his hand, and wondered. And he kept wondering long into the day and night. The next day, with diminished effect, thoughts recurred of the dusty streets of Zaria, of lightening forking from lowering clouds over his thatched roof house, of the awful, final scene with Daphne, and those thoughts flickered through memory the following day and the day after that until, with an effort of will, he put the trauma of Africa from his mind.

Not long thereafter, about a year after leaving Nigeria and much to Dick's surprise, he received another telephone call. He was in his office. It was Walter, and he asked if they could get together. They agreed to meet in a week in the afternoon on the village green in Woodbury. Walter's tone was very cordial and friendly. He said how very sorry he and Carol were to hear that Dick and Christine had separated, and he did not ask how or why it had happened.

When they met, it was a warm summer day. Both were dressed casually for the season. Dick noticed that Walter had more gray hair at his temples and had lost weight. Because he was genial and cheerful, Dick's trepidation eased. Walter suggested that they take a walk, and they ambled in the direction of the high school and the high, grassy hill behind it.

On the way, Dick inquired how Walter liked living in Marblehead and whether he missed Woodbury. To both queries, Walter gave affirmative responses. "Of course we miss Woodbury," he said, "and the friends we had here. But Marblehead is a wonderful place to live, right on the water, and we've made many friends." He added that he now had an easier commute to his office.

Dick had no further questions, and Walter seemed disinclined to talk, so thereafter they strolled along in silence. Dutch Elm disease had destroyed most of the large, wine glass-shaped elms that had flanked the roads and whose boughs had covered each street like roofs over the naves of cathedrals. Oaks and maples still provided shade, however, and they walked along a gravel path that served as a sidewalk past colonial and Victorian houses, set back behind lawns and shrubbery, that baked in the still, quiet warmth of a mid-afternoon summer day. When they reached the high school all was peaceful save for shouts from children enrolled in a summer camp who were using the nearby football field as a recreation area.

Puffing from exertion and the heat, they climbed the hill and found a grassy patch on which to sit. The sky was a dome of cerulean blue with scattered, fluffy clouds. The spires of three churches poked through the leafy canopy of mottled green that mantled the buildings beneath them. In the distance, near the horizon, smoke spiraled upward from a factory on the outskirts of an adjacent town.

At first there was further silence as they both absorbed the view. Walter remarked how beautiful it was. Then they sat, staring outward, saying nothing.

Eventually, clearing his throat, Dick said, "I think I should start by saying how sorry I am about the loss of our friendship. I'm not sure any words can repair the damage, but I want you to know that I recognize… and regret… the hurt that I caused."

Walter swiveled his head to look directly at him. "Dick, this is pretty much what I wanted to talk to you about, in fact, to clear my own conscience, what I had to talk to you about. That's why I called."

Dick was surprised. Clear his conscience? Of what? Walter continued: "You probably didn't know it… how could you unless Carol told you, that I was having an affair with an old girlfriend from Philadelphia at the time Christine first got sick with cancer. It went on for quite a while, and Carol found out about it. Oh, I tried to deny it, but she knew."

"She said something about it once, but I didn't believe her."

"Well, you should have. It's over now, a long time ago. Do you remember that walk we took at night down to the bridge, and I left you two alone together?"

"Sure," Dick said, "I remember. You've got to believe me, nothing serious happened, and Carol and I never had an affair. But that's probably when all the trouble started."

"No, Dick, it started before that. It started with me. That's what I want to tell you. I know Carol, and I had a good idea how she would try to repay me. I just didn't give a damn."

"So what you're saying…"

"What I'm saying… look, it's like links in a chain. Because I was involved with another woman, I turned around and went home, and everything that happened afterward would not have happened, at least in Woodbury, if I'd stayed with you." Frowning, Walter picked at the grass between his legs. "One thing just led to another. In a way, I suppose, you were an unwitting actor in a play composed by others."

"Wait a minute," Dick protested. "Carol and I knew the roles we were playing, and I wasn't innocent."

"Maybe not, but whatever happened that night, innocent or not, you didn't know the context. Carol did, although I won't deny that you and she probably cared for each other. All I'm trying to say is that you didn't start all the gossip and foolishness that came later. Don't blame yourself." Walter paused. He was staring out at the landscape before him. "Why do you think I never got angry? I knew whose fault it was."

"I still want to apologize."

"Apologize all you want, Dick, just don't blame yourself for being human and – I believe you – for something that never happened. But what if it had? Hell, we all have our faults. Lord knows I have mine… you, Carol, me… even Christine."

For possibly half an hour they again said nothing. Dick listened to the children shouting on the football field below and the faraway ding-ding-dinging of crossing gates descending as the Boston and Maine commuter train approached the Woodbury station.

"I'm not Lancelot after all," he said finally.

Walter grimaced. "For Chrissake, no. And neither am I King Arthur." He stood up, brushing stray bits of grass from his trousers. "I'd better get going. It's almost time for rush-hour traffic."

"Would you like to stay for dinner?"

"Thanks, Dick. I promised Carol I'd be home by six."

Rising slowly to his feet, Dick stretched his back, swiveled his neck a couple of times and also slapped new-mown grass from his pants. They stumbled down the hill and retraced their steps back to the village green and Walter's car, this time with shadows slanting across the roads.

"There's one more thing," Dick said, "but I feel a little

awkward, out of place, asking it." He could feel his Adam's apple rising and falling. "If you don't mind my inquiring, and say so if you do, how is Carol and how is your marriage?"

"No problem, Dick. Really, no problem. Carol is fine. She goes to church a lot. Not Unitarian anymore; she's back to being an Episcopalian, and… damn, I should have mentioned it. She said to give you her very best. As for the marriage, we've been to marriage counseling and it seems to be stronger than ever. We've both made adjustments. I don't drink as much, and you may have noticed I've lost a lot of weight – over forty pounds. My paunch really bothered Carol."

Dick wanted Walter to say more, to hear by some slip of the tongue that Carol still had affectionate feelings for him, but he was glad she and Walter were together and presumably happy. When they reached Walter's new Porsche – the accounting business, he noted, must be doing well – Dick said, "You're a good man, Walter. I always knew it. To be honest, I wasn't at all sure what to expect from this meeting. It meant a lot to me."

"And to me, Dick. I hope we both feel better for it." They shook hands, and Walter reached forward with his free hand and squeezed Dick's shoulder. "I'll convey your regards to Carol. And again, I'm sorry. I'm sorry about your… current situation. I hope things work out for you."

Walter got in his car and started the engine. He pulled slowly out into traffic and was gone.

Dick stood for a long time gazing after him, doubting that he would ever see Walter again.

Chapter 36

California
1981

Slightly over a year later Dick moved to Stockton, California, a small city in the San Joaquin Valley. A nearby law school had offered him a tenured faculty position at higher pay. He decided to leave behind all his memories of Woodbury. Molly was enrolled in a private school, thanks to the generosity of her grandparents, and he assured himself that she could visit him on vacations. Allen was doing very well in his new job in New York City. Dick's parents had died, and David, his brother, was a five to six hour airplane ride away instead of a four-hour drive by automobile. He loved New England, but California, being so very different in topography, promised to be an interesting and healing change. Having learned to survive on his own in northern Nigeria, he doubted that he would have any trouble making his way there. Other Penelopes and Peters would appear in his life, but with luck no one like Matt or Daphne. Moreover, he had heard that Cathy had moved to San Francisco to become the copy editor of a magazine. A secretary in the law school's career planning office had given him her new address and telephone number. If he cared to stir that ember, she would be, as she had said in her farewell in New York City, "Just a phone call away."

Malcolm and Alice invited Dick for a farewell dinner. Several friends were there, including Bob, who had separated from Mary several months before. Malcolm and Dick had become very close friends, and the leave-taking was a bittersweet combination of joy for Dick on his new position and sorrow occasioned by his pending move so far away.

Shortly before his departure, Dick met with Molly before she left for a summer job in Maine. The silence from Christine had continued, and thus he was surprised when Molly handed him an envelope with his name on it in Christine's distinctive handwriting. Molly told him that her mother had asked that Dick open the letter after his arrival in California. Dick was not, in any event, eager to receive a letter that he feared would contain vituperative accusations. He placed it, unopened, in a file with some of his personal papers.

A week after his arrival, when he had finished a late supper, he was sorting through boxes piled high in the front hall and living room of the condominium that he had rented. In one of them he found a file, and in the file he found Christine's unopened letter. Carefully, he removed it and tapped it in the palm of his hand. He walked into the kitchen, found a knife and slit the envelope open. He had almost forgotten it and yet had always known it was there. Retreating to an overstuffed chair in the living room, he sat down and nervously extracted a single sheet of paper. There it was in Christine's rounded handwriting. After reaching into his pocket and putting on his reading glasses, he started to read:

Dear Dick,

This is a difficult letter for me to write.

I've spent hours, days, months and years thinking about what happened to us, and I've come to understand the difficult – no, nearly impossible – situation we were both in. Some was my fault, some yours, and a lot was chance circumstance and bad luck.

Do I love you? Yes, deeply. You have been and still are the only man in my life. Do I forgive you? I now realize that that's the wrong question. Rather, I should ask if we can forgive ourselves and each other, and I'm trying.

My cancer has returned, and I'm not sure what, if anything, can be done.

Now for the really hard part. I want you to come home, wherever home may be. Or at least we could talk about a reconciliation. I know that you're going to California – that's what finally spurred me to write – and it may be too late. But we can think about it and, when/if you're back here visiting, we could discuss it. There's plenty of time – well, there may not be, but I hope so.

I know this may sound confusing and slightly crazy. That's because it is. And it may be impossible. Too much time may have elapsed, and too much hurt and bad feeling may have occurred.

But for both our sakes, and the sake of our children, please consider it.

Your ever loving and forever faithful wife,

Christine

Still holding the letter, Dick slowly lowered his hands into his lap. He closed his eyes, his thoughts cascading discordantly through his mind. Could they reconcile? So much time had elapsed. He could not return, nor could Christine – it was much too late for that – to earlier versions of themselves. The stream had carved a new channel, and those versions had ceased to exist. Yet surely he had compassion for his companion of so many shared years now afflicted with a fatal disease. His presence would unite the family again in adversity. But what if she survived? Would he be vaulting himself back again into the same tangle of righteous morality and unrequited desire that had already torn them apart?

And what, in the final analysis, is enduring love – not infatuation but committed, marital love? Is it sexual longing, but much more? Or duty, but not that alone? Could they really fashion a relationship of mutual forgiveness, of companionship, of shared thoughts and ideals, as if they were sturdy columns at each end of a portico to a sacred inner sanctum, both holding up the same roof but with space between them for individual needs, thoughts and feelings?

Pondering, Dick sat hunched in his chair while shadows deepened in the room. Finally, he rose, turned on another lamp, and continued unpacking boxes.

A Poem by Dick Blodgett

Christine

We quarreled
And the word-wounds
Left bitter scars.

That was yesterday morning.

In late afternoon it snowed.
A weave of anxious traffic flowed
Past decorated shops and stores.
From a leaning trolley's side,
Bell clicking in the sudden cold,
I stepped with slow, uncertain stride
Through the flakes of dancing white
Cast mutely on the falling night.
The crunching pavement, worn and old,
Led by lamps and shuttered doors
To our apartment's faded gloom
Where words were flung in foolish pride
And love and hope together died.
Silence sounded in the room.

Drawers open,
Dresser bare,
Dishes unwashed and unclean.
A search for a note,
A call to a friend,
No, she hadn't been seen.

Railroad stations at night
Are tawdry, lonely places;
Drunks sprawled on benches,
Graffiti scrawled on walls,
Piss smell in rest rooms,
Waiters and watchers
Bundled cheerlessly
Against the cold
And themselves.

The nine o'clock train was late.
Snow-hooded, it panted
At the platform, steam rising,
Passengers and porters
Swirling briefly at its doors.
Yet soon, too soon,
Shuddering forward again,
It slowly became beads of light,
Gently curving, dying into darkness.

In the station
The ceiling's iron tracery
Flickered cold mockery of hope.

I walked alone behind a candy stand
And held my crumpled face within my hand.